GRAY'S LAKE

JOHN HANSEN

GRAY'S LAKE
Published through Summit Creek Press

Cover design: http://www.selfpubbookcovers.com

ISBN: 979-8-218-13264-4

CHAPTER ONE

The day was near half gone when they'd come. The sheriff and six men, five of them having become deputies not four hours ago. Their bravado, loud and bold, was infectious. *They robbed the bank in Soda Springs. Killed Bessie Perks. Just for spite it appeared.*

She'd whispered as if she could override his sense of obligation, his ego, *This isn't your job. For sure it's not the boys' calling.* But they went, her husband and sons. Josh was a grown man. He'd done such things before. Pursuing men that wouldn't listen to reason because, to do so, would get their necks snapped courtesy of the state. And Caleb and Noah, they were boys even if their facial hair and the guns they wore said otherwise. To Sarah they would always be boys.

It'd been just yesterday that she'd watched Josh pedaling the stationary grinding wheel down in the old weathered log building that served as their shop. Sparks flew as the sandstone ground the metal to a keen edge. He held the hoe up for her inspection. *Figure that'll do ya?* She smiled and nodded. He was her fixer of all things. Always had been.

Between the rows of waist high corn and a potpourri of shin high vegetables were occasional intruders. They never lasted long. Sarah took pride in her garden. It was situated on the south side of their house next to a little trickle of water called Papoose Creek. Quaking aspen and tall, lush grass defined its course. Her garden was good sized, maybe close to an acre. To irrigate it, Josh had cut a shallow ditch from the creek. A small wooden headgate diverted the water whenever the board was inserted. Sarah had just done that and was not quite out of the trees when she saw them, three black dots that briefly sky-lined themselves before dropping down into scattered timber. Sarah knew the slope well. She knew the reason the trees were not thick there was because, years ago, her and Josh had cut down a good many of them to build their cabin and out buildings. She knew too that beyond that ridge was rough country. An unlikely place for three men on horseback to have come from without a pack animal. Having lived in the Grays Lake country for almost twenty-two years had made her real savvy about things that didn't seem right.

From beneath the brim of her tattered black felt hat she looked out at the approach of the riders. They were coming slow. Even though there were storm clouds building, she cupped her hands at eye level to see better. It became apparent then that one of the horses was lame. In that instant, before her mind could process the potential ramifications of this, her eyes shifted to their horses in the pasture next to the barn. There were seven of them, all good animals broke to ride. A surge of adrenaline caused her legs to move. She stepped over the little ditch with the water probing its way towards the garden. On she went at a quick pace now. Their back porch was screened in. Sarah let the spring-loaded door slam behind her. She brushed past the old faded green couch with white stuffing sticking out of the arm nearest her leg and opened the door to the kitchen. She did not slow her heart beating far faster than need be. *Oh Josh, why aren't you here.* From the wooden pegs on the wall near the front door she took down her "skunk getter," a double barreled 12

Gauge shotgun so named for the skunks she'd dispatched who'd gotten into the chicken coop near the barn. Her hands were trembling as she broke the action to make sure of the gun's readiness. Her mind flashed back over twenty years to the time she'd killed a man to save Josh's life. Back then there'd been no doubt what to do. Today, it was a bad feeling mustered from afar. The naysayer in her mind kept reminding her their place was almost two miles off the main road that led to town. There were other ranches, not many, along that road. And these men come here.

Sarah stepped to the window in the front room. It was four panes. Special order from Salt Lake City. Each piece of glass 12 inches square. *Got to be big enough to let the light in so I can grow flowers*, she'd told Josh. A slab board table the width of the window sat in front of it. Three tin lard cans bearing wildflowers were evenly spaced there. They bore colorful upright blue and white blooms that did nothing to disguise the fact that the buckets once contained "Morrell's Snow Cap Pure Lard."

She could see them more clearly now. They were on the wagon road that led right up to the house. They were pointing to the horses in the pasture, no doubt discussing which ones they would take. Sarah grimaced while suppressing the desire to whimper. She looked across the room to the rock fireplace and the Winchester lever gun that hung above it. *Holds more shells*, she thought. And then she laughed, outright laughed aloud. "You silly woman. If both barrels of the skunk getter doesn't discourage these boys, you're in trouble."

Several of the pasture horses trotted over to the worm fence, so called because its interlocking wooden poles zigzagged slightly to give it stability. There were lots of one-time lodgepole pine trees in the fence that the horses were now reaching over to nicker. The riders stopped next to the inquisitive animals. Sarah could hear bits and pieces of their banter.

"The bay's mine."

Laughter. "Not if I get my saddle on him first."

"The hell you say."

The third man who'd been mostly silent since they'd stopped at the fence said loud enough so as to cause them to pay heed, "Why don't you fools just holler over to the house there and tell them of your intentions?"

Slow to comply, one of the two talkers who wore a tan colored felt hat with a peaked crown and a red shirt that had a large stain on the left side proclaimed, "They're ours for the taking."

The man with some common sense, the cautionary man, shook his head. "Walter, one of these days that empty spot between your ears is gonna get you turned under."

Walter laughed and spate a stream of tobacco juice off to the side of his horse before coming back at the man reprimanding him. "For 37 years I've said what I like and done what I like and ain't no one put me in the ground yet."

For a moment, the common sense man said nothing. Just sat there on his horse with four good legs. Then he turned to the other talker, a pudgy man with a graying beard shaded by a black felt hat with a wide flat brim. "Pete," he said in a voice decidedly mocking in tone, "It has come to me that since Walter is the one with the lame horse that maybe you and me have no business here. I believe the prudent thing to do would be for us to ride on and let Walter, with his good luck, secure a new mount on his own accord. What say you?"

Walter cut in. "Fine, Hooper, you think you're such a smart sonovabitch then ride on out. The both of ya, but don't you forget the water in this crik flows both ways. There'll come a time when you'll need my help."

"Your help? Shootin' old ladies isn't the kind of help I need."

"It was an accident."

Hooper scoffed. "Those kind of accidents will make people chase you, chase us to the gates of hell.

Sarah gasped. Her suspicions were proving true. She began to slowly shake her head at the cavalier behavior of the strangers. Knowing what was likely coming caused her face to scrunch up with fear. She whispered, "Of all the days for you to be gone, Josh, why today?" And then, in her mind's eye she saw herself going out the back door and hiding in the woods. *Let them take what they want and leave.* For a moment she seriously considered this option. She'd even started for the door but then she heard him. The one called Hooper. "I'll do the talkin'. Ya hear me?" His voice struck her as smug and confident. Like he knew she was the only one on the place. A schoolmarm and Sunday school teacher to boot. That she was better suited to dealing with ten-year old boys than grown up killers. Like he could violate her family and all they'd worked for because he fancied himself a smooth talker that could ply her with politeness until he gauged the time right to reveal his intentions.

They stopped their horses next to the waist high split rail fence that bordered the grass surrounding the house. Hooper got down and began walking up the flat rock path that led from the opening in the fence through the rain-starved brown grass to the front door. His pace was like that of a deer wary of coming to water rather than a man with legitimate business.

Sarah stood still, far back in the room. The knock was solid. Three or four raps and then it was quiet. In her ears she could hear her heart pounding and she thought Hooper's spurs, just faintly. Nonetheless, she stood dead still. It wasn't that she'd changed her mind about confronting the men. Her paralysis was due more to the naïve hope that the men weren't evil and they'd go away if they couldn't raise anyone. But then the knock came again. "Anybody home?"

Sarah's heartbeat quickened. The naysayer in her mind shouted the impossible, the unreasonable. *Oh Lord, please in the name of Jesus make these men go away. Amen.*

From atop his lame horse, Walter called out, "Appears it's our lucky day."

Hooper glanced at Walter, said nothing and then knocked again, harder and louder.

Walter, feeling the tension between him and Hooper had eased some, shouted, "Hell, let's just go on in. See what's for breakfast."

"No Sir. You're not welcome here."

The robber's heads jerked in the direction of the voice. At the very instant they did so, their expressions of fear and surprise suggested they expected to die. Seconds later there was only mild relief when they saw it was a middle-aged woman who'd gotten the drop on them.

Hooper was first to recover. "Mornin', Ma'am."

Sarah had decided in the time it had taken her to slip out the back door and come up along the side of the house that she would capture these men. She knew what they'd done and that they would not go away without the fresh horses they'd come for. She knew too that because she was a woman, they'd likely not respect her authority, shotgun or not. She was committed now. She stepped out from the corner of the house in full view of them so that they could see both hammers of the Skunk-getter were cocked. She took a quick breath to steady her voice and said, looking mostly at Hooper, "You men need to unholster your pistols and drop them on the ground."

"Like hell I will," snarled Walter.

Sarah glared at Walter. "It would be a grievous error on your part to misjudge my abilities with this gun."

Walter ran his eyes over Sarah and the revelations her man attire provided. She was buxom and slender otherwise. He laughed. "I don't doubt your ability to do some things, female things, but using that shotgun takes moxie. You ever kill a man?"

The memory of that day nearly twenty-two years ago when she had killed two men as wicked as Walter flooded her mind. It angered her that she was being forced to recall that incident. Suddenly, she found herself moving towards Walter aiming both barrels at his face. She stopped maybe twenty feet away and seethed the words, "You will not get the better of me. Now, either throw down your pistol or I will send a load of buckshot your way."

In moving closer to Walter, Sarah had also given Hooper a better view of her face. It was this new perspective that caused an epiphany in him which he blurted out. "I know this woman, Walter. She means what she says."

Sarah instantly shifted her focus to Hooper searching his face for recollection of him in another time and place. And then he provided that.

"This woman's a whore from up in Montana. A little place called Bear Creek. She killed a crooked sheriff and one of his cronies up there years ago." He paused and laughed. "You better do what she says Walter, or she's liable to blow you right outta your saddle."

Sarah brought a hateful look to her face. "Mister, you're mistaken about who you think I am."

Hooper grinned. "A man tends to remember women that he's laid with."

A different Sarah, more like the Bear Creek Sarah, took hold of her tongue. "You're as full of shit as a Christmas goose."

"Spoken like a true whore."

Walter and Pete laughed.

Hooper went on. "I'll bet people think you're respectable being married and living here in a nice house. It'd be a shame if they was to find out who you really are."

Sarah felt helpless. She wanted to shout out, *Josh knows my past.* But he was the only one. Her boys didn't know nor did the school board or the church people. Not anyone here in her new life. Tears welled up in her eyes.

Hooper's look became cruel, gloating almost at his good fortune. Still in possession of his pistol, as were Pete and Walter, he said in a calm voice, "Here's what we're gonna do. We're going to swap our horses for some of yours. And out of the kindness of your reformed whore's heart you're going to fix us some food to take with us." He paused and smiled. "That sound good to you, cause if it doesn't, I'll tell all your neighbors who you really are."

Sarah felt helpless. The temptation to pull the Skunk-getter's trigger loomed in her mind. She could see Hooper being blown off his feet and, in the next instant, Walter tumbling from his horse. And then logic, or her conscience, crowded into the scene. After she had emptied her second barrel Pete would spur his horse rather than shoot her. So, there'd she be with two dead men that would join those from her past and together they would taunt her nightly. Or, maybe they would not wait until nightfall and her dreams but would come on a bright sunny morning like they had just last week. It was, of all things, cherry pie filling that gave them a nexus to her mind's eye. Red and pulpy. Double OO buckshot does nasty things to human flesh. And that cherry pie, it was their pastor's favorite. If he only knew. Sarah lowered her gun. She looked hatefully at Hooper. "Alright, but I pick which horses you take."

Hooper laughed. "No, we pick 'em."

"Some of those belong to my boys."

Hooper scoffed. "A whore with kids."

Sarah raised the shotgun again towards Hooper. "You bastard. I should just shoot you."

"Go ahead but you won't live to touch off that second barrel. And then who would tuck in your boys at night, or more importantly, pleasure that man of yours. As I recall it was pleasurable." Seeing the instant anger in Sarah's eyes caused Hooper to laugh some more as did Walter and Pete.

Walter glanced first at Hooper, maybe to gauge the receptiveness of what he was about to say, and then looked at Sarah. "Maybe me an' Pete should take a turn. See for ourselves if she's good as you say."

Sarah shifted the gun back to Walter and sighted down its barrels directly at his chest. "It's time for you guys to leave. Just take the horses and leave. If you step down with other intentions, I've got nothing to lose. So, you've got ten seconds to rein your horse around and head for the pasture or I will kill you."

Walter's eyes were fixed on the dark openings at the end of the Skunk getter's barrels. The bravado in his face melted as he jerked the reins of his horse and started away. Over his shoulder he shouted. "You'll get yours, Bitch."

Saying nothing, Pete fell in behind Walter.

Sarah brought the gun to bear on Hooper. "Your turn."

"Not without our food."

"I'll bring it to you."

"Alright, just know that I'll be knockin' on your door if you don't. And know too, my patience with you and that scattergun has run out."

Sarah frowned. "You'll have your food."

They singled out the biggest and strongest horses. Those that looked like they could outrun a posse. And true to her word, Sarah came to the pasture with a Blue Bird flour sack filled with sandwiches, dried fruit and a couple of quart Mason jars full of coffee. She set it on the ground near the fence where they had tied the horses so they could saddle them. She briefly made eye contact with Hooper and then started to walk away.

Hooper called out in a disingenuous tone. "Much obliged, Ma'am." And then he laughed.

Sarah thought to keep on walking, but her anger wouldn't allow it. She paused and looked Hooper in the eyes. "There will come a day when my husband will kill you and your friends. When that day is all depends on how far you go from this place." She then continued walking towards the house. In the pasture to her left a Meadow Lark called out and a gentle breeze rattled the leaves of the Quaking Aspen next to the house. Behind her, it was dead silence.

The muscles in Sarah's back were taut as if they could deny a bullet access to her internal organs. She envisioned it, felt it plowing through her flesh. Saw herself stumbling and falling there on the road and bleeding out. When Josh and the boys came home she'd be lying there, likely minus her eyes and any exposed flesh courtesy of the ravens and turkey vultures. But the bullet did not come. Only when she had reached the front porch did she dare turn around. They were riding off, Hooper and the others, on fresh horses headed east to Wyoming. It came to her then, as she stood and watched until they disappeared in the dark timber, that she would not tell Josh. She wouldn't, she couldn't tell anyone how she'd bargained her reputation for their horses. Horses that had been born on the place and had been given names by her boys and cared for by them and would now cause tears to come to their eyes because they were young men with feelings. There'd be no understanding that.

CHAPTER TWO

Other than some biscuits and elk jerky, Josh and his boys had nothing to eat. It was more, however, than most of the posse had as they'd followed Tom Percy's lead. As sheriff he dictated how things would work and right from the git-go it was evident that they would be sleeping in their own beds tonight whether they caught the robbers or not.

They'd gone a good ways on the road to Eagle Rock inquiring of folks if they'd seen three men, one of them on a paint horse. *No, can't say as I have*, or some such was the standard reply. Each encounter, however, required Tom to explain his reason for asking by telling how the bank in Soda Springs had been robbed. Around three o'clock they met a man driving a wagon loaded with barbed wire. Two stout looking chestnut colored Belgians were pulling it. The driver, a middle aged man who had the sleeves of his sweat stained blue denim shirt rolled up to the elbows, reined the team to a stop. He spied Tom's badge right off. "Afternoon, Sheriff."

"She hot enough for ya?"

The man laughed, his tobacco stained teeth barely showing through his black walrus moustache. "Just the way I like it."

Tom bobbed his head and grinned. "Yeah, it don't do any good to bitch about it I reckon."

From beneath his sharply peaked Stetson the man's eyes roved over the posse before settling on the sheriff. "What brings you and yer friends out this way?"

"Lookin' for some fellas. Three of 'em. One's ridin' a paint. You seen anybody like that?"

The wagon driver came back as quick as if he was swatting a fly. "Nope. Ain't seen nobody that looks like that."

Josh, who was sitting on his horse straight out from the guy at eye level, could see the uneasiness in the man's green eyes. It ignited a flame of doubt in his mind that flared up considerably as the man glanced down at the Winchester leaning across the seat beside him.

Tom went on. "Well, if you see these ruffians be wary of them. They robbed the bank in Soda Springs and killed Bessie Perks for no good reason. Shot her right in the face. They're scoundrels of the highest order."

"Hell, Sheriff, I had my money in that bank How much did they make off with?"

"About $12,000. Purty much everything. Lotta folks lost their life savings."

"Helluva note, Sheriff. Hope you catch those boys."

"You come from Eagle Rock this morning?"

"I did. Left about ten."

The sheriff nodded. "Good to know."

And then the wagon driver tightened his grip and rippled the reins over the horse's backs. "Giddup. Hope you catch those boys."

The Sheriff turned in his saddle and began talking in a low voice to his permanent deputy. While they decided what to do some of the posse watched, some did not, as the stranger's wagon rattled on down the road. Caleb was among the watchers. Before the wagon was out of sight he nudged his horse alongside his father's and whispered, "I don't believe I care for that fella."

Josh nodded but remained focused on the Sheriff and his deputy's conversation. And then it was decided.

"Alright, men. We're gonna start working our way back to town."

Josh thought to challenge the decision. *Shouldn't we go on to Eagle Rock. Let the law there know to be on the lookout for these boys.* But then he thought of Sarah being home alone and how that worried him and how he could sleep in his own bed tonight with her safe and sound. And besides, he banked in Eagle Rock. And then his conscience thrust Bessie Perks into his mind's eye. Shame flooded over him for thinking the way he was. He was forming up the words to object to going back when he realized his horse was standing alone. Even his sons were lined out with the others.

They soon caught up with the wagon and passed him. The Sheriff waved. The wagon driver merely looked over and back. Over the next several miles they encountered a couple of less traveled roads going off from the one they were on. At the time, Josh thought it would be logical that the wagon man might live down one or the other of them. After a while, when they'd gone maybe another five miles towards home through sagebrush parks bordered by aspen groves that often gave way to dark timber, they came to a faint, seldom used road. The Sheriff reined his horse in so he could share with the others what he and his full-time deputy had been discussing for the past mile. "Men, I got a gut feeling about this country to the west of us. I believe it might prove worthwhile if we was to make a swing through it. Just a hunch and we'll still be headed in the direction of town."

A skinny man sitting a bay horse in front of Josh and his boys came back. "Sheriff, we ain't had a for certain track to follow from the start of this goose chase. To me, chasing outlaws on a hunch is kinda like playing roulette and I ain't never had much luck at that."

The crow's feet at the corners of the Sheriff's eyes bunched up in a way that suggested he felt insulted. He made no effort to hide his displeasure as he scrutinized his critic. The man was wearing a slate-colored Stetson that was curled slightly on the right side, not like he'd done it on purpose but rather it was due to having been blown off or thrown down and left for a time. And he had a six-shooter in a cross-draw position on his left hip and dark brown chaps and spurs. A real buckaroo, in appearance. The men waited, thinking what the skinny man had dared to say but holding their tongues. A horse snorted wearily, impatiently. A Steller's Jay screeched in the big pine tree next to the road. Finally Tom Percy, Sheriff for the last ten years, spoke. "Gimme your badge and you can be on your way."

The skinny man snorted. His adrenaline filled fingers fumbled to remove the deputy's badge he'd gotten just that morning. At last, it came free of his gray shirt and in that same motion he tossed it from about 15 feet away. It was the Sheriff's arthritic hand that failed to catch it. He looked down. Most of them did. The badge had come to rest in a fresh pile of horse shit. The Steller's Jay screeched again and again as if to verbalize Tom Percy's thoughts, *You sorry sonovabitch. If I was a younger man, I'd whip your ass.* He looked at the skinny man and shook his head in disgust. "You're free to ride on."

Zeke, the Sheriff's only real deputy, jumped down from his horse and retrieved the badge. He rubbed it in some dirt and then grass and then on his pant cuff before handing it up to Tom who nodded his appreciation. The skinny man, who'd spurred his horse to a canter to distance himself from his shame, was already rounding a bend in the tree lined road.

Tom looked at the rest of them. "You're free to follow that fella if you're of a mind to."

To his surprise and disappointment, another man, middle-aged, a farmer whose only weapon was a Winchester in a saddle scabbard spoke up. "I'm sorry, Sheriff, but I got chores to do."

Tom nodded. "Thanks for your help." The farmer rode off. "Anybody else want to quit? Now's your chance."

The men looked at one another. Some, hopeful that if there was another quitter amongst them the Sheriff would call off this extension of the goose chase he was now proposing. Josh was never good at keeping his thoughts from bleeding through to his eyes. Knowing this, he took the fixings from his shirt pocket and went about rolling a cigarette mostly as a disguise. By and by he blew smoke into the air feigning disinterest in the apprehension that gripped the Sheriff's face.

After a while, not a long time, the Sheriff took their silence, their downward looks as approval of how he'd conducted the day. However, in that dark corner of his mind where a person sees themselves as they really are, he knew that he was wrong in thinking he could save face with this last minute detour. Nonetheless, he declared, "Alright, men, let's move on."

And so they did, with the Sheriff and his real deputy leading the way riding side by side in a wagon road that led to an abandoned homestead. The road saw little use. In places it disappeared all together beneath the encroaching carpet of sage and yellow grass. To either side of it were Ponderosa pine trees.

In less than a mile they came to a log cabin that Josh knew had been there almost twenty-one years. He knew this because the German couple who had built it did so about a year after he and Sarah had settled here in 1870. After three years of trying to grow wheat and burying their first born behind the cabin, the Germans gave up and moved away.

As they rode by, Caleb pointed to a raven perched in the frame of the window to the right of the door. "I don't know why people have to be so mean spirited bustin' out windows like that."

Noah conjectured mostly serious, "Same reason they steal people's money and shoot old ladies, I reckon,"

Josh said over his shoulder, "I suspect the fella that shot Bessie Perks ratcheted his meanness up several notches above whoever busted those windows."

Undeterred in his belief, Noah came back. "I'll betcha, Pa, the fella that shot Mrs. Perks and the ones that busted the windows are cut from the same bolt of cloth. One of 'em's wickedness has just had a little more time to cure."

And so they rode on, the lot of them, without regard for the noise they made. It was pointless anyway. No savvy person, least of all a bank robber and killer, would sit on their haunches and ignore the warning cries of Steller's jays and pine squirrels. The posse made their loop through the timbered low hills. Josh guessed less than two miles, but enough off the main road to ease the Sheriff's conscience.

CHAPTER THREE

Sarah was not a practiced liar. She wasn't a liar at all but, in this situation, she feared the truth would not serve her well. She knew her neighbors. She taught their kids through the eighth grade and Sunday School too. They were God-fearing and sometimes generous to a fault. Forgiving a whore though, that would be different. She was certain of it. Even if they did, their forgiveness would pale in comparison to her son's shame and disappointment in her. She had no choice.

Sarah allowed the back porch's screen door to slam behind her. The sound of it caused their black and white mutt dog to come bounding out of the trees along the creek. He stopped just short of her and began prancing about in anticipation of going someplace.

With an empty lard bucket in her left hand and the Skunk-getter in her right, she could not pet him. She paused, however, and surprisingly mustered a happy voice. "Oh, Buster, I'm glad to see you too. Have you been off chasing squirrels again? You wanna go get some chokecherries? Well, let's go."

She'd already made one batch of jam and syrup. Making another had not been her intention when she'd gotten up this morning but concocting a lie for her family hadn't been either.

It was common knowledge that the best chokecherries were a half mile or more up the creek. A little past noon Sarah had filled her bucket. Close to two gallons worth, she figured. Time to go home. Continue the ruse by making syrup and practice her lie. That would be the tough part. She'd never lied to Josh. Not even a white one. Her allegiance to that fact wasn't due only to his having rescued her from a mining camp saloon. It was more. They both recognized the futility of building anything based on lies.

Buster snapped the air trying in vain to exact revenge on the deer flies that pestered him. Sarah reached over and ruffled his ears. "Alright, let's go home. I'm tired of the flies too."

Had it not been for the flies, she would have stayed on in the shade beneath the aspen trees. As it was, they'd lingered another hour after she'd filled her bucket in a kind of erroneous self-delusion. *The horses were gone when I came back from picking chokecherries..*

In spite of the house being shaded somewhat by aspens on the south side and Ponderosa pines to the west and north, the kitchen had heated up under the August sun. It had been helped along too by Sarah boiling the chokecherries on their wood burning cook stove. She was in the process of swabbing the beads of sweat from her forehead with the back of her hand when Buster began barking out front. Her heartbeat quickened as she knew Josh was likely home. She paused at almost the same place in the living room where she'd stood this morning looking out at Hooper and his friends. As she expected, Josh and the boys stopped at the barn next to the pasture. They'd not even gotten down from their horses when Caleb, their oldest son, yelled, "Something ain't right here, Pa."

And then Noah, the one she feared would hurt the most from having his horse stolen, chimed in, "Snookers and Baldy are gone. And Boots too. He ain't here either."

Unable to take anymore, Sarah backed away from the window and went to the kitchen like she hadn't heard Buster nor her sons. The time when she'd have to tell her story, her lie, would come soon enough without her walking down to the barn. She hoped the tears in her eyes would be gone by then.

They went horseback searching the woods on the far side of the pasture for their horses and looking for a hole in the fence that might explain what they were seeing. After about a half hour their wishful thinking gave way to reality. It was Caleb who assembled the bits and pieces of speculation they'd tossed out while searching. "Pa, you think it was those bank robbers that did this?"

Josh shot a stream of tobacco juice from beneath his salt and pepper moustache off to the side into the powdery dirt. He then brushed away the drop that clung to his moustache with the back of his hand. "I wouldn't bet against it, Son. Stands to reason those robbers rode their horses hard, probably through the mountains avoidin' the roads."

"That paint is gimpin' purty bad," said Noah.

"All three of'em is played out."

Caleb tossed his head. "Guess that's why we couldn't catch 'em."

"Naw, I thought all along we was pissin' in the wind staying on the road to Eagle Rock until late in the day."

"I know, Pa. I was of the same mind. Too damned many tracks on that road to make sense of who made 'em."

Josh nodded. "Maybe that's what the robbers were counting on."

"Or maybe the sheriff's just yellow."

Josh frowned at Noah. "Those thoughts are best left unspoken."

"It ain't my thought, Pa. That came from one of the posse deputies. I heard him say it not long after those fellas quit us."

"Don't matter. That's a serious accusation."

Caleb came back. "Hell, Pa, the man's being paid to do a job. All we did today is go for a ride."

"I know. Just the same, calling a man a coward is serious business."

Noah hung his head. "Sorry, Pa."

Josh came back forcing his voice to be cheerful. "The important thing is there's smoke coming out the chimney, so your Ma is alright."

"And supper is on the stove," said Caleb.

"What about our horses?" pined Noah. "We gonna go after 'em?"

Josh sighed. The sun was down causing a huge shadow to cover the land. "Not tonight. We'll see what morning brings."

They brushed and grained their horses before starting for the house. In spite of its ineffectiveness, the goose chase had been arduous. Taking care of your horses, before all else, was something Josh insisted on.

Sarah knew full well what the routine of Josh and the boys would likely be upon their return. And vice-versa, they would expect her to meet them at the door if not come to the front porch and wave from afar. Tonight, none of that was the case.

Immediately upon opening the door the sweet smell of the syrup enveloped them.

Josh looked to the empty kitchen and called out. "Sarah."

For a moment there was silence punctuated by the pendulum of the clock hanging above the couch and the snapping and popping of the stove. He was about to call again when he heard the whirring of the cream separator through the open door to the back porch. He said, his voice prideful of the woman he'd married, "Your Ma's been busy milkin' Deary and makin' syrup too."

"And she'll probably be churnin' that cream into butter come mornin'." said Caleb.

Josh kept on across the kitchen towards the back porch leaving the boys to hang their gun belts and hats on wooden pegs near the front door.

Sarah had heard them come in but pretended that she hadn't, cranking the heavily geared separator with her back to the door. Cream trickled out one pour spout splashing gently into a metal bowl while next to it a larger stream of fat free milk cascaded from another spout into a larger bowl. She was intent on watching the level of raw milk falling in the main bowl when she felt a playful slap on her butt. She twisted her head around to give Josh a kiss while continuing to turn the crank.

And then it began, his green eyes were soft and clear and not in the least condemning. "I take it you ain't been by the horse pasture lately."

Before she'd had time to consider her response the words began to pour out like the raw milk when, in fact, she would have been better off trickling a few words like the cream. "No, I haven't. I was gone for a good while today. Buster and I went up the creek to pick chokecherries. We didn't get home till late. I don't remember when exactly, close to milking time, but I worked the cherries before I got to Deary and, oh my, I guess I never gave much thought to the pasture."

Sarah's avalanche of words caused Josh's expression to become curious, puzzled almost. "You never noticed anything odd when you brought Deary in from the pasture?"

"No, she was right near the barn."

Josh laughed. "Well, remind me to never leave you to guard the chicken coop."

Sarah's heart jumped into her throat. "Why's that?"

"Somebody swapped three played out horses for three of ours."

Sarah looked quickly back to the separator. "Oh, for land sakes. That would take a lot of nerve."

"And time. It's good that you were gone this afternoon. I would hate for you to have to deal with them."

Sarah knew that Josh would wonder why she wasn't more angry, incensed that someone would steal the boy's horses. She knew too that she should say something condemning. To do so, however, would only immerse her deeper into the façade she was perpetuating on her husband of almost 22 years. Fortunately for her, the last of the raw milk drained from the biggest bowl allowing her to stop cranking. As if she'd forgotten what they'd been talking about she picked up clean cheese cloths from a small table next to the separator and covered the metal bowls with the cream and fat free milk. She did not look at him when she spoke. Her paranoia and shame wouldn't allow it. "You want to help me take these to the icehouse?"

Josh nodded and picked up the bigger bowl with the fat-free milk. He held the screen door open for her.

Always the gentleman, she thought, *and I'm lying to him.* The door slapped shut behind them.

They walked in silence for a moment before Josh called out from behind her. "The boys are pretty pissed off their horses being stolen. They're chompin' at the bit to gittem back."

The image of Hooper telling on her, should they catch up to him, came to mind with startling alacrity. "No Josh, there could be gun play if they were to do that. I don't want my boys getting killed over horses."

"Hon, you know in these times and in this country, you got to defend what's yours or folks 'll run rough shod over you."

"Report this to the sheriff. It's his job to catch these men."

Josh laughed. "Hell, I may as well go tell Santa Claus as Tom Percy."

They went quiet walking past the garden towards where the root cellar and icehouse sat side by side. Sarah's conscience jabbed at her. *He knows my past. I should just tell him.* The naysayer within her scoffed. *Yeah, tell him that your past came to visit today and that he threatened to tell how for two dollars anybody in Bear Creek could ride your loins.*

From the outside they looked the same. Inside, below ground level, they were different. The root cellar was for storing potatoes, carrots, onions, apples and such while the icehouse, whose walls were lined with blocks of ice cut from Papoose Creek in the winter, was for keeping meat and milk and butter cold.

The darkness inside the icehouse was the consistency of molasses. It necessitated leaving the door ajar so they could see to place the bowls on a shelf to their right. Hanging from the ceiling on the opposite side of the room were the quarters of a mule deer buck that Josh had shot not quite a week ago. In the near darkness Sarah looked at the meat. "You want venison steaks for supper?"

"Ain't nuthin' better. That an' some fried spuds and biscuits."

Sarah stepped to the small table along the back wall and lit the kerosene lantern sitting on it. In the pale yellow light she saw to pick up the knife from the table being careful to not make eye contact with Josh. "I'll cut some steaks if you'll fetch me a platter from the house."

Josh sensed the usual Sarah was elsewhere. *Got to put her mind at ease about us going after those horse thieves.* He said aloud, "I'll send Noah with the platter."

Sarah purposely began carving a steak with her back to Josh. "You need to think again about going to the sheriff on those horse thieves."

"Maybe we can talk some more on the matter after supper."

And then the door closed. The outside light went away. Sarah could barely hear the ravens perched in the trees outside. She laid the first steak on the table and turned back to the hanging meat hoping that her tears would stop before Noah came.

CHAPTER FOUR

It wasn't dark when they rode into Freedom, Wyoming but close to it. The timber covered mountains behind them were contrasted by a faint glow on the Idaho side. A brown dog was trotting along in front of the drab log and clapboard structures to their left. To their right a couple of horses were tied to the hitching rail in front of the Antler Saloon. Its front door stood open in hopes, more so, of drawing in the cooler night than the improbable customer at this hour in this little spit of a town. Yellow light spilled out the door and dimly through dirty four paned windows to either side of it.

Walter broke the silence. "I could do with a drink. Been a long ass ride here."

In another hundred yards or so was a large barn like structure made of rough lumber and devoid of any paint except on the façade over its big double doors. Blocky white letters about two feet tall read: LIVERY. A pole corral was attached to the barn's going out of town side. Hooper nodded towards the stable. "Let's settle the horses in first."

Pete frowned. "I still ain't real good with the notion ah stayin' here."

Hooper came back with casual indifference not even looking at Pete. "Gonna be alright. Nobody knows us here and I seriously doubt they know what happened on the other side of the mountain."

"I'll remind you of that if we end up in the hoosegow."

Walter cut in. "I ain't going to nobody's jail."

Hooper whispered angrily. "You two shut-up."

Walter and Pete, somewhat surprised, looked his way. Hooper nodded to his left and a small log building with bars on the window looking out to the street. A white wooden sign with black lettering that read, CITY MARSHAL hung above the door. Light from inside sliced through the bars.

Hooper hissed again, "You fools." His words were barely audible above the rhythmic creaking of their saddles and the weary plodding of their horses' hooves in the soft dirt and manure. In another fifty yards they came to the livery katy-corner to the marshal's office.

Walter whispered sarcastically. "Well, ain't this handy."

They'd just stepped down from their horses when a voice called out from the cavern of darkness through the open doors. "Can I help you boys?"

Hooper shouted back to a shadowy form of a man in a chair. "We need to put our horses up for the night."

The old man grunted as he rose from the rocker, he'd dragged out between the two rows of stalls so he could look out at the street and, it appeared, pick and choose who he revealed his presence to. He began hobbling towards them. When he was nearly to the doorway he said in a gravelly voice, "Be four bits a head." He paused and added like he'd been stiffed before, "In advance."

Hooper dug two dollar bills out of his pants pocket and handed them to the man. "You got a good place to eat in this town."

"Nope."

"Walter cut in, "There ain't no place to eat?"

The old man paused, still frowning at having to apply his stiff bony fingers to one of the dollars that was wadded up, "I didn't say that. Your friend asked about a good place. What we got ain't worth a shit."

Hooper sighed. "Well, where is this place?"

"Hotel, but it's closed."

Pete, who'd been counting on sleeping in a bed, blurted out, "It's closed?"

"Eatin' part is. Be open at six in the morning if you wanna take yer chances."

Walter scowled at Hooper. "You shudda made that whore girlfriend ah yours fix more food for us."

"Maybe if you'd been nicer to her she would have."

Walter scoffed. "Maybe if she'd have put that damned scattergun down I wudda."

Pete laughed.

Walter went on. "Once a whore always a whore. I don't care if she's married or not. Those kind never change."

Hooper sensed the old man was taking a reading of their moral compass and it wasn't good. "That's enough."

The old man pivoted off of the alarm in Hooper's voice and feigned momentary confusion. "Let's see. Three horses, right?"

"Right. You owe me four bits."

The old man neatly folded the bills in half and stuck them in the breast pocket of his blue cotton shirt whose sleeves were rolled to his elbows. He then came back wanting to put distance between what he'd just soaked up and they're thinking he might see fit to mention it to the marshal since it involved a whore and a shotgun. "Four bits ya say?"

Hooper scowled and shook his head. "Yeah, you owe me four bits."

The old man exaggerated putting his hand in the pocket of his Levi's and pulling out some coins. He stared at the money for a few seconds before finally picking up a quarter and holding it out to Hooper."

"I need another two bits."

The old man looked at the coins in his hand carefully taking one at a time, two dimes and a nickel and handing them over. "There ya go."

Hooper looked at the old man as if to gauge what was behind his watery blue eyes and droopy white moustache. It was his own stupidity that might have given the man reason to question their character. He thought to dilute the suspicion. "We're lookin' for work. You know of any ranches that might be hiring."

The old man shook his head. "You night ask down at the Antler. The bartender there would probably know if anybody does."

Hooper continued the ruse. "Much obliged. We'll hunt that fella up after we find us a room."

The old man's uneasiness with these strangers that he judged to be south of the law had been building since the talk of the whore with the shotgun. At the time he'd immediately wondered if this woman, whore or not, had good reason to pull a gun on these men. It worried him now that they might take him for some busybody with nothing better to do than walk the fifty yards to the marshal's office and spin a tale of speculation as to why it was a whore threw down on them with a shotgun. He'd been wishing hard, just short of the voice in his head breaking into prayer, when salvation of a sort came riding into town from the east. It was obvious the riders, a middle-aged man and a teenage boy, were coming to the livery. The old man looked their way. "Well I'll be go to hell. I ain't had this much business since I can't remember when."

Behind the old man, Hooper and the others removed their rifles and saddlebags from their horses. Hooper called out. "Hey Mister, we'll be back for our horses 'bout seven in the morning."

The old man did not look at Hooper. He tossed the words over his shoulder. "They'll be ready."

The stolen horses stood patiently where their reins had been dropped. The new strangers stopped next to them and dismounted. The old man spoke first. "Evenin'."

The bigger rider, who had a coiled lariat hanging on the right side of his saddle partially obscuring the curved butt stock of a Winchester in a scabbard, came back. "Got room for two more?"

"I do. Run ya four bits a piece."

Without prodding the rider pulled a dollar bill from his Levi's and stepped towards the old man, the rowels of his spurs jingling as he did. "Here ya go."

The old man took the dollar and stuffed it in his shirt pocket next to the two dollars he'd collected from Hooper. He came back. "Where do you boys hail from?"

The rider nodded towards the dark silhouette of the mountains at the far end of the street. "Idaho. Grays Lake country. Got a ranch over there."

The old man noted the heavy sweat stains surrounding the crown of the rider's gray Stetson. "So, what brings you to our side of the mountains?"

"Bulls. Purebred Angus bulls."

From the other side of their horses came the voice of the boy. "Pa, come look at these brands."

Alarm seized the old man's face. He mumbled, "I knew it."

The boy's father glanced at the old man but kept walking with the old man trailing after him.

The boy was pointing to a haired over but still legible brand on the left flank of the horse with the four white leggings. "Look, Pa. It's Josh Morrow's brand."

The old man cut in. "Fella ridin' this horse is kinda short and chunky. Older, but not as old as me."

The boy snorted. "That ain't none of the Morrows."

There was concern that bordered on fear of where this might go on his father's face. He laughed nervously. "Well, you know mister detective, it could be Josh sold this horse."

The boy shook his head. "No, Pa. I know these horses. This is Boots. It's Noah's horse. He'd never sell it. And this one is Snookers and that big bay is Baldy. They both belong to Caleb. There ain't no way in hell those guys would sell these horses."

The old man offered. "The fellas ridin' these horses claimed to be lookin' for ranch work but my take on 'em is they've got an aversion to honest labor. They was quibbling about some woman they said was a whore who pulled a shotgun on them. One of them groused about her not fixing them enough food."

The boy's father came back. "They say what color hair this woman had or anything about her?"

"No, but just the way they talked I took it she was a looker."

The boy said it. "Sounds like Mrs. Morrow."

The father said, "They say what kind of shotgun this woman had? Was it a pump, double barrel, single barrel?"

"They didn't say."

The boy became cocky. Like when it came right down to poking this sleeping bear he would be the one to do it and not his father, which he knew wouldn't be the case. Hence, he pointed out his father's reluctance stopping short of calling it what some people might. "Pa, you need to get the law after these fellas. Call 'em on what they've done."

The man looked at his son. He had a lot of spunk for sixteen. Right now, he wished that he didn't. It had put him in an awkward spot. Not his son. Not the old man. Just him.

Even to an outsider looking at the situation it would be only logical that he should be the one to get the marshal and go with him to the Antler. And so it was, the boy waited with the old man and tended to the horses while his father did what a man is supposed to do.

The marshal, whose name was Herb, walked with a slight limp. The boy's father, whose name was Orville Duke, slowed his pace to accommodate him. Orville said, "Do you often get ruffians like this in town."

"Not since I been marshal."

"How long has that been?"

"Almost six months."

Orville was taken aback. His surprise was such that he stopped dead in his tracks and looked at Herb. Where minutes ago, in the Marshal's office, he had seen wisdom and confidence in the deep wrinkles that cascaded away from Herb's cheek bones, he now saw the old livery man's twin. He said straight out, "How is it you became the marshal?"

"Well, didn't seem like anybody else wanted the job and I'd reached a point where all the ornery broncs I've tangled with over the years was makin' it purty damned tough to get up in the morning. So, I said to myself, why the hell not?"

Orville's insides had begun to betray him right when they had stepped out of the marshal's office and started up the street. He suddenly felt like he needed to take a piss and was wishing he'd done that before now, and he was wishing too that him and his son had just camped along the trail somewhere. Him and Jeremy would likely be sipping coffee now and looking at the stars. But they'd not come equipped for that. He'd decided at Jeremy's urging to "town it". And so, here he was about to walk through an open door and maybe the end of his life. He looked at Herb, who seemed unphased by what awaited them inside the Antler, "You know accusin' these boys ah bein' horse thieves is likely to get 'em purty riled up."

Herb laughed indifferently. "Yeah, I figure it will."

Orville looked down at Herb's holstered Army Colt. "You ever shot anybody with that?"

"Not since I left the Army I haven't."

The marshal's stove up posture and deeply wrinkled face tempted Orville to press him on the matter. He was a few seconds into pondering this when Herb fired back at him. "What about you?

Regret that he'd ever opened this can of worms took hold of Orville. He said, barely above a whisper, "No, no I never have."

Herb did not lord it over him that he'd killed men some thirty years ago, as someone might have if their abilities had been questioned. He let it go. "I'm the one drawing the paycheck for enforcing the law, so I'll ask the questions. They go for their guns though I'd appreciate some help."

Orville nodded. He was seeing Herb in a different light now. Knowing that he would be going into the Antler with an experienced man killer to face men who might want to do the same to him eased his fear somewhat. They started walking. The Antler's door not more than twenty-five feet away. Orville could hear voices and now laughter. He thought, a *laughing man wouldn't kill somebody.*

Herb whispered. "Stay by the door with your back to the wall."

Orville made eye contact but said nothing. And then they were inside. The talk stopped about the same time as the jingling of Orville's spurs did. Hooper and Pete were seated at a table about halfway into the long skinny room. Across from them was a smooth cherry wood bar. A short fat man with receding brown hair and a bushy moustache stood behind it. Two cowboys, real working cowboys that smelled of sweat and manure and the pungent odor of burnt hair and hide of calves they'd branded just that day, sat in front of the bartender. They could see themselves in the big mirror above the liquor bottles on the back bar. They could see too that Herb and a stranger had come in and that the stranger was acting peculiar, leaning up against the wall to the right of the door like he was. Hooper and Pete took note of the strangers as well. It was Pete who was dumb enough to outright point at Herb's badge. "There comes John Law."

Hooper frowned at Pete before taking another drink of his beer and trying to ignore Herb's approach.

"Evenin' boys."

For a few seconds silence, save for the ticking of a clock on the wall above Hooper's table, engulfed the room. The clock's bold black Roman numerals read 10:15. As if the decorum of potential violence required it, nobody moved or spoke. The cowboys did not spit in the brass spittoon next to their stools. Nor did they take a puff from the smoldering cigarettes they held. Nor did they dare take a drink. At least five seconds of ear ringing quiet went by before the smirk on Hooper's face gave way to a response. "What can I do for you, Marshal?"

"Your horses, the ones you and your friends just left at the livery, how'd you come by them?"

"Bought 'em."

"When was that?"

"A long time ago. Coupla years back I reckon."

"Who'd you buy 'em from?"

"I don't recall."

"You got a bill of sale?"

Hooper snorted sarcastically. "Would you carry around a bill of sale from two years ago?"

Herb's heart began to pound faster, painfully fast. He wondered if he might have a heart attack and be free of saying what came next. Soft yellow light flooded upwards from a chimney lantern perched on a shelf beneath the clock. The big hand clicked rigidly forward one notch to 10:16. Herb wondered if he was going to see 10:17. And then he lit the fuse. "Well, Mister, I got reliable witnesses that say these horses belong to some folks over in the Grays Lake country of Idaho. And this was just last week, not two years ago."

From deeper in the room, just beyond the light cast by the lantern on the end of the bar, Walter shouted, "I told you we shouldn't have done business with that whore."

Herb looked towards the shadowy figure of a man that had apparently came in from the privy out back. "Why don't you come over and join our little parley?"

"I'm good where I'm at, thank you."

Orville shifted his attention to the voice at the rear of the room. There was a half dozen lanterns scattered about the front part of the bar but nothing by the back door. He sensed if there was trouble it would be this shadow man that would start it. By the tone of his voice, Orville surmised, *that fella doesn't give a shit about the law.*

Up to this point, the cowboys sitting at the bar had watched the drama unfolding in the mirror straight across from them. There was no need for them to turn around on their stools and gawk, lest they get drawn into something they wanted nothing to do with. They were nervous now. It was like they were watching a tornado approaching and had just decided it was time to go to the storm cellar. They had waited too long.

Herb stood, his arms hanging loose to his sides, not ten feet from the table where Hooper and Pete sat. He said, his voice beginning to falter, "Boys I wanna believe what you're tellin' me but I got folks that knows the horses your ridin' and they're convinced that the owners would never sell 'em."

Hooper sneered at Orville. "That fella huggin' the wall one of 'em?"

To his credit, Herb came back, "It don't matter who he is."

"Like hell it don't," shouted Walter from the shadows.

Hooper was angry now. "Stealin' horses is serious business. We got a right to know who it is that's accusing us."

It was easy to see that Herb knew he was in over his head and that he likely regretted signing on for sixty dollars a month to deal with the Hoopers of the world. Nonetheless, he stood his ground thinking back to when he'd had the moxie to fight the Sioux. He said, ignoring Hooper's demand, "In the morning I'm gonna send a telegram to the sheriff over in Soda Springs concerning this horse business. Hopefully, I'll get an answer in a day or so. Until I do, I don't want you boys leavin' town."

Enraged, Walter stepped from the shadows. "No Sir, that ain't gonna happen."

Herb looked straight at Walter, now able for the first time to see in his eyes the cold killer he was. "You can either walk the streets a free man until we clear this matter up or you can wait in our little jail. The choice is yours."

It may have been that the importance of time in situations like this caused Orville to notice the big hand clicking down to 10:18. And then, as the saying goes, all hell broke loose. Walter was not particularly quick in pulling his pistol but there was no hesitation in pointing it at Herb and pulling the trigger. The .44 Caliber bullet struck Herb solidly in the chest causing his knees to buckle. Fortunately for him, and less so for Walter, the moxie, the tenacity that he was hoping to recall from his days as a cavalry trooper flickered one last time. The look on Walter's face was more insult than surprise. He would have time to second guess why he hadn't shot the old marshal again instead of shooting their accuser.

Hooper had already shot Orville right through the heart. He'd never even gotten his gun out of his holster.

The acrid smell of gun smoke filled the room. The cowboys and the bartender remained still as statues, uncertain if the highly agitated men with drawn guns would see them as a threat to their escape.

Walter was gut shot, bleeding bad. He was laying on his back, looking up, his pistol hand outstretched. For a moment, Hooper stood over him just looking. There was no question that he was going to leave him to die. They'd never liked one another. And then to make sure that hatred didn't result in his getting shot in the back, Hooper kicked the gun out of Walter's hand. Pain tempered Walter's words. "You're a real sonovabitch, Hooper."

Hooper flashed an arrogant smile. "And you're not?"

The two of them, Hooper and Pete, then walked out the back door. They started running behind the mercantile next door and a café whose food must not have been worth a shit either as the old man at the livery hadn't even bothered to mention its existence. On they went in the direction opposite the livery rousing sleeping dogs as they ran. A cacophony of barking and at least one, *shut the hell up*, permeated the night air. At last, they came to the stairs at the rear of the hotel. It was none too soon as Pete's generous belly and the fear of being caught and hanged had him sucking wind. Although he knew why they had come to the hotel instead of straight to the livery he whimpered, "We gotta get outta here, Hooper."

Hooper abruptly stopped on the steps that led to the second story entrance. He leaned down close, within a few inches of Pete's face. His breath stank of cigarettes and beer. He whispered through clenched teeth. "You wanna leave the money behind?" He then shook his head. "Not another word."

Surprisingly, the gunshots at the Antler had not attracted much interest beyond the dogs and the proprietor of the hotel who stepped outside in time to see one of the cowboys at the bar walk across the street and disappear in the darkness to the side of the funeral home on his way, he supposed, to the undertaker's cabin behind it. The proprietor, a teetotaler and regular church goer, scoffed, "Those people." He then went back inside and locked his front door while some of *those people* went out the back door.

At about the time that Hooper and Pete found their way to the rear of the livery, Walter ran out of blood. To his mother it would have been a sad ending, laying there on the dark wood floor of the Antler. Wide eyed, staring up at the ceiling he was. Laying where, not more than a week ago, a sheepherder had puked on his way to the back door. It was questionable even if God would have felt sorry for Walter. Certainly not the cowboys. He'd killed the marshal, who was one of them until six months ago, and ruined their night in town. And the bartender was mad. Never mind that it was a despicable thing that Walter had done. *Somebody's gotta haul his sorry ass outta here and those bloodstains don't cleanup good. The sonavabitch.*

The old man and Jeremy heard the gunshots, muffled as they were inside the Antler, and had run out to the street in front of the livery. They searched the darkness, hopeful that some fantasy would play out where Orville and Herb would emerge unscathed from it. After a time, Jeremy got the sniffles. He turned towards the door of the livery. "I'm gonna get my rifle and go down there."

The old man grabbed Jeremy's left arm. "No son, your pa wouldn't want that. Wait here like he told you. Things 'll be alright. You'll see. "

A lantern hung from a beam just inside the door. It cast enough light on the old man's face that Jeremy could see he didn't believe what he was saying. He pushed the words out with a sob. "But it's my fault."

Ever since Orville and Herb had left, the old man had wrestled with his conscience on the rightness or wrongness of what they were doing. Not from the law's perspective. It was more common sense and self-preservation. He'd talked to those ruffians. Seen the look in their eyes. Never mind being a coward. No way in hell would he go down there. Just him and a broken down old cowboy looking for rocking chair money. No sir. He lied again to the kid. "You done the right thing, Son."

From deep inside the livery one of the horses nickered. And then, big as life, there came Hooper pistol in hand.

Jeremy cried out. "Where's my pa?"

A wry grin surfaced on Hooper's face. "Down at the Antler, I reckon."

"Well, why isn't he here?"

Hooper shrugged. "I don't know. Last I saw he was standin' at the bar, him and that marshal having a drink."

Beyond Hooper, Pete was busy saddling Snookers and Baldy. Jeremy took note of it causing the fear within him to surge. "Why are you leaving?"

"This ain't a friendly town. We no sooner ride in and we're falsely accused of being horse thieves."

"Well, you are."

Hooper stepped close to Jeremy. "You know we just settled this matter with the marshal and your pa. I'm in no mood to plow that same ground with you."

The old man could see the futility of the conversation as well as he could see the gaping hole in the barrel of Hooper's pistol. He mustered a non-threatening tone. "Let it go, Son. We'll go check on your pa later."

Jeremy glanced at the old man before looking hatefully at Hooper. "This fella is a liar through and through."

Hooper stepped to within arm's length of Jeremy and rested the barrel of his pistol on the boy's lower lip. The hammer was back. His finger was on the trigger. Jeremy began to cry and tremble. It appeared Hooper was going to blow the kid's head off when Pete, who possessed a modicum of decency, came up behind Hooper with the horses. "Ain't no point in making things worse."

Hooper laughed. "They can only hang you once."

"Maybe so, but leavin' another dead body in this town might just make 'em more determined to do that."

Hooper relaxed the hate in his face for a second or two, almost like he was sorry for shaming the kid, and then, quick as a snake bite he cold-cocked Jeremy with the barrel of his pistol. The kid went down like the earth had been jerked from beneath him. He was limp. Dead quiet. The right side of his face in the dirt. Blood was oozing out of the short dark hair on his left temple. The old man and Hooper's eyes lifted from Jeremy at about the same time. Hooper said, "I believe your years has made you smarter than this boy. Am I right?"

The old man came back quick, real quick. "Oh, yes sir. You won't get no trouble from me."

Hooper grinned and at last lowered the hammer on his pistol.

The old man, having already surrendered much of his pride, continued on in that vein. "You want your money back since you won't be staying?"

Hooper looked down from his saddle. "Naw, you can keep that for any inconvenience we might have caused you." He laughed again and then, reining his horse to avoid Jeremy's unconscious body, he and Pete rode east deeper into Wyoming.

CHAPTER FIVE

The difference of being on the right side of the law and having the appearance of a respectable citizen, as opposed to being an undisputed sonovabitch like Walter, was that the undertaker prepared Herb and Orville for a decent funeral. Walter, on the other hand, was buried in a plain pine box made of rough lumber. His grave was situated in Freedom's little cemetery well away from those people destined for heaven. A scrap piece of lumber leftover from making his coffin marked Walter's grave amongst the rocks and weeds. Black paint had been used for the lettering which hadn't been applied with concern for neatness. It read: WALTER – AN EVIL MAN. GOT WHAT HE DESERVED. August 5, 1892. For his efforts the undertaker kept Walter's pistol and gun belt, $7.53 he rifled from his pockets and all the tack necessary to ride the stolen horse he came to town on. To some it was shameless greed when he proposed keeping Orville's horse as a guarantee that he would be paid for getting him ready to go in the ground. It was mid-morning of the second day after the debacles at the Antler and the livery before Jeremy regained his wits in sufficient quantity to be credible. After some telegraphing and messages being delivered, it was decided that Josh and Caleb, Orville's neighbors, five miles distant, would come for him and Jeremy and Boots.

It was the fourth day after the killing when they got to town. A pinch of sun lingered on the horizon towards Idaho. It proved light enough to see the incessant horse flies pestering the gray Percheron team pulling the big blue Studebaker wagon. Josh had bought the wagon surplus from the Army years ago. He'd hauled lots of things in it but never a body. Now here he was going to bring his neighbor home to his widow all on account of him trying to get Josh's horses back. It had been wearing on his conscience, like a leaning tree rubbing on another in the wind. Nonetheless, here they were, him and Caleb sitting beside one another high up on the wagon's seat elevated by the heavy leaf springs beneath it. They drove on knowing that the livery was on the far end of town. A buckboard drawn by a single bay colored horse was parked in front of the mercantile. A man and woman had just come from the store with their arms full. On first impulse they smiled politely towards Josh and Caleb. And then their faces suddenly became sad. Josh suspected that it had just occurred to them why he, this stranger, was there. What he didn't know was that some of these smilers on the street had learned through the rumor mill that he was the husband of the whore with the shotgun. *Oh, that poor man. To have lived such a deceitful life all these years.*

Josh pulled back on the reins. "Whoa, team."

As was his custom, the old man was sitting in his rocking chair just inside the livery doors. He'd been privy to the telegrams that Jeremy and the sheriff from down at Afton had sent. He stood up. "You the fellas that come for the boy and his pa?"

Josh nodded. "We are."

"Got your horse inside."

Josh set the brake on the wagon before he and Caleb jumped down. Caleb was first to reach Boots. He immediately began talking soft to him and stroking his neck. "He looks ok, Pa."

The old man cut in, "It's good you got him back. The fella that was ridin' him was no good."

Josh nodded. "Horse thieves usually ain't."

"Well, he's where he belongs now."

Josh moved on. "Can we put our horses up here for the night?"

"I reckon so. Be six bits each."

A sign just beyond the old man on the wall of the stable read: HORSES BOARDED. $.50 A DAY PER HEAD. Josh pointed to it. "Your sign says four bits."

"That's for saddle horses. These big fellas will eat more."

Josh was about to agree when he saw the old man's eyes shift away. Coming from the direction of the hotel was Jeremy. They watched his approach. The old man said in a low voice, "That kid's lost without his father. Thinks it's his fault that his pa got killed."

"His fault?"

"Yeah, it was him that called attention to your horses. Badgered his pa into going for the marshal." The old man hesitated, not wanting to speak ill of the dead, but then he went ahead anyway so as to get it said before Jeremy got within earshot. "Just between me, you and the fence post I don't think the boy's pa had the stomach for it."

Josh kept quiet letting the old man's conscience, what little there was of it, wallow in the shameful silence surrounding his gossip. In Josh's opinion, Orville Duke had made an unwise and mostly unnecessary decision to carry a sidearm. He'd ignored the message that it sent to ignorant, reckless men that hadn't yet succumbed to civilization. Nor had he considered that his son would believe him far more capable than just shooting an occasional rattlesnake or animal with a broken leg. And so now, here he was lying on a hard table in a strange place pumped full of embalming fluid.

Jeremy's face was sullen. He called out, "Hello, Mr. Morrow."

Josh stepped towards the boy and briefly hugged him. "Sorry about your pa."

Caleb, who'd come alongside the old man, made eye contact and nodded as if to parrot his father.

Jeremy stepped back from the embrace. "They got Pa over to the undertakers. He's all ready to go."

"We'll head out first thing in the morning."

The sadness in Jeremy's eyes begged to be fixed. He went on, almost like his father was of the feeling world. "That'll be good. Pa has spent enough time in this town."

For a time, they continued to waltz around the fact that Orville was dead and taking him back to Grays Lake wasn't going to change that. It was like they could keep Orville alive by talking about him. Finally, Josh said, "It's been a long day for the horses. We need to tend to 'em."

Sensing the lull, Jeremy suddenly realized how he was. He spit the words out. "Sure, sure. See you at the hotel for breakfast?" He then turned and began walking away.

Josh called out. "Six o'clock?"

Jeremy raised and lowered his right arm in acknowledgement but didn't break stride.

It had been a coincidence that Josh had given in to Sarah's plea that he report their missing horses to the sheriff in Soda Springs. He was sitting in the sheriff's office mid-afternoon of the day following the gun fight in Freedom when the man from the telegraph office brought word that Orville Duke had been killed and his boy hurt bad. Right then and there Josh's priorities were reshuffled. To avoid riding the fifteen miles to tell Irma Duke that her husband was lying dead in the funeral parlor in Freedom Josh instructed the sheriff, *Tell 'em I'll come tomorrow to fetch Orville and the boy.* And so here he was sidetracked not once, but twice, from going after his horses on his own.

In spite of paying the old man six bits a head, in advance, to care for their horses, Josh and Caleb did most of the work themselves. They even *grained* them with oats they'd brought from home. It was just how they were. They were walking out when to their right, near the entrance to the livery, the door to the old man's living quarters opened.

"Got 'er done, do ya?"

Although he had not told the old man yet, as he didn't think it was necessary, he now thought better of it. "We're headed out to find some chuck. If it's no never mind to you, we'll roll out our blankets under our wagon."

The old man glanced at their wagon parked to the side of the livery like he briefly considered how much it was worth to let them sleep on the ground there. Fortunately, his conscience or Josh's stern look won out. "Sure, help yourself."

"Much obliged."

Josh and Caleb started to walk away only to be stopped by the old man's inquiry. "You going to the Antler?"

"The Antler?"

"Yeah, that's where it happened. Folks been flocking in there to hear George tell about it."

"George?"

"The bartender there. He saw it all."

The nagging thought that he was doing Tom Percy's job flared up again in Josh's mind. It may have been that Percy was so relieved to have the horse thieves and killer of Orville Duke in Wyoming and out of his jurisdiction that he just couldn't keep that emotion from his face. He feigned regret at not being able to get Josh's horses back. *It's too damned bad those scoundrels got across the state line.* Josh, however, would have no restrictions once he got Orville and his boy home. By then, he knew the trail of the killers would be cold. He knew too, that the killers would not have been stupid enough to say but he asked anyway, "These fellas ever mention where they was headed too?"

The old man laughed. "Shit, like anything they'd say would be the truth."

Josh felt like the stupid one now. His momentary discomfort caused the old man to admonish him. "If you're wantin' to know where these fellas went with your horses you might be well advised to talk to George. He's got ears like an elephant, and you know how whiskey can loosen a man's tongue. Could be he heard something."

Josh nodded while thinking that going to the Antler would be as futile as talking to the old man. He said anyway, "Well, maybe we'll swing on by there after we get a bean under our belt."

CHAPTER SIX

A toothpick protruded from beneath Josh's bushy moustache suggesting he'd just finished supper. As he and Caleb approached the bar George honed-in on the tiny bobbing sliver. "Been to Molly's poison palace, I see."

Josh grinned but not real big. "We have. I believe she left the hide on our steaks."

George snorted derisively. "I think she's in cahoots with the dentist."

"Well, I can see that. I don't know that a fella's teeth would hold up long term eatin' her chuck."

"What'll ya have?"

"Better give us a coupla Olys," said Josh as he and Caleb took their seats at the bar.

George nodded and reached into the cooler behind him. After rummaging for a moment and grumbling about his ice melting, he came away with two cans of Olympia beer that were dripping cold water. He set them in front of Josh and Caleb and levered two V shaped holes in their tops. "That'll be twenty cents."

Josh placed the coins on the bar and went right to his reason for being there. "Hear you had some gun play in here the other night?"

Anger came to George's face. At the same time, a lone cowboy at the end of the bar looked over as if to gauge who was asking. George sneered. "The sons-ah-bitches. I got bloodstains on my floor and two bullets in the wall over by the door."

Caleb swiveled on his stool in the direction that George was looking. There was just enough light that he could see where one of the bullets had splintered the board. He said, "Somebody miss?"

"Hell, no. Two bullets went clear through that do-gooder from Idaho that came in here with the marshal."

Josh gave George a hard look. "That do-gooder was our friend. He was here to get our horses back."

George forcibly eased his state of agitation slightly to allow momentary contrition. "Sorry to hear that."

Josh tossed his toothpick in a dirty tin ashtray to his left before taking a long drink of his beer. Its hopsy quality caused a gentle belch that he made no effort to suppress. He gave himself a few seconds and then went on ignoring George's disingenuous condolences. "These fellas that done the shootin', they regulars in here?"

"Hell no. What kinda place you think I run?"

"Sorry, didn't mean to step on your toes."

"I never saw those assholes before the other night when they came in here."

"You by chance hear 'em say where they might be headin'?"

"No, never heard anything about that. It was mostly the mean one, the one the marshal killed, badgering the bigger guy. About your age I reckon."

"Badgering, about what?"

"Well, I just got bits and pieces of it. Had a coupla customers at the bar, you know."

Josh nodded.

"Like I said, I didn't catch all of it but this guy, Walter something, was razzing the big guy about his whore girlfriend with the shotgun."

At the mention of the shotgun a pang of adrenalin surged through Josh. It took him aback like George would know the significance of the shotgun or, for that matter, that the woman was a whore. But more importantly Caleb would know about the shotgun part. Josh dared not look at his son for fear that his eyes would give credence to what was already likely spinning in his mind. It didn't matter. Caleb said, "This woman, she have a name?"

George remained oblivious to the trail he was headed down. He laughed. "No, the mean one, the one that bled out where that stain is on the floor behind you, that one, he kept chidin' the big guy. Told him if she hadn't been his two-dollar girl he would've shot her."

Josh came back trying to hold his anger in lest he draw attention to the two-dollar whore and cause George to speculate as to why that would be. "The big guy have a name?"

"Hooper is what I believe they called him."

"What'd this fella look like?"

"Little bigger 'n you. Six foot or so. Stout lookin'. Dark moustache but startin' to show his age. Short hair. He's probably old as you."

"Close to fifty?"

"Yeah, I reckon. You going after this fella?"

From the corner of his eye Josh could see that Caleb was looking at him with an expectation that appeared to be a given in his mind. Josh sighed. "Don't know. Gotta take my neighbor home to his widow first and then I got a ranch to run."

Caleb cut in. His voice was angry. "We ain't got no choice, Pa."

Josh looked sideways from his beer but more at the bar than Caleb. His tone was soft and patient. "We do have choices. Knowing which one won't come back to bite you is the problem."

"People 'll talk, Pa. Start all kinds of rumors. We can't have that."

As if to set the example, Josh took a long drink of his beer. "Drink up. We'll flesh this out later."

Caleb frowned but followed his father's lead. Within a minute or so they'd finished their beers and were heading for the door. George watched them go. He didn't call out. *Good luck on your trip home. Thanks for coming.* Nothing. He just let them ease out with their shame.

They walked a ways before Caleb broke the silence between them. "Whaddaya thinkin', Pa?"

Why would she lie? After twenty-two years of being together why now? He said aloud, naively thinking or hoping that he could pass off the whore part of what they'd said as drunk talk, but the shotgun part was another matter. "I ain't certain what happened but it sounds like your ma got the drop on these fellas with her skunk getter."

"That's what I was thinkin' too, but if she did how is it these guys get away with our horses? Why would Ma lie about not seeing who stole the horses?"

In that instant it came to Josh to spin his own lie. "I suspect she did what she did out of concern for us."

Caleb looked at his father like he was talking nonsense. "How's that?"

"There was three of them. At least one of 'em was lookin' at getting his neck stretched by the state if the law was to catch up to him. I think your ma figured there'd be gun play if she tried to stop these guys from taking the horses and that she'd come out on the short end of things. And, she knows too that if anybody was to hurt her that I'd chase 'em to the end of time. My guess is she was afraid I'd get killed in the process."

They walked on, Caleb digesting what his father had just said. After a time he came back, reluctant to say the word. "But why call Ma a whore? And this Hooper guy's two-dollar girl? That's a lotta bullshit, Pa. You know it and I know it but they go talkin' that around and there'll be people that'll want to believe it. You know how folks are."

The lie slid off Josh's tongue like it was coated with melted lard. It had to. It had to be quick to be believable. "It's just bar talk, son. Your ma was a schoolmarm and had been for some time before I met her."

Caleb eyed his father suspiciously. "I don't get why men would say such hurtful things."

Josh continued the deception shrugging his shoulders. "Who knows? Men get liquored up and they'll start teasing out some fantasy and, well, there ya go."

Caleb shook his head. "You know if the bible thumpers back home get wind of this it'll not bode well for Ma."

Josh laughed sarcastically. "Let the one among you who is without sin cast the first stone."

Caleb frowned. "You know what I'm saying is true, Pa."

Josh knew Caleb was right. He also knew that it was a sin to lie to your son, even if you thought it was for his own good.

CHAPTER SEVEN

Herman Snyder was a neighbor to Orville Duke. He lived about a mile south of the Duke Ranch, much closer than Josh Morrow. The first he knew of Orville being killed was the day after it happened when his son encountered Josh on the road from town. He could have gone over to the Duke place that night and offered his condolences and the usual, *is there anything I can do for you*? But he did not go. His wife, Thelma, put her foot down. *I don't give a shit if it does look bad. You ain't going over there.* She was not without justification for being so cold hearted. It'd only been just last fall that she caught him, or rather them, in the act. For some time she'd not liked the looks and friendly banter between him and Irma Duke at church and community socials. Especially the dances. She didn't care for the way they seemed to waltz perfectly together. It was on an Indian summer day in mid-October that Herman had announced, *I'm gonna check on the cattle.* Thelma's gut told her something wasn't right. The day before, when church was letting out, he and Irma had stopped short of where most of the buggies and buckboards were parked. She watched them from a distance. Their faces were intent and serious until Herman saw her out of the corner of his eye. He then gestured toward a big ponderosa pine tree as if to point out a bird or squirrel to Irma. There was nothing there. So, on that day last fall, Thelma played dumb. *Okay, Hon, I'll have supper ready when you get back.* Lest he leave with even a hint of suspicion, Herman kissed her on the lips. *Elk steak for supper?*

To which she replied, knowing full well there might not be any supper if her intuition panned out, *Yeah, and all the fixings with peach cobbler for dessert.* Herman kissed her again and then rode off confident that she was none the wiser. She, on the other hand, waited until he had disappeared into the aspen trees along the creek that ran past their ranch buildings before catching a horse and trailing after him. She was proud of her stealth, but regretted instantly surprising them in their naked embrace. Nonetheless, she stood and stared at them in their little meadow hideaway. It would have been romantic if it would have been her and Herman. Lush, knee-high blue grass. Aspens overhead. Their yellow leaves rustling. The tattling cries of ravens and Steller's jays. It could have been so good. Irma was first to see her. She shrieked. *Oh no!* Herman rolled to the side and looked back. A charging grizzly bear would have caused less terror than was on his face. Irma sat up trying to cover her naked breasts. She began to cry. *I'm sorry, Thelma.* Thelma gave them no reprieve as she stared at them.

Herman scowled at her like he had a right. *Dammit, Thelma, look away.*

She came back, cold and hateful. *Your boys will be home from school in a couple of hours. If you're not home by then, I'll tell them where to find you.* She then turned and started to walk away.

Herman called out his voice frantic, fearful. *Wait, Thelma. I'll ride back with you.*

Sensing she'd gained the upper hand, she said, *You can lay with your whore for all I care.*

And so, Orville Duke's grave was dug not by Herman alone. His two boys, in spite of the fact they had hay that needed to be mowed and buck-raked went along to help.

CHAPTER EIGHT

Although Josh had seen it, perched on the wagon seat as he was, he said nothing. Jeremy, who was riding behind with Caleb saw it next. "There's Pa's grave. They got it dug."

It was that time of day when the sun has called it quits and the moon, bright and full, was rising over the mountains behind them. Josh looked to his left. About fifty yards away, in the shadow of two big ponderosa pines, was a pile of dirt that had not yet lost its color. Cobble rocks, sufficient in number to make Josh grimace slightly in deference to the grave diggers, were clearly evident. He said only, "Pretty spot." And then he wondered to himself if pretty grave sites were more for the living than the dead.

Even though Orville was nearly home the road showed him no mercy. His coffin bounced in response to the wagon rolling over big half-buried rocks and in and out of badger holes. In response to one particularly hard jolt, Jeremy frowned hateful and cried out, "Damn."

Josh looked back at the boy. He thought to say he was sorry but didn't.

Caleb, who was riding Boots, said in soft a tone as his patience would allow, "It can't be helped, Jeremy."

Jeremy acted like he hadn't heard.

Shortly, they came to the Duke's white clapboard house. An old brown and white Collie dog got up from the porch and began barking. Momentarily, the door opened. Irma stood there looking out. Her long hair, black as a crow's wing, glistened just slightly in the lantern light that poured from inside. She stepped out followed by Ruth, her teenage daughter and a spitting image of her mother, buxom and petite.

The Percherons were standing wearily in place. Josh called out over their backs. "Evenin', Ma'am."

The women gathered their skirts, plain and drab, as they descended the two steps from the wooden porch to the trampled bare ground that comprised the yard. Irma was stoic, dry eyed almost. Ruth not so, sniffling now. Tears trickling down her cheeks. Irma gestured off to her right. "Let's put Orville in the barn."

The naysayer in Josh's mind shouted out, *Shit, you'd think we'd been huntin' and needed a place to hang an elk.* In that same instant he thought too, *I got no problem bringing Orville in the house.* The untowardness of her request left him speechless just long enough for Jeremy to bring his horse forward, quick like, so that he blocked Josh's view of Irma. "That ain't right, Ma."

"It's where he'd want to be. Close to the stock."

Jeremy scoffed. "It's where you want 'em. Away from you."

"Mind your tongue, Jeremy. You don't know what you're talking about."

Josh looked on, uncertain what to do. He dared not ask lest he make things worse butting into Duke family matters. And then, the intense looks between mother and son ended and the women started toward the barn. Josh rippled the reins over the Percheron's and followed after them. They walked briskly with King, the dog, trotting alongside. They said nothing, not even to King. And then they came to the big double doors. Irma swung back the left half and Ruth the right. Josh pulled on the reins. "Whoa boys." He briefly looked toward the women purposely not making eye contact. Beyond them was a shadowy tunnel. A tack room and stalls to either side. He could see no animals before darkness choked out his view. *Orville's gonna be by his self.* He jumped down from the wagon only then looking at Irma to speak. "Where would you like Orville?"

She hesitated, like Josh had seen something that would preclude the obvious, before turning sideways into the cavern and pointing to the barn's pulverized manure and dirt floor. "Right here will be fine."

Josh thought to ask, *Have you got some sawhorses so we can keep him off the ground?* Aloud he said, "Yes, Ma'am."

Caleb jumped up into the wagon and dropped to his knees at the end of the coffin. "I'll shove it out to you, Pa."

Josh stood ready to take hold of the wide end, the heavy part where Orville's torso with the bullet holes was at. As the coffin edged past the end of the wagon he took hold of it, lifted and slid the rest until about a foot remained in the wagon. He'd already noted that Jeremy was content to unsaddle his horse and untie Orville's from the back of the wagon. He wanted no part of putting his father in the barn like he was a load of oats. Josh stood patiently holding his end of the coffin while Caleb jumped down from the wagon. His face showed no strain. At almost 200 pounds he was stronger than most men his size. Almost 22, Caleb was near his father's equal. He took hold of his end. "I got it, Pa."

They began to take short deliberate steps towards the women and Orville's resting spot for the night. Ruth grimaced thinking no doubt that the pine box was heavier than it really was. She'd seen, like most folks, where it took six men to carry a person to their grave. She'd never considered that was mostly for show and not necessity. Regardless, she cried out, "Jeremy, why don't you help these men?"

Jeremy scowled in her direction and then pulled his father's saddle from the back of the wagon.

As Josh walked heavy footed past Irma and Ruth, he wondered how it was they came to be like they were. His inclination that read like a cow track in soft mud was that Irma had become a bitter woman. Had he known her dark secret and the fact that Ruth knew, and Jeremy didn't, might have helped explain things.

Irma caught Josh's eye. "Right there is fine."

They set the coffin down. Light from a full moon perched above the mountains to the east flowed into the barn's entrance. It illuminated Orville's box. Plain pine boards, knots and all, no better than Walter's. He said, wanting to be free of the Duke's acrimony but respectful of their grief, "The service, gonna be tomorrow?"

Irma nodded. "One o'clock." She paused before asking. "I'd like you to drive our wagon to carry Orville to his grave."

Jeremy, who had a two-hand grip on his father's saddle and was taking limp steps toward the tack room, shouted in a breathy voice, "No, I'll drive it."

Irma frowned as Jeremy heaped more sadness on her plate. "Thank you for bringing my boys home. You're a good neighbor, Mr. Morrow."

In that instant, Josh saw the Irma he'd come to know over the years. He came back, "I know Sarah will want to help with after the service. Anything she can bring?"

"A pie would be nice."

"I'll pass that on."

CHAPTER NINE

The road, just two well-worn wagon tracks in a sea of grass and sagebrush, stood out in the bright moonlight. The horses were tired. They cleared their nostrils in a fluttery, snorting way, much more frequently now. Josh needed to ease his conscience for the twelve hour pull he'd required of them yesterday and again today. He called out as if they understood. "You boys get tomorrow off and extra oats tonight."

Thinking they would talk before they got home Caleb had tied Boots to the rear of the wagon and was sitting next to his father. "They're a good team."

"None better."

"I'm glad that Hooper bunch didn't steal them too. They'd be worth some money to the right fella."

"They would."

"You think we'll ever get Snookers and Baldy back?"

Josh looked away. The night was warm. To their left several nighthawks darted and soared just above a grassy meadow. Their distinctive whirring call was a welcome distraction to the pestering of the events in Freedom. "Too bad there ain't more of those hawks. They're hell on flying bugs."

Caleb pretended to study the birds while, from the corner of his eye, doing the same to his father's face. By and by it came to him that he was elsewhere in thought, most likely what had been said about his mother in the Antler bar. It bothered him too. "So, whaddaya make of that story those fellas was tellin'?

"Drunk talk."

"Purty coincidental, don't ya think? A woman with a shotgun."

In the distance, the lights of the house were visible. The sight of it appeared to have rendered Josh speechless.

Caleb knew exactly where he was going with what he was saying. So did his father. Caleb pushed on. "I think there's more to this, Pa, than just drunk talk. If you know the straight of it, I think I got a right to know it too."

Josh looked over at his son. "There'll be no good come of bringing that Wyoming business back here."

"It can't be helped, Pa. Jeremy knows it. He prodded me a coupla times on the ride back. He didn't come right out and say it but I know he's got it in his mind that Hooper bunch is callin' Ma a whore."

Josh sighed angrily. He spit the words at his son. "That was a long time ago."

Shock, disappointment, a potpourri of nothing good came to Caleb's face. "She was a whore?"

Josh snorted. "You're the one pickin' that scab off."

It got quiet between them. The whirring call of the hawks had been replaced by the chirping of the crickets and the creaking of the wagon. Way ahead at the house, Buster had detected their approach. His barking was sure to bring Sarah and Noah outside.

Caleb came back. "Why didn't you ever tell me?"

"What the hell for? So you or somebody else could judge her? People change. She did what she had to at the time to survive."

"It's just – well, not how a guy sees his mother."

"She was a good mother before we went to Wyoming. Am I right?"

"Yeah."

"Ain't nuthin' changed, but if you go in that house and tell about this I guarantee it will and it won't be for the good."

Caleb shook his head. "Well Pa, I doubt that it'll be up to me to tell about this."

Buster was to them now, barking excitedly. And then yellow light replaced the door to the house. Sarah and Noah came through it and into the darkness meeting the wagon close to the barn. Caleb jumped down from the wagon. It wasn't his usual practice to give his mother a hug when greeting her. Tonight, he did.

It was long after the supper dishes were done. They were lying in bed. Sarah cuddled next to Josh resting her head on his hairy chest. Their bedroom window was open to the cool night air and the sound of the wind rushing through the big pines outside. They'd made love and now lay there with thoughts of their own. Josh was replaying the supper conversation. It was only natural that her and Noah had wanted to hear about what happened in Freedom. He told it, with Caleb throwing in too. They were careful to leave out the whore and shotgun part. It was Caleb, though, who gave names to the horse thieves. *This Hooper fella left his partner, a scoundrel named Walter, to die right there in the bar. No honor among thieves I reckon.* Josh saw the look on her face. He knew it was all true. *But why would she let these guys go if she had the drop on them? Why would she lie about seeing them?* His mind vacillated between the obvious that her past would be revealed if she held them for the law and a fringe thought, *maybe she has feeling for Hooper?* It troubled him, troubled him a lot that she would lie to him.

CHAPTER TEN

There was no viewing of the body. Irma didn't see a need for it. Some folks in attendance thought it strange to which Irma responded, *Would you want me to come to your house tonight and watch you sleep? Just stand there and study your imperfections?* The woman to whom she had said this, a God fearing, church going person strutted off in a huff. The real gossip mill, however, started after Orville was in the ground and mostly after people had stuffed themselves on the plethora of food that had been brought for the meal afterwards. It was Jeremy, of all people. He had an audience of three teenage boys in the shade of some ponderosa pine midway between the house and the privy. He was keeping his voice low. "Now, if you was to ask Caleb he'd tell you this is all bar talk. That these ruffians were just calling this woman a bad name cuz that's how drunk men are and that none of this happened cuz his ma never saw anybody the day their horses was stole. Sounds purty damned fishy to me. All the pieces fit except it being Mrs. Morrow. What do you boys think?"

It was a red-haired kid, about fourteen, wearing black suspenders to hold up his pants whose eyes suddenly grew to silver dollar size. Jeremy spun around. "Caleb."

Caleb came on around the edge of the tree stopping face to face with Jeremy. He ratcheted up a disgusted look and shook his head. "You're an ungrateful little shit. If I ever hear of you

talking bad about my mother again I'll whip your ass good."

Jeremy, being a head shorter and thirty pounds lighter than Caleb, turned pale. "I'm sorry, Caleb. I was just repeatin' what I heard."

"And why would you want to do that?"

"Just talk. That's all."

Caleb gave Jeremy a hateful look before glaring at the other boys and walking away. When he was definitely out of earshot, Jeremy whispered, "He wouldn't be so mad if there wasn't something to it."

Anger, the intense kind that has reached a peak boil barely able to stay within the confines of its kettle, is hard to hide. Such was the case with Caleb. His quick deliberate strut validated the look on his face. *Ungrateful little shit. We haul him and his pa home from Wyoming and here he is talkin' bad about Ma.*

"Caleb, where are you going in such a hurry?"

To his left, Pastor Tom Combs deviated from the well-defined path to the privy on a course to intercept Caleb. Their eyes met. He paused. "Oh, hello, Pastor." He lied. "Didn't see you there."

Combs, thin, middle-aged, clean-shaven, wire rim glasses, black suit and Bowler hat to match stuck his hand out. "How are you?"

Caleb shook the pastor's hand feeling as he always did with him, that it was more about gauging his soul than a social formality. "Doing good, Pastor." It crossed his mind to ask Combs how he was, but didn't. Men of God are always doing *just fine.*

"You look upset?"

"It's a sad day, Pastor."

"Yes, it certainly is. Orville's demise will leave his family in a precarious spot."

"Be up to Jeremy to take over, I reckon."

"Yes, I saw you and him having what appeared to be a brief but fairly intense exchange. It was surprising to me given the assistance you and your father have rendered the family."

Caleb studied the Pastor's expectant eyes. *He's worse 'an these old busybody hens that quilt and gossip all day.* Aloud, he lied again. "We was talkin' about those thieves that killed his pa and stole our horses. It gets me purty worked up."

Although Combs' expression said he knew he'd just been lied to, he had the good sense not to probe the matter further, at least not with Caleb. There'd be a time, he knew, when any one of those boys would give up the truth. It was his belief that a good pastor was like a sheriff in that it was prudent to keep tabs on your flock. To that end, he went along with Caleb's diversion. "I can well imagine. If it's any solace though, those men will have their conscience and God to answer to."

Caleb scoffed. "Pastor, I think you've confused these men with someone who might have a smidgeon of decency."

Combs smiled. "God knows their true character."

And then they saw that Sarah was coming toward them. Combs was first to speak. "Mrs. Morrow, I heard that apple pie was your creation. Delicious. Very tasty."

Sarah smiled. "Thank you, Pastor. I'm glad you enjoyed it."

"I need to pay you another compliment as well. You're doing a fine job with our Sunday school class."

Sarah blushed slightly. "Oh my. They're a joy to teach."

Caleb looked on, proud of his mother yet fearful of the gossip brewing. *Combs 'll sing another tune if he catches wind of this whore talk.*

Combs had already thought it out. He'd continue on to the privy and on his way back he'd find Jeremy or one of his audience. He smiled broadly, mostly at Sarah. "See you Sunday."

"Yes, of course, Pastor. We'll be there."

Combs turned and took a few steps towards the privy before pausing and looking back at Caleb. The distance required him to speak louder. "Caleb, Ecclesiastes 7:9 tells us, *Be not hasty in thy spirit to be angry: for anger resteth in the bosom of fools.*" He did not wait for a response from Caleb, instead he abruptly walked away.

Sarah said, "Pastor weigh in on all this business?"

"He did."

"That was probably good advice he just gave you."

"Ma, I've been wronged. Our family's been wronged. I don't see being upset with that as being foolish."

"Anger needs to be controlled or it can get you in trouble."

He looked into his mother's eyes, confident that her secret was safe. He came back like a schoolboy being reprimanded for fighting on the playground. "I know, Ma."

"Have you considered these men did leave their horses."

Caleb snapped sarcastically, "Oh, so I should just look at this like it was a swap?"

"No, but you do have their horses and you got Boots back."

Her son looked incredulous. "Are you defending these guys?"

Fear, not anger, showed in Sarah's face. Fear that maybe he'd learned her secret. She sensed it in Josh. You don't sleep with a man and not pick up on such things. He'd been different since coming home from Wyoming. She came back, "I'm just saying it isn't all bad."

Caleb looked down at his mother and shook his head. "Maybe you should tell this to Combs. I think he's more in line with your thinking." He then walked away, saying nothing more. His sudden departure, however, did not go unnoticed. Thelma and Herman Snyder, sitting beside one another at a picnic table between two aspen trees, saw it all. They saw too the hurt look on Sarah's face. For a moment, Sarah stood there in the midst of the bare dirt and sporadic tufts of brown grass uncertain where to go. She felt exposed, vulnerable to the truth. Finally, her feet began to move.

CHAPTER ELEVEN

Sarah looked around the room taking a head count as she did. It was on the Sunday following Orville Duke's funeral. The Morrow family had come to church just like she had told Pastor Combs they would. Normally, she had eight kids in her bible study class. None of them over twelve years. Today there were seven. Patsy Jenkins was late. Through the wall of their small room, Sarah could hear the adults singing. *Amazing Grace, how sweet the sound that saved a wretch like me. I once was lost but now am found* ;;; She'd seen Patsy earlier, sitting with her folks before the kids were dismissed for Sunday school. Generally, she was one of the first ones in the classroom. Wilma Jenkins, not to be denied her place in the hereafter, made sure of that. The kids sat on benches to either side of the room. For some, their feet dangled above the dark wood floor while others touched. In another year Maggie Reeves' feet would likely touch. Maggie and Patsy were best friends. Sarah knew this from her observations at church and the one room school where she taught them second grade. The kids in their nice clean church clothes were getting fidgety. Sarah glanced down at the handout material in her lap and then back at the kids. "We'll give Patsy another minute and then we'll start. We're going to talk about forgiveness today."

A window on the outside wall of the room was half open. A Steller's jay screeched in the pine tree shading the church. Through the wall behind her, Sarah could hear that Pastor Combs had begun to preach. He too was talking about forgiveness, "Ephesians 4:32, Be kind and compassionate to one another, forgiving each other, just as in Christ God forgave you."

And then Maggie offered, "Patsy's not coming today."

Sarah looked at her, not doubting the seven year old's credibility. "Why's that?"

Maggie's innocence was pure and genuine. "Her mama says you're a bad person."

The class, mostly older than Maggie, instantly got quiet. Their faces shared Sarah's embarrassment. Ethel, a twelve-year old in a yellow dress whose obesity made her look older than she was, nudged Maggie. "Be quiet."

Sarah was torn. Afraid to ask why, at least in front of the class she was. But they were waiting. They'd know she had something to hide if she didn't ask. Seven sets of eyes looking at her. Her mind frantically spun the possibilities. *How could Wilma Jenkins know?* She gathered her courage. "Are you sure that's what she said, Maggie?"

The child nodded emphatically.

Sarah's face flushed red. A hint of tears came to her eyes. Her voice quivered. "Well, I guess I'll just have to talk to Mrs. Jenkins after class. See if I can clear this up."

Thirty minutes can be a long time when you've been humiliated. It can seem even longer dreading what comes after it.

She did not tell Josh or the boys what had happened. Instead, she waited until after the service when people were outside chatting and laughing prior to going home. It galled her that Wilma Jenkins had ruined her day. *She's a vile hateful woman. By day's end there'll be seven more kids repeating to their parents what happened this morning. Come next Sunday how many of them won't show up.*

Caleb and Noah, who'd ridden their horses, had already left when she saw Wilma walking toward the privy. Sarah smiled at Josh as she gently unhinged herself from his arm. "I'm gonna visit the privy before we head home."

He nodded. "I'll wait for you at the buggy."

Sarah stopped short of the privy like she was waiting her turn. She could hear Wilma's feet scuffling on the plank floor inside as she likely was turning around and hiking up her paisley dress to sit. She could hear too the flies buzzing incessantly, the tinkle of urine splashing in the sewage beneath Wilma and her mumbling that became hatefully distinct, "damned flies". And then the door creaked open belying the recent coat of white paint to disguise the need for a new privy. The look on Wilma's face was immediately uncomfortable. Her mousy brown hair and premature wrinkles made her look too old to have a second grader. And they did nothing to hide her irritation with Sarah's presence. "What do you want?"

It flashed in Sarah's mind, *What a bitch!* She then gathered her church voice. "We missed Patsy today. Is she ok?"

Wilma scoffed. "You know why she didn't come."

"I have the word of a seven year old."

"Well then, why are you bothering me?"

Anger pooled in Sarah's eyes. "You're alright with having a seven year old be your messenger of gossip?"

"If it's true it ain't gossip and my boy Frank got it from Jeremy Duke that it's all over Freedom how you were a whore once and a killer too. And he heard too that one of the fellas that shot his pa was an old boyfriend of yours. A paying customer. So, you wanted to know why Patsy didn't come to your class, there you have it."

Had she been innocent of Wilma's accusation Sarah would have lashed out at her. As it was, she stood there struggling to not cry. Her mind was awash with the potential consequences of what Wilma had just revealed. *If Jeremy knows, Josh and Caleb must know too. They know I lied about not seeing Hooper. Oh, that sonovabitch. Why now?*

Wilma sneered at her. "I'm surprised you would even show your face here."

Sarah told herself, *Don't let her see you cry. None of them.* She watched Wilma in her haughty manner walk away, the rise and fall of her plump buttocks beneath her dress clearly evident.

From where the buggy was parked, Josh could see the rigid behavior of the women. Their body language suggested to him that, had they been men, blows would have been struck. He was sitting in the buggy, reins in hand, when Sarah reached it. She climbed in without speaking. He rippled the reins. "Giddup, Bruiser."

Tom Combs and his wife were standing on the church steps waving at the departing parishioners. Josh nodded in their direction while Sarah pretended to not see them. They were barely on the road going home when Josh broke the ice. "I take it things didn't go well with Wilma?"

For a time, she allowed the clip-clop of Bruiser's hooves and the rattle of the buggy to fill the silence between them. Finally, she met his stare. "Why didn't you tell me what they were saying in Freedom?"

"I guess I was hopin' it would die."

"Gossip like that is too tempting for someone like Wilma Jenkins to not make hay of it."

"So, that's why Patsy was snugged up to her today."

"The woman's poison. She's gonna tell all she knows, or thinks she knows."

Josh hesitated but then said it. "Kinda hurts that you didn't think you could tell me the truth about how it was when they came to the place."

Tears overflowed Sarah's eyes. She sobbed. "I wanted to, but Hooper said if I told about them being there and they were caught he'd tell everything about Bear Creek. I didn't want the boys finding out."

Josh did not hold back. "Caleb knows."

A flood of anguish and shame enveloped Sarah as she buried her face in her hands. Her crying caused her shoulders to tremble. Josh put his arm around her. "It'll be alright, Hon. He's a clear-headed boy."

Sarah shook her head. "I just wished he'd never known about my past."

"I've talked to him. I believe he 'll do alright with knowing it."

"And Noah?"

Josh sighed. "He doesn't know."

Sarah looked at Josh, her blue eyes now red and blood-shot. "He's going to be mad when he finds out. He's going to feel like we kept it from him and not Caleb."

Josh nodded. "I know. I've thought about that."

"And what?"

"Probably need to sit him down. Maybe the both of them and explain how it was 22 years ago in Bear Creek."

"I don't know that young people will understand."

Josh shook his head. "Hon, they're good boys that love their mother."

"And everybody else around here?"

"Well, if those bible thumpers had their ears open this morning they'll forgive you, if not I reckon they can just go to hell."

CHAPTER TWELVE

It was about three miles from the church to their house. Josh had purposely allowed Bruiser to take his time so that Sarah could compose herself before having to confront the boys. As it turned out, it wasn't necessary. Sabbath or not, the boys had changed from their church clothes and went to work. Noah was mowing hay with the Percherons in the meadow to the south of the barn and across the road from the horse pasture. He gave his folks a big wave as they drove by. They waved back. "He's a good boy. You can always count on him." said Josh.

Sarah looked at Josh wondering if he meant that Noah could be counted on to be ok with her past that was no longer a secret or was it that he was cutting the hay. She concluded that it was probably the latter. "He is."

Josh glanced left and right in a cursory way. "I don't see Caleb around. He must of already headed for Mink Crik."

Sarah asked rhetorically, "He going to check on the cows?"

"Yeah, I suspect it's gittin' purty short up there. We'll see what Caleb reports but more 'n likely the four us will have to move them out of there in the next day or so."

The worry in Sarah ebbed slightly. "There's good grass up there. We should get a good price for the calves."

Josh sensed her spirits had lifted a little. "Maybe this 'll be the year we can afford the material to develop the spring. No more hand pump. Just turn the spigot right there in the kitchen."

Some joy came into Sarah's eyes. "And a sink too."

Josh fed her happiness. "Oh yeah, nuthin' but the best for my queen."

Sarah smiled. For a few seconds more, she was unfettered of the doom in her future. And then she noticed Noah, his broad brimmed hat shielding his face from the hot sun. Sitting on the hard metal seat of the mower. The Percherons moving briskly along. The hay before the mower's sickle bar falling like dominoes. He appeared to be at peace with life. She thought, *not today, maybe tomorrow I'll tell him.*

It was late afternoon. Caleb was riding along Mink Creek. Mosquitoes and horse flies, two of his least favorite living things were pestering him, his horse and Buster. He slapped at the back of his neck, too late to get revenge. "Damned flies." The feed, as he and Josh had suspected, was used up. He was musing to himself. *Need to gather these tomorrow and push 'em over to Taylor Basin. Finish out the season there.* This thought was still perched in his mind's eye along with a vision of having to deal with the insects tomorrow when he heard it, a gunshot on up the canyon. He guessed a half mile. Pausing to listen for more shooting, his heart thumped in his ears and a pine squirrel scolded him for being there. The shooter was silent. Caleb nudged his second favorite horse, Pickles, in the direction of the shot. It was slow going meandering through the aspens and pine trees that crowded them. In places, Pickles stepped over fallen trees. In others, where the dead branches created a barrier, they went around. Although he was 22 years old and a good shot with either a pistol or rifle, Caleb wished that his father was there. His apprehension grew as he considered the scenarios that would account for the gunshot. Either someone had shot a deer, in which case it was none of his concern, or it was a replay of what happened last fall. And then the speculation ended. Pickles pushed through a stand of young aspens into a small clearing. On the far side of it, maybe 75 yards, stood two saddle horses their reins hanging to the ground before them. To their right was a big bay horse with a packsaddle. Its lead rope laying on the ground as well. Between them was what Caleb had feared. Two men were butchering a fat Hereford calf. A fifty-dollar bill come November. Caleb felt of his pistol, a .45 Colt, before urging Pickles forward. Buster, good dog that he was, fell in beside them. He was undetected halfway there when two ravens, who, in anticipation of the offal that awaited them had landed nearby, flushed at his approach. That did it. The men stood, each holding a knife, their hands and arms to the elbow coated with blood. Caleb recognized the bigger one from last fall. Same black slouch hat. A wispy moustache and his black hair in two long braids. Tony Bear Killer was his name. The other guy, an Indian too, wearing a black flat brim Stetson with an eagle feather stuck in a rattlesnake hatband was a stranger to Caleb. The Indians were nervous. So was Caleb. He called out rhetorically. "Tony, what are you doing here?"

Tony's smile was absent one tooth on top and two on the bottom. "Just like last year. Come for beef."

Caleb shook his head. "That was one time only. My father felt sorry for you."

"You no feel sorry for Tony. I got wife and kids to feed."

Caleb felt a sudden pulse of anger towards his father. *I told him there'd be no end to it if he gave them that beef.* Caleb shook his head again. He pointed west toward the reservation. "You've got a lot of land, good land with wild game. You don't need to be over here shooting slow elk."

Tony grinned. "We take calf this time. Never come back."

Caleb frowned. "That's what you told my father last fall when he let you take the calf you killed then. And now here you are Tony, going down that same road. We can't have it."

It was at this point that Stetson guy stepped between their horses. He was mostly hidden to Caleb but clearly next to the butt stock of a rifle protruding forward from a scabbard along the saddle. Caleb noted it. Adrenaline swamped his senses. He took a breath even though he was sitting still. He shouted. "Tony, tell your friend to get away from that gun."

Tony grinned again. "We take beef."

Caleb saw his family repeating this again if he said yes, or more likely they'd just come upon gut piles and horse tracks headed back to the reservation. If it wasn't Tony, it'd be his neighbors. *Easy meat*, they'd say. Beyond telling Tony he couldn't have the calf Caleb's mind was frantic with indecision. *If I try to disarm them and take them to the sheriff, that's likely to blow up. But if I let 'em go back to the rez there'll be no justice.* And I'll be out a day's ride each way to the BIA at Fort Hall, likely for nothing. It was a situation with no good outcome, that Caleb could see anyway. He looked down from his horse. "Tony, you and your friend head on home."

A wry smile came to Tony's face. "We take beef."

Caleb frowned. "No, I'll not reward your thievery. You went back on your word. My father and I are going to tell the BIA police about this."

Tony laughed like Caleb's threat meant nothing to him. But to Stetson guy it was a different matter. He was tugging on the rifle in the scabbard of the far horse. His intent was clear to Caleb. Use the first horse for cover. Shoot over its back and kill him. In that instant Caleb went for his pistol while shouting, "Gittem, Buster."

It happened quick. Caleb vaguely remembered hearing the lever of the Winchester being worked and seeing the near side cover horse bolt, Buster biting at its hooves. And the immense fear he felt when he saw through the smoke from his pistol that Stetson guy was drawing a bead on him. And the wait. Less than a second. Wondering if his bullet would get there in time but then, crowded into this milieu of terror, the Winchester bucked and roared. *Oh shit, I'm dead.* Stetson guy stumbled backwards. The Winchester fell to the ground. The ravens cawed their approval from the trees overhead and Tony stood dead still with his arms raised. "Don't shoot."

It was fortunate that Caleb did not need to fire again. His hand was trembling such that any attempt to kill another man would have been futile. His father's "talk" came back to him. He told him several years ago when he'd insisted on wearing a sidearm that it was serious business carrying a gun. It would send a message to other men that could be misinterpreted. That killing a man would haunt you forever. Now, here he was seconds into that prophecy knowing full-well that his father was right.

A relative calm came over Tony's face. It may have been that he had resigned himself to dying and being buried with his friend in a shallow grave never to be heard of again or it could have been that he could see Caleb was not the kind to shoot an unarmed man. He locked onto Caleb's eyes hoping to drain away the wild fear that resided there. "My friend is dead."

"You saw what he did."

An awareness of what he was seeing came to Tony's eyes. His voice was absent any emotion close to compassion. It was mostly indifferent. "He almost won."

It was only now, after Tony's eyes called attention to the blood trickling from beneath his hat and down his left temple that Caleb became aware of it. He dabbed at the moistness he could now feel. His fingers came away dark red. It wasn't particularly alarming to him. He was still standing and he was the one holding the gun. He looked away from his bloody fingers to Tony. "Look what you've caused."

Tony appeared to accept the blame. "I should take my friend home now. Never come back."

"And his family? They'll be upset."

"They know how he was."

"What about the BIA police?"

"It's none of their business."

"If they find out it'll be your word against mine what happened here."

A sarcastic smile came to Tony's face. "White man word or Indian word, who you think they believe?"

"But I'm in the right, Tony."

"Maybe today you are."

The consequences, both moral and legal, of killing a man was hammering at Caleb's conscience. He wanted to believe Tony. That he would take Stetson guy home to his family and explain away their desire to get even. Deep in his mind, or maybe not so deep, he knew the right thing to do would be to go to the law right now and explain what happened. To try and bury it along with Stetson guy somewhere out on the reservation was not, he figured, what his father would approve. He was certain of that. Nonetheless, he eased the hammer down on his pistol and holstered it. He looked hard at Tony like he could see inside his head and what his real intentions were. Momentarily, Tony succumbed to the scrutiny. "I tell truth. You see."

Caleb sighed. "I believe you. But don't forget the water in this crik flows both ways."

In the end it cost Caleb his lariat and the calf. He helped load Stetson guy onto his horse, belly down, across the saddle lashing his feet and hands together with a loop under the horse. And the calf. *Pa would just give it to 'em.* But before he helped Tony load it on his pack horse, he analyzed his options. He wondered if in this heat and flies, with his head aching like it had been split open with an ax instead of creased with a .44 Caliber bullet, he could get the calf to their icehouse without a pack animal before it started to spoil. He wrestled with the decision all the while they were tying Stetson guy to his horse. And when they'd finished, even though blood was still oozing from under his hat down to his jawbone, his conscience won out. Like he could square it with God for having killed a man.

CHAPTER THIRTEEN

The events of Mink Creek were so disconcerting to Josh and Sarah that the idea of having their "sit-down talk" with the boys to explain her past seemed inconsequential. They had another secret to hide which was more secure, as far as they knew, than Sarah's cancer. However, on the third day after the shooting Caleb's secret appeared to be in jeopardy.

"It'll be alright, Pa. I just need a little more time."

Josh shook his head. "You've gave it time and it ain't gotten nuthin' but worse."

Caleb looked up from where he lay on the couch in the front room. "Well, you know old Doc Hale is gonna know this for what it is. He'll go to the law. He's got to don't he, or risk gittin' himself in trouble?"

Josh hesitated as if to acknowledge his son was right before coming back, "Well hell, you can't just let the left side of your head rot off."

"So, you're proposin' we go to town this morning?"

"We'll take the buckboard. Make you up a bed in the back of it."

"Hell's fire, Pa. You parade me down Main Street like that you'll have every tongue in town waggin'."

Josh snorted. "Well, mister tough guy, you think you can sit a horse there and back?"

"Got to."

Within the hour they set out, just the two them. From atop his horse Josh had shouted, mostly to reassure Sarah, *don't take our plates off the table. We'll be home before sundown.* And then they started at a trot causing Sarah to grimace, knowing that it had to be causing Caleb pain.

At about five miles into their fifteen mile journey the thin scab on Caleb's wound had cracked open. Blood was seeping from under his hat onto his temple. Even though they stopped at a little creek with cold clear water just outside town and cleaned his face the bleeding was such, that by the time they dismounted in front of Doc Hale's office Caleb was drawing attention.

"For land sakes, young man. What on earth happened to you?"

Caleb half-turned to face a portly gray-haired woman wearing a blue dress and sun bonnet of the same color that tied beneath her chin. Black pointy shoes were barely visible beneath the dress. Caleb was working up a lie to account for his appearance when his father beat him to it. "Horse went down in a badger hole. He took a bad spill is all."

"Oh, those dog-gone badgers. My father lost a good saddlehorse to a badger hole when I was just a girl. Broke its leg. Had to shoot it. Only time I ever saw my father cry."

Caleb, feeling woozy now and wishing he'd come prone in the buckboard, placed his right hand on the hitching rail to steady himself. Ever the gentleman, Josh patiently nodded. "Yes Ma 'am. Nuthin' worse than losing a good animal."

And then the woman noticed Caleb's distress. "Oh, my goodness. I'm keeping you. I'm sorry."

Josh smiled and touched his right hand to the brim of his hat as if to doff it. "You have yourself a good day, Ma'am."

The old lady shifted her eyes to Caleb. "Good luck to you, young man."

Caleb mustered a polite smile that contradicted the rivulet of blood creeping toward his jaw. "Thank you, Ma'am."

Josh waited until the woman was beyond hearing distance before speaking. "Probably ain't no point in trying to fool Doc Hale."

Fear abruptly overrode the pain in Caleb's head. He hissed, "Shit, Pa, I don't know that I want to open that can of worms today."

"Today, tomorrow, next week. I think the lid is already off and the minute we go through that door the can will be upside down."

Caleb whispered like his father had forgotten. "I killed a man, Pa."

"You shot a thief in self-defense. No right-minded lawman is gonna lock you up for that."

Caleb frowned. "I suspect over on the rez the story will go different than that."

"Maybe we should just tell our side first."

"I don't know, Pa. That ain't the way I left it with Tony Bear Killer."

Josh's eyes suddenly became fixated beyond Caleb. "Tom Percy is comin' our way and it don't appear to be coincidence. You be straight with the man."

Caleb turned around just as the sheriff finished crossing the street. Before he could speak the sheriff called out, "My horse and my ass is thanking you boys for saving me the ride out and back to your place."

Caleb pretended they still had the element of surprise. "How's that, Tom?"

Sheriff Percy laughed wryly and then launched a stream of tobacco juice onto the boardwalk where minutes ago the old lady had been standing. He stepped close to Caleb and lowered his voice. "Got a telegram from the U.S. Marshal over in Pocatello this morning. Seems the tribal police are claiming you killed an Indian up on Mink Creek a few days ago. Any truth to that?"

Caleb suddenly felt weaker than he already was. The Sheriff's silver star pinned to his black vest was intimidating. It represented Caleb's ticket to jail should the Sheriff lose his common sense. Caleb nodded. "Yeah, I caught a couple of Indians butchering a steer. Told 'em I was gonna turn 'em into the BIA and the one pulled a rifle on me." Caleb paused and removed his hat to give Tom Percy a better look: "He damned near put me under."

The Sheriff peered at the angry red furrow in Caleb's scalp. He whistled low. "He sure enough parted your hair." And then he added real quick, "He shot first I take it?"

Caleb's mind flashed back to that Sunday afternoon. In truth his bullet was on its way before Stetson guy fired. Caleb described the image in his mind. "He was aiming at me when my bullet hit him. He still got off a shot though."

Percy nodded. "I can see that." He paused and then casually added, "His family is claiming you caught him and another guy with a beef. You got mad and just up and shot this guy."

Caleb exploded. "That's horseshit, Tom. A bald-faced lie is what it is. That sonovabitch didn't want to answer to the BIA police so he went for his rifle."

Percy took a step back from Caleb and raised his hand. "Calm down, son. I ain't accusing you of lying. I'm just tellin' you what this dead guy's family is saying."

Josh came to his son's defense. "Tom, that marshal needs to talk to Tony Bear Killer. He was there. He knows the straight of it."

Caleb sneered. "If he'll tell it."

Percy came back like he was sympathetic. "Well, you know how those damned Indians are."

"Tom, Caleb even gave Tony the calf they'd butchered."

"Yeah, I know that. They're saying Caleb tried to buy their silence with a beef."

Caleb saw things getting all twisted. "It was Tony who wanted to keep this quiet. He didn't want to get in trouble for butchering our beef."

Percy glanced to his left and the red brick building that housed the doctor's office. A young woman with shoulder length brown hair was looking out the picture window at them. He turned back to Caleb. "We're becoming a spectacle. When you get done here, I want you to come by my office and write down exactly what happened so I have the facts when I talk to this marshal."

Caleb came back in an agitated tone. "I just told you how it happened."

Anger flared in Percy's eyes. Josh cut in before it boiled over. "We'll be there, Tom, just as soon as the doc is finished with the boy."

Percy glared at Caleb. "I ain't the sleepy old dog that you and some of these other folks think I am."

Josh said again before Caleb could respond. "We'll stop by, Tom."

CHAPTER FOURTEEN

Doc Hale stitched up Caleb's wound and sent him home with a bottle of laudanum for the pain. The day following his trip to town, Caleb stayed on the couch per Doc Hale's advice and Sarah's insistence. He took liberal amounts of the laudanum not only for its intended use but because it took his mind to a place where he wasn't worried that Tom Percy and the Marshal from Pocatello would come for him. On Saturday, or day two of his convalescence, a buggy being pulled by a paint horse that Caleb recognized came out of the pine trees on the far side of the hay field and continued on up their lane. Caleb shouted to his mother, "Pastor Combs is coming."

Sarah was standing at the stove with a spatula in her hand probing the spuds she was frying. She looked Caleb's way. "Alright." She then took up a tattered blue potholder and grasped the handle of the iron skillet with the spuds and slid it to the cool part of the stove. She suspected why Combs was there. He wouldn't be coming inside and her spuds would burn if left unattended. She walked to the front door and opened it saying nothing more to Caleb who was looking out the window at Combs' approach. As she usually did on the ranch, Sarah was not dressed like a lady. She'd often said, *As often as I go to the barn or corrals, makes no sense to trail a dress through that muck.* So here she was dressed in Levi's, a man's green cotton shirt and cowboy boots. It was attire that outwardly Combs was obliged to disapprove of but inwardly he was like any other man who took in its revealing qualities. She purposely feigned pleasure in Combs arrival. "Good morning, Pastor. How nice of you to stop by."

Combs sat in his buggy looking out from beneath its canopy. He looked uncomfortable like he was suppressing his anger. And then he launched into it. "I'm sorry it has come to this, Mrs. Morrow."

Sarah continued the façade, taking some satisfaction in it. "Come to what, Pastor?"

Combs, seeing that he was being played, allowed his embarrassment to morph into anger. "I believe you know."

"Wilma Jenkins complained to you?"

"And others. As it stands now, there won't be any kids in your class tomorrow."

The words, the rejection hurt. Sarah wanted to cry but she did not. She stared intently at the Pastor hoping to cause him shame. To point out his hypocrisy. She thought to remind him of Jesus and the prostitute he forgave, but she did not. She thought to plead her case but knew it would do no good. Self-pity seized her. *They think I'm a whore without feelings.* Hooper came to her mind's eye. *That bastard.* Her retaliation, feeble and impotent, tumbled from her mouth. "Well, Pastor, you've seen the last of the Morrow family in your church."

She waited for it. Even naively expected it. *I'm sorry to hear that. We'll miss you.* Instead, Combs looked away and rippled the reins over the back of his paint horse causing his buggy to clatter away. For a time, she watched him leave thinking, hoping that she was having a bad dream. And then the melodic call of a meadowlark perched on a fence post near the barn reminded her of what she did have. And, as if that wasn't enough, the door to the house opened behind her. "You alright, Ma?"

Sarah wiped the tears from her eyes and turned around. "Just fine, but I won't be if I don't finish frying those spuds before your father and brother get here."

Caleb knew he'd just been lied to. Nonetheless, he stepped aside to let his mother pass. It was obvious that she needed to believe she was ok.

CHAPTER FIFTEEN

The Morrows had two hay fields. One, across from the horse pasture in plain view of the house and the other a natural meadow hidden in the timber about a half mile west. Had Josh and Noah been working in the one next to the house they would have seen Pastor Combs come and go and would no doubt have asked why he was there. Instead, when they came in at noon for dinner there was no talk of it. Caleb did not betray his mother's silence on the matter. The two of them allowed the good-natured banter, even participated. There was conjecture on when they would have the 20 acre field cut and put in the stack. And they groused too about how hot it was with it being, *damned near September*. And there was talk about school starting next week. Surprisingly, to Noah anyway, Sarah had little to say. He'd asked, *are you excited for school, Ma*? To which she'd barely smiled, *oh, I don't know. It wears on me.* Already she was paving the way for her exit. She'd reasoned, *if they don't want me teaching their kids scripture, reading and writing can't be far behind.*

It was at supper that Noah's protective bubble was burst. The boys were finishing their rhubarb pie and Josh was rolling a Bull Durham cigarette to have with his coffee when Sarah cleared her throat. She looked at Josh as if to apologize for springing this on him. And then she shifted her attention mostly to Noah. "Pastor Combs paid me a visit today. He informed me that I won't be needed to teach Sunday School any longer."

Josh and Caleb, in the know about Patsy Jenkins, pretended outrage while Noah's was genuine. "Well, what in the world is that all about?"

Sarah looked almost ill. "There's been talk about my past."

"Your past?"

Sarah looked to Josh holding his unlit cigarette. He said in an even, calm voice, "Vicious gossip from your mother and I's time up in Montana."

Noah looked perplexed. "That was a long time ago."

"It was before you were even thought of."

"So, what's this about?"

Caleb sat mute as a rock like he was hearing this for the first time. Josh went on. "Your ma worked in a saloon there."

A hopeful grin came to Noah's face. "Peddling drinks and dancing with the customers."

Sarah cut in, her voice trembling. "And more, Noah, not a lot but there was more." And then she began to quietly sob.

The legs of Josh's chair grated across the wood floor as he pushed back from his place at the table and went to Sarah. He knelt beside her chair and put his arm around her shoulders. He looked at Noah. "People do what they have to do to survive, son."

And then Noah ended the dance around it. "A whore?" The words came like they repulsed him even more so than they did Wilma Jenkins.

Josh thought to rebuke his son but stopped short realizing he had no where to go with that argument.

An unmerciful glint came to Noah's eyes. "Why now? Why is this coming up now?"

Sarah recovered enough to come to her own defense. "One of the thieves who came here is telling it around."

Noah sneered. "He knew you back then?"

Sarah nodded.

A mean spirited arrogance came to Noah's face. "You lied about him being here?"

"I had to."

"Or he'd tell that he slept with you in the back of some sleezy saloon. *Ma*?"

Josh scowled at Noah. "Don't be a shit. Your ma feels bad about all this."

Noah looked incredulous. "You're not mad about this?"

Josh squeezed Sarah's shoulder. "Your Ma and I put this behind us before we ever left Montana."

Disappointment came to Noah's face. "You're a better man than me, Pa."

Sarah pleaded. "I'm sorry, Noah."

Unphased, Noah stood up. "Believe I'm gonna go outside and have a smoke."

CHAPTER SIXTEEN

It was the third day of school. The kids, what there was of them, had all gone home. Sarah was sitting at her desk grading papers. A big clock with dark Roman numerals hung on the wall at the back of the room. Save for its methodic ticking, the room was dead quiet. There weren't many papers, 13 to be exact. Had Wilma Jenkins and Pastor Combs not poisoned other parents there would have been 21. The chalkboard behind Sarah reflected how the class was organized. It extended across almost the entire width of the room. Close to 20 feet. The left half, for grades one through four, had simple math and simple words to use in a sentence. The right half was for the older kids in grades five through eight. Math problems there required long-hand division and they were to write one page on, "What did you do over the summer? What were your favorite and least favorite things that you did?" And they needed to know that Benjamin Harrison was the current president. The younger kids' papers were quick and easy to grade while the older students took more time. This was especially true for a fifth grade boy. His least favorite part of summer was when his dog "Bones" had died. Sarah was genuinely saddened. She took time to write a note on his paper. *Bones has gone to heaven. He'll be waiting for you there.*

Sarah looked up at the clock. It read 4:20. *Ten more minutes*, she thought. *We'll have deer steaks and boiled spuds and fresh carrots.* It was a 30 minute ride to home. She'd fix supper and finish grading papers afterward. Josh and the boys were good to clean up and do the dishes. Even Noah, who'd become distant since her confession, still helped.

She heard Buttons, her horse, nicker outside. Not once but several times. Sarah rose from her chair and went to the window on the north wall. Buttons, who was picketed on a hundred foot rope near the creek, was looking at an approaching rider. Sarah's apprehension was such that a sudden fluttery sensation commandeered her heart. She took several deep breaths. After a few seconds it went away. There was no mistaking the rider. *First Tom Combs and now him.* She thought to greet him at the door. *No, better that he walk in. See me working at my desk.* Moments later, Eloy Hunsaker, president of the Grays Lake school board came through the door.

He called out the obvious as his spurs jingled across the wood floor towards her. "You're working late.:

Sarah smiled. "Yes, another school year."

"It is indeed."

Sarah watched his approach as she might a student coming up front to read to the class. His stride was slow and casual but his green eyes, always easy to read in the past, were invasive. They had settled on her breasts like he had the right. Her yellow cotton dress, full to the neck, showed nothing to invite such an obvious stare. It was a struggle to not show her discomfort. "So, Mr. Hunsaker, what brings you by today?"

He stopped directly in front of her desk. Sarah looked up, more so than usual, him being a big man. His gray sweat-stained Stetson and Colt on his right hip made his physical stature even more intimidating. Words somehow escaped from beneath his black walrus moustache. "Since we last talked, things have changed."

"They have?"

"You know what I mean."

"I'm still the same person. The same teacher."

"Maybe so, but that's not the way parents are seeing it."

Anger was on the verge of replacing Sarah's common sense. "Well, what is it these parents fear?"

"You're not a good role model. Your moral character is lacking."

"You're judging me for what happened 22 years ago? Do you think that's fair?"

Hunsaker said it slow and deliberate. "You're a whore and a killer. Most folks just don't want to associate with someone like that."

And there it was, her second claim to infamy. Two men, evil, wicked, scourge of the earth men, seconds away from killing Josh and an old miner who had befriended them. She had no choice. Somehow, Hooper had learned of that too. It was pointless, she knew, to try and explain her past. She said, barely able to contain her shame, "So, what is your intent today, Mr. Hunsaker?"

"Just know, it's not what I prefer to do."

Sarah sensed what was coming. The $75.00 a month she received for teaching was important to them. That aside, she feared the humiliation would destroy her family. Her eyes had become tear-filled. "You won't change your mind?"

Hunsaker shook his head. "I've already made arrangements for your replacement."

"Please, Mr. Hunsaker, my family needs this job."

Hunsaker paused, looking at Sarah like he had when he first came in. He smiled. "Maybe you could convince me otherwise."

Her anger was instant. "You're pathetic."

Hunsaker snorted in an arrogant way. "I was going to allow you the rest of the week, but I've had a change of heart. Give me your key."

Sarah opened the drawer where she kept her purse and retrieved the key. She held it up to Hunsaker. "I'll finish grading these papers and go."

"No, leave them. Mrs. Duke can tend to them."

A less than favorable image of Irma Duke came to Sarah's mind. It was due mostly to Josh telling her of Irma's lack of emotion, almost indifference, to the return of Orville's body. Now here she was an accessory to Sarah's ruin. Sarah collected her purse and stepped from behind the desk. She thought to offer to meet with Irma and explain her system and what the kids were studying. Their individual strengths and weaknesses, their needs. But she did not. Only one thing mattered to the president of the school board. And he didn't say a word as she walked out.

CHAPTER SEVENTEEN

Summer had finally quit the country. Most of the grass had turned yellow and a golden hue peppered the aspens. The Morrows no longer attended church, went to community potlucks and certainly not dances. It was like they were lepers.

Elk had knocked down some of the barbed wire fence surrounding the hay field west of the house. Two of the posts that were likely rotten below ground owing to having been there for nearly twenty years needed to be replaced. Noah had a two-handed grip on the iron digging bar as he raised it head-high and then drove it into the ground beside the broken off post. "You'd think," he said trying to catch his breath, "that these damned things wouldn't be so hard to take out."

Caleb laughed. "Appears Pa found the only sliver of dirt in this rock pile to wedge a post into and now you're stuck with the cobble around it."

Noah grunted as he slammed the bar down hard again. Sparks flew from the rock in the hole less than a foot deep. The collision with the rock caused the bar to vibrate in Noah's hands while producing an audible twang. "Listen to that shit, will ya. Don't know why Pa didn't put up a worm or jack fence. Damned rock pile."

Caleb looked at his brother's beet red face and the trails of sweat running down it. He grinned, knowing better not to laugh. "Pa said another guy gave him a good deal on the wire. Said at the time he thought diggin' the post holes would be easier than cuttin' all those poles for a worm fence."

Noah paused to catch his breath and allow the burning in his arms to subside. He caught the tail end of Caleb's smile. His tone was curt. "You know, you still gotta cut the trees for the posts."

"Pa said that occurred to him too late. Course, he reminded me too that Ma never groused half as much as we do about fixin' fence."

Noah looked at his brother like he'd resorted to some underhanded tactic and went back to digging. He drove the bar and grunted three times before Caleb checked his silence. "You know, you've got to let this thing with Ma go."

Noah frowned. "Thing? It don't bother you that she was a whore? Every time I look at her now I see one of those painted trollops down in Pocatello or Eagle Rock."

"She's our mother, Noah."

Noah shot Caleb a hostile look. "And that doesn't bother you?"

"Don't be an ass."

Noah shook his head as he leaned on the digging bar. "I can understand her killing those two guys to save Pa and that old miner. It sounded like they had it coming anyway. But for Ma to have sold herself in a saloon. In my mind that puts her on the same level as the guys she killed."

Caleb's first thought was to call out, *oh, bullshit.* And to parrot their father, *you ain't being fair.* But those words wouldn't come. Instead, "If I had my druthers, I'd as soon Ma was as sweet and pure as a mountain meadow filled with wild flowers." He paused before adding, "From afar, she is that meadow. We should let it go at that."

Noah scoffed. "I can't live a fantasy when I know there's weeds in that meadow of yours."

"So, whaddaya aim to do?"

"Leave. It ain't right Ma and me being strangers in the same house. I know it's eatin' her up just as much as it is me and it's pissin' Pa off."

"So, where will you go?"

"Been thinkin' I'll go down to Fort Douglas and join the Army. The Army was how Pa started out in life."

Caleb felt a hollowness in his chest. "You'll be busting up the family."

Noah frowned. "Like it isn't already?"

"We'll be short-handed."

"It's best if I leave."

"How soon you figure to go?"

"Next day or so."

Caleb looked surprised. "Damn, so soon?"

Noah grimaced. "You see how it is with the neighbors, people in town. I want no part of it. These people can go to hell for all I care."

CHAPTER EIGHTEEN

That night at supper Noah announced his plan to join the Army. Had there not been a collective awareness of the broken feelings between him and his mother there would have been looks of shock and arguments made to dissuade him. There were sad faces all around. If grades had been assigned Sarah, being close to tears, would get an A. Caleb, already in the know, a grade of B. Josh, on the other hand, was out of patience with his youngest son's unreasonableness. His pragmatism scored a D. He paused, fork in his right hand, steak knife in his left. He chewed and thought. *How can that little shit want to hurt his ma more than he already has?* He took a noisy sip of his coffee. They were waiting on him, he knew, to give the opinion that would matter most, if any did. He glanced at Noah. "Army 'll be good for ya." He then began to cut another bite of deer steak. "Indians are mostly settled down. Ain't no wars. Be a good time to be in the Army."

Noah was taken aback by his father's response. Starting tomorrow they were trailing their newly weaned calves, all 117 of them, to the railroad in Eagle Rock. Two and a half days if all went well. But that was with four riders. Now there would be three. *He ain't gonna ask me to stay.*

"When you leavin'?"

Noah looked at his father who was focused on buttering a biscuit. He recognized the purposeful indifference. *It's good that I'm leaving.* Aloud, he said simply, "In the morning. I figure to take one of the thieves' horses and sell it and my tack to the liveryman in Pocatello for train fare to Salt Lake."

Josh thought to counter. *You could help us drive the calves down to Eagle Rock and catch the train there.* But he was not about to prolong his wife's misery. He came back. "Yeah, I know that fella that owns the livery in Poky. He'll give you a fair price."

A hateful look came to Noah's face. To his credit, he was careful not to look at his mother. "I'd still rather have my own horse. Course I wouldn't sell him."

"Well, if you had Snookers you probably wouldn't be joining the Army." Caleb realized his blunder even before his mother got up from the table and left the room.

His father scowled at him and shook his head. "Ain't none of this your Ma's fault."

Noah glared at Josh, not wanting to accept the blame he was seemingly tossing out. Now, it was his turn to stand up from the table. "I'm gonna have a smoke."

Josh had the words loaded on his tongue, *sit your ass down*, but then he thought better of it. *He's leaving and that's all there is to it.*

Caleb looked at his father. "Sorry, Pa."

Josh said nothing as he pushed back from the table and his unfinished meal. His body language suggested he was at a loss as to how to fix what had just happened. Pausing, he said, "Your mother is hurtin'." He then went out the door to the back porch closing it quietly behind him. He expected that she would be sitting on the couch, but she was not. Through the screen in the near darkness enveloping the garden he could see her standing like she was taking stock of what had grown there. He purposely let the screen door slam behind him so as to not startle her. He expected her to turn around, but she did not. Within a few steps he could hear her quietly crying. He stepped next to her and put his arm around her shoulder. For a few seconds they stood there, both focused on the stalks of corn that had been picked some weeks ago. She shivered, maybe from the October night air, or maybe not. Josh squeezed her right shoulder. "It's gonna be all right, you'll see."

Sarah turned into him burying her face in his chest. And then she began to cry, just a little harder.

It was not a restful night for any of them. At breakfast, no mention was made of Noah leaving for the Army. Their talking all around it made for an awkward situation. They'd barely finished eating when Josh announced, "Well, let's go catch the horses." He and the boys stood up from the table while Sarah remained seated. Her expression was tired but hinted expectation. She looked at Noah, wanting so much to hug him goodbye. Fear of rejection kept her where she was. She said loud enough to force his attention. "You'll write when you get there?"

He paused, reluctantly, to make eye contact with her. "Sure, Ma. Just as soon as I get settled in." And then he took his gun belt from the peg on the wall and walked out the door followed by his brother.

Sarah rested her elbows on the table to either side of her plate and rubbed her forehead with the tips of her fingers. Her eyes were closed. "Am I that bad, Josh?"

Josh, who'd just finished stoking the fire to heat dish washing water stepped behind her chair and placed his hands on her shoulders. He gave her a gentle squeeze. "No, you're not. You're a good person. On God's tally sheet, I dare say you've got far more checks in the good column than the bad."

Sarah reached up and took hold of his hands. "I can always count on you."

"Yes, you can. And Caleb too."

Sarah shook her head. She had begun to quietly cry. "I guess I can't blame Noah, with so many folks feeling the same way."

"Yes, you can. You gave him life. He knows you better than these other people."

Sarah became silent. They both did, their fingers interlocked on her shoulders. They savored the moment. It was soothing, if only for a short time. Near silence, save for the prickly meowing of the dishwater starting to boil atop the popping and crackling stove. They were secure in knowing they had each other. Sarah was first to emerge from the good place. "Do you think we'll ever see Noah again?"

"I don't know. The Army will grow him up."

"Lots of grownups around here."

"I'm hoping he'll be different."

Sarah hesitated before letting go of Josh's hands. "It's a long way to Eagle Rock."

He bent down and kissed the top of her head. He said teasingly, "Yeah, I reckon it ain't moved any closer since we were last there. But on the bright side, we'll spend the night we get there in a hotel. I hear it's got running water. And we'll eat town chuck, not that it's any better than yours."

A surge of feel good came over Sarah. She stood and kissed Josh on the lips. "You better skedaddle."

For a moment they held one another. He whispered as he patted her on the back, "It's gonna be alright."

By the time he got down to the barn and corrals, Caleb and Noah had the horses caught and saddled. The team, which would be pulling the buckboard with their bedrolls, cooking equipment and food, was not yet hitched. Noah, on the other hand, had just climbed onto his horse. Josh called out. "Hold up, Noah."

Regret that he'd not left already was clearly visible on Noah's face.

Josh looked up at him. Maybe with too much anger. "You need to give your Ma a hug. Give her a proper goodbye. She don't deserve how you're being."

Noah frowned, exasperated with it all. "Let it go, Pa. I'm leavin' and that'll be the end of it."

Josh shot his son a hateful look. "By hell, if you don't go up to the house and give your mother an apology and a proper goodbye, I don't know that you need bother ever coming back here."

Hurt flashed in Noah's eyes as they shifted up the road to the house and then back to his father and brother. He then grimaced and shook his head before spurring his horse.

Josh watched until Noah was out of sight. Without looking at Caleb, his eyes being moistened as they were he said, his voice as distant as his departing son, "Let 's get the team hitched."

CHAPTER NINETEEN

It was the morning of the third day. They were in the sagebrush foothills south of Eagle Rock. Threads of quaking aspen and chokecherry bushes lined some of the draws. On the flatter ground were irregular shaped patches of yellow grain stubble. The weather was cold. Tops of the mountains towards Wyoming were already dusted with snow.

They missed Noah. Even though they'd stayed on the road the trip had not been without some difficulty. Right from the git-go the newly weaned calves balked at leaving the home place and their mothers. That first day Josh and Caleb had to work their horses hard, and Buster too. Sarah helped as best she could while driving the buckboard. It had been a full-time job keeping the calves gathered and moving away from the only home they'd ever known. There'd been a few times the men cursed the fact Noah had deserted them. Inwardly, their hearts ached. Josh's maybe more so on account of how he'd left it with Noah. It wasn't that he regretted saying what he had, it was the fact that it had to come to that.

Caleb shouted, "Pa, coupla fellas coming our way."

Josh spotted the riders who had apparently been watching them from a patch of aspen up on the hill to their right. A spring there bled a trickle of water and green grass downslope fifty yards or so before petering out. The men were allowing their horses to meander through this lushness before plowing into the waist high sagebrush that spread up from the road. The one wearing a red mackinaw pointed toward Josh and said something that was purposely beyond hearing to anyone on the road.

Caleb looked again at his father who was riding a short way out in the sage on the other side of the road. "You know these men?"

"Not from here, I don't"

"Well, they seem intent on talking to us."

"Being neighborly, I guess."

By and by the strangers intercepted the road just short of Caleb, but close enough for the one wearing the mackinaw to call out. "She cold enough for ya?"

Caleb came back, "Yes sir, just the way we like it."

Mackinaw man took note of Josh working his way towards the social gathering. "Good looking bunch of calves you got."

Caleb nodded. "Yes sir, had good graze most all summer."

"Where do you folks hail from?"

"Grays Lake country."

Josh emerged from the sage onto the road. "Mornin'."

It was at this point that the strangers, both of whom were wearing six-shooters, became uneasy. Mackinaw man shifted his attention to Josh. "Mornin' to you, Sir. Good lookin' horse you got there."

Josh was riding a buckskin that Hooper had left behind due to it being lame back then. He sensed something was afoot but said, "He's a good animal."

"How'd you come by him?"

"You might say it was a trade of sorts."

And then with one sweeping motion Mackinaw man pulled his pistol and thumbed the hammer back. "That RS/ brand mean anything to you?"

Josh left his hands resting on the pommel of his saddle. "Sit still, Caleb. We just need to explain this."

"You damned right you do," said Mackinaw man. "That's my horse. You stole it several months back."

Josh replied, his voice calm but a notch beyond stern. "You don't know that to be fact or you wudda come got your horse."

Mackinaw man jabbed the air in Josh's direction with his cocked pistol. "You're in no position to be gittin' smart-alecky"

"Well, if that gun of yours goes off, intentional or not, I will do my damnedest to kill you."

Mackinaw man laughed. His tone cavalier, "In my experience dead men ain't too good at doing anything."

Josh deliberately spate tobacco juice to the side of his horse before addressing the stranger again. "Mister, you holster your weapon and I'll tell you how it is that I came by this horse."

The second stranger, his mouth surrounded by black whiskers, had become fearful of what was about to happen. He scowled. "Dammit, Bill, put your gun away."

"And allow him to gain the advantage on me."

"You fool, the man has got upwards of a hundred head of calves here. You think he'd need to steal your horse?"

From her seat on the buckboard, Sarah called out, "An outlaw named Burt Hooper stole that horse. He came by our ranch when it had gone lame running from the law and left it behind after stealing some of our horses."

An awareness, like someone had just struck a match in a mine shaft came to Mackinaw's face. It caused him to rove his eyes over Sarah in a none too subtle way. "I heard about you."

Josh cut in. "Mister, you'd be well advised to consider real careful what you say next."

"So, these stories I'm hearing are true."

Josh nudged the sides of the buckskin and rode to within ten feet of the gunman. He looked into Mackinaw's eyes with as hateful of an expression as he could muster. He seethed the words, "Here's what I'm gonna do. We're gonna push these calves on into Eagle Rock. Your horse will be waiting for you at the stockyards. If that don't suit ya, well, I guess we'll go to it right here."

For a long, long time, maybe five seconds, Josh stared into the cavernous barrel of Mackinaw's .45 before Sarah cried out, "Mister, if it's going to make your day to trample my reputation get to it. You won't be the first, nor probably the last. But you leave my husband of 22 years out of it and count your blessings that you've snookered him like you have. In a fair fight he'd kill you in a heartbeat. So, go ahead. Tell how you heard I was a whore that killed two men. Go on, tell it."

Mackinaw was taken aback to the point there was a hint of shame in his eyes. But he was far from saying he was sorry. He continued to wave the pistol in Josh's direction in a vain attempt to salvage his ego. The others, his friend included, looked on being almost embarrassed for him. At last, he said in a voice much louder than necessary, "Well alright, I'll be by the stockyards 'bout four o'clock today. My horse damned well better be there or I'll come lookin' for you and we'll have that fair fight your missus seems to think you'd win in a heartbeat."

From the corner of his eye Josh could see Sarah. Her eyes were pleading for him to set aside his pride. He said, letting

Mackinaw feel like he'd been justified in being the way he was, "Four o'clock. Your horse 'll be there."

"He better be." And then Mackinaw spurred his horse riding past Sarah. He knew better than to look her way.

CHAPTER TWENTY

The night in Eagle Rock had been good for their spirits. They were not well known there so the Grays Lake gossip did not haunt them. They'd gotten a good price for their calves and surrendered the buckskin at the stockyards without incident. And they ate town chuck, steaks with all the fixings. They took hot baths and slept in soft beds. For a little while life was good as it should have been.

It was late afternoon. Josh and Sarah were in the buckboard with Caleb following on horseback. To either side of the narrow dirt road were sagebrush parks scattered amongst patches of pines and aspen that climbed their way up gentle hills. The sky was full of ash gray clouds that had just started to tease of what was to come. Snowflakes, not a lot of them, were floating down.

Sarah sat close to Josh. She was wearing a dark wool coat and a red stocking cap pulled down over her ears. Her left arm intertwined with his right. "It's good that it's not sticking."

He came back, it having gotten cold enough in the last few minutes to see the horses' breaths. "I suspect it won't be long though."

For a little while, maybe a half mile, they went on without speaking in the cushioned silence of the falling snow.

Coupled with their good night in town, it was soothing to listen to the squeak and rattle of the buckboard and the occasional snort of the horses. And then Sarah revived their conversation from last night. "So, you think we really can use some of the calf money and get tap water and a sink in the house?"

Josh had been looking forward to the day when he could do this for her. They'd made their payment on the note at the bank and there was money left over, but it had to last until next year when they sold their calves that hadn't even been born yet. There would be no other income owing to the fact Sarah had lost her job. From the corner of his eye he could see that she was prepared for disappointment. *She's been hurt enough.* Aloud he said, "I hope to get started on it tomorrow. Get the spring developed and the pipe in the ground before everything freezes."

Sarah looked up at him. "Are you sure? I know I've put us in a money bind."

"It wasn't you that put us where we are. We'll get by."

Her eyes filled with tears just short of overflowing. She thought to say *thanks.* Instead, they squeezed one another's leather gloved hands.

By the time they were approaching the road to the schoolhouse snow had made the ground mostly white. Irma Duke's buggy was coming at a good clip. Following behind it at a slower pace was an old blue Studebaker wagon with black wheels that, at one time, had belonged to the Army. Most everybody around Grays Lake recognized it now as Herman Snyder's. Josh slowed the buckboard to allow Irma to enter the main road ahead of them. She not only didn't acknowledge his courtesy, she didn't even look his way. Her rudeness caused Sarah's good mood, her flirtation with happiness, to evaporate. She sighed. "Is there no end to these people's hate?"

For a few seconds, Josh stared at the fresh tracks Irma's buggy had made in the snow. Its wheels spraying bits of snow and moistened soil as she got farther and farther away. He wondered how she could be the way she was. *Was she even bothered by it*? Rudeness did not come easy to him or Sarah, but their neighbors embraced it like life itself. They'd laid in bed talking, too many times, the wetness of her tears on his chest, rationalizing it long into the night. In the light of day, he still had no answers.

Sarah offered an excuse for Irma. "Do you suppose she blames us for Orville getting killed? After all, it was our horses he was trying to get back."

Josh stopped the wagon just short of the schoolhouse road. Sarah looked at him like she truly thought this possibility needed hashed out yet again. Josh came back, his voice flat, tired. "Orville did the right thing. Most men's conscience would have bothered them if they had done nothing."

"It's too bad Irma can't see that."

Josh scoffed. "I don't think she's lookin' too hard in that direction."

"You don't?"

Before Josh could explain himself, Herman Snyder's wagon rattled to a stop part way onto the main road and within talking distance of the Morrow's buckboard. He called out, cordial enough, "Looks like winter's come early."

Josh briefly looked at Herman like he was some sort of anomaly. Since everything had blown up at church and the school, he'd not had much neighborly banter. He was hesitant to come back in that tone but decided to roll the dice. "Well, if it ain't winter it sure as hell could pass for its twin brother."

Snyder laughed politely. And then, as if to account for the uneasiness in his eyes he said, "Took a load of firewood to the school."

Sarah could hear herself laugh and join in, *that drafty old place will keep you busy hauling wood.* She kept quiet.

Josh couldn't help but take a swipe at the man who'd fired Sarah. "I thought it was up to Hunsaker to get wood for the school."

Sarah squeezed Josh's arm like he was in danger of making things worse.

Snyder's look became even more uncomfortable. "I got some bug killed pine on my place. Needed to get rid of it."

Josh knew in past years that Hunsaker had hired a couple of Indians to cut firewood for the school. He probed that assumption. "What happened with the Indians bringing wood?"

Snyder's face was a chameleon of change. It'd gone to fearful. He stammered. "Well, they still are. I'm just bringing a little extra."

Josh said on purpose, knowing that his words were loaded with intent. "Why, you'll be deserving of one of Irma's pies or something."

Snyder came back quick, too quick. "Oh, no. I hardly see her. Just drop the wood off and leave."

It was at this point that the suspicion way in the depths of Josh's mind bobbed to the surface. Here it was going on 6:30. School had been out for several hours. Snyder had come by himself to unload the wood and now he and the shapely widow Irma Duke were leaving at this hour. Josh said simply, thinking to end the conversation, "Well, I'll bet Thelma will have something good for supper."

Snyder hesitated long enough to draw attention that he had and make a person wonder why. "Guess you ain't heard. Thelma is in Phoenix caring for her dying sister."

Josh's voice became sympathetic. "Oh, sorry to hear that."

"Not sure when she's coming back."

Sarah piped up. "Tell Thelma we'll be praying for her sister."

Snyder shook his head. "I don't think it'll help. She's pretty bad off."

The conversation stalled. The awkwardness grew with the Morrows knowing, or thinking they did, why Snyder and Irma were at the school so late in the day. Snyder, on the other hand, was certain he'd been found out. And then from behind the buckboard, Caleb's horse snorted wearily. Snyder seized the cue. "Guess, I better let you folks get on home."

Josh kept his team idle until Snyder had put some distance between them. And then he shook the reins. "Giddup."

All three of them were thinking it. Perhaps Sarah most of all. *Hypocrites. Irma Duke on her backside right there in the school. Hunsaker. What a damnable fool.*

Sensing where her dead man's stare into the falling snow and encroaching darkness had taken Sarah, Josh squeezed her hand. "They'll get their come-uppance one day."

The anguish, bitterness was evident in her voice. "Like I'm getting now?"

"Can't say."

"No, you can't. Cuz maybe they'll waltz along through life and never have to account for today."

"They'll have to answer to God."

"And I won't?"

Josh had no come back. He floundered in the silence.

And then Sarah added, "God can't punish me anymore than he already is."

CHAPTER TWENTY-ONE

In the morning there was three inches of new snow but there was sunshine too. It being the 21ˢᵗ of October suggested there might be enough of it to melt goodly amounts of the snow. Caleb was among those hoping for that to occur. "It's too damned early for winter, Pa."

Josh stomped his right boot down on the shovel driving it into the ground just short of covering its blade. He then pried a scoop of dirt up and dumped it to the side of the trench. His breathing was labored. "It won't last."

Caleb, swinging a pick ahead of his father, came back, "You sure of that?"

"Well, if I ain't we're in deep trouble cuz we ain't got enough hay to last from now till spring."

Caleb abruptly stopped digging. He was looking downslope towards the house. "Speaking of trouble, here it comes."

Josh stepped to the side of his son to see what he was looking at. He sighed. "Now, what could he want?"

Caleb called out, his stomach already on edge. "Mornin', Sheriff."

Tom Percy paused his horse, a big bay all of 16 hands. He came back cordial, as folks were wont to do even when they had bad news. "I thought you boys would've been smart enough to stay by the fire today with a cup of coffee. Guess I gave you too much credit." And then they all laughed as the decorum in these matters required. The Sheriff went on, delaying why he was there. "So, what the hell are you fellas up to here with all this dirt slingin'?"

Josh stabbed his shovel in the ground and removed his gloves. He nodded to a small gathering of water maybe six inches deep next to a big clump of willows. At present, as the little pool overflowed, the water fell off into a natural grassy depression that ended at the creek a stone's throw away. "Gonna box in this spring and run water to the house."

"Seems to me that wudda been a better idea last summer."

"Well, if I had me a cushy lawman's job with a regular paycheck I might have done that. But I only get paid once a year and now that our neighbors have saw to it that my wife is out of a job, we can't afford to buy the materials to pipe water to the house just whenever the weather suits it."

A sudden pall descended over the group. Magpies, perched in the willows behind Josh cackled as if to throw in their two cents. It had not been Josh's intention, but he'd spent another night in bed holding his wife trying to reassure her that their lives would get better. The effects of his uncertainty in that regard lingered yet this morning. He now proceeded to roll a Bull Durham cigarette. He glanced up at the Sheriff still sitting on his horse. He said, purposely calling him by his first name thinking the familiarity might mend any damage he'd just done. "So, Tom, why is it you're out here pestering folks engaged in honest labor?"

Percy tossed his head to the side. His look was serious. "Well, Caleb has pissed the Indians off."

Caleb jumped in. "How's that? The Marshal over there said it sounded like self-defense to him."

"That ain't cuttin' it with that dead guy's family. Talk on the rez is they're gonna get even."

Josh raised his right leg so as to tighten his Levi's. He then zippered a stick match across the back of his thigh until it burst into flame. His cigarette seesawed between his lips as he lit it while asking, "You figure these folks to be serious or are they just blowing off steam?"

"According to that Marshal in Pocatello there's some hotheads in that bunch that wouldn't lose any sleep over bushwhackin' you and leavin' ya for the coyotes. If it was me, I wouldn't go out alone or unarmed."

Josh drew pensively on his cigarette, held the smoke briefly in his lungs before exhaling in a hard forceful stream that, given the situation, might be correctly perceived as angry. "And if there's gun play, what's your take gonna be?"

"As long as you don't start it, you'll be ok."

Caleb flared up. "Hell, Tom, I didn't start nuthin with this fella and that marshal was primed to throw me in his jail."

Percy frowned. "For a while he wasn't hearing both sides of that affair."

"Well, I hope his hearing improves if we get crosswise with these boys."

"I believe he's got some town folk twisting his ear."

Josh threw in, "Well, I sure as hell hope they ain't got a mouthful of beef steak while they're grousing."

Percy shook his head. "They got money and they know politicians."

With his cigarette hand, Josh poked the air in the Sheriff's direction. "A man's got a right to defend his property."

Percy turned his head to the side and arched a stream of tobacco juice onto the snow beside his horse. Several drops failed to escape his moustache. They glistened in the noon time sun. He came again. "Ain't sayin' ya don't. Just make damned sure if you shoot one of these fellas, he has it coming."

Josh drew on his cigarette before catching Percy's eye. "Nobody here wants to shoot anyone. If we're left alone, it'll stay that way."

"I know that, but there's folks on the rez and in town that think otherwise. So, be mindful of that."

Josh shook his head and took a final puff of his cigarette before tossing it into the snow and stepping on it out of habit. As best he could, he bled off the angst in his voice. "Care to stay for dinner. Sarah's got a pot of chili on and cornbread. And apple pie just baked this morning."

It was clear that Percy was tempted but he said otherwise. "Told the missus I'd be home in time for supper. Appreciate the invite though."

Josh thought to try and convince the sheriff to stay. He knew that it would make Sarah happy. They'd not had any real social interaction since she'd been shunned at church and school. He watched as Percy reined his horse around. *Damn him. He knows how it is for her.*

Percy waved casually, not even making eye contact. "Be seeing you boys." And then he nudged his horse giving the house a wide berth, Josh figured, so as to not have to explain himself should Sarah come out.

From inside the house Sarah watched the sheriff leave. Her mind spun the worst. *He'd rather ride 15 miles on an empty stomach than break bread with a whore.*

CHAPTER TWENTY-TWO

It had been almost two weeks since the snow melted and God had denied Sarah's request to spare Thelma Snyder's 42 year old sister. And so it was that Thelma found herself being rhythmically jostled inside the stagecoach from Salt Lake City to Pocatello. It was not her preferred means of travel, but the train did not run north every day. As luck would have it, a stagecoach was departing for Pocatello this very morning.

"They say," said Thelma to the man sitting across from her, "the stage is likely to go out of business within the coming year."

The man, dressed in a dark suit with a matching bowler hat and a neatly trimmed black beard smiled. "I suspect they are right. We are ample proof of that."

A blank look came to Thelma's face.

The man added, "There's just the two of us. You can't make money on that."

Thelma flushed slight embarrassment at being so ignorant of what the man thought so obvious. "Well, how do you suppose they stay afloat?"

"Mail contract. If they lose that they'll be finished."

"Oh, I wasn't aware of that."

"Yes, it's like any other entanglement with the government. It can be lucrative."

Thelma thought of the letter she'd sent Herman last week telling him that she would be coming home today. "It's an important service though. Don't you agree?"

"Yes, however, I'm of the mind that the mail service should keep pace with the times and go by train."

Thelma smiled. "If we applied that standard to ourselves, we'd still be in Salt Lake."

The stranger appeared to take offense at being one-upped by a woman. He came back curtly, "In the long run trains make the most sense."

Thelma acquiesced. "No doubt you are correct in that belief." She then looked out the window deliberately pausing the conversation. The early November air had a bite to it. Snow crowned the peaks of several big mountains to the northwest, but around them the sage and juniper hills were devoid of it. The road had begun to climb now, slowing their progress. Outside, she heard the driver crack his whip and curse at the horses. She felt bad for the horses and thought to shout out the window to not do that on her account. But she kept her place. By and by the coach leveled out and the driver proved himself to not be quite the ogre Thelma had concluded he was as the stage came to a stop in a flat grassy area.

The shotgun messenger, who was sitting next to the driver, jumped down. He opened the coach door and stuck his head inside. "Gonna rest the horses a bit. You're welcome to get out and stretch your legs."

Thelma had just raised from her seat to take the messenger's hand in helping her out when a surly voice sounded outside. "This is a holdup. Keep your hands off your guns and nobody will get hurt."

Thelma immediately sat back down. She looked out the window on the right side of the coach. Two men with rifles stepped out of an aspen patch. They were coming toward the coach. In that instant, the stranger across from her reached inside his coat and came away with a packet of money. He hissed the words, "Put this in your bosom."

Thelma hesitated. The outlaws were getting closer by the second. Her heart was pounding. She felt as if she was going to be sick.

The stranger scowled at her. "Dammit, do what I say. You'll be rewarded."

And then a shot rang out from the trees to the left of the coach. This was followed by the whomp of a bullet striking flesh and a moan. "Oh, I've been shot, Hank." And then the driver's lifeless body pitched off the top of the coach landing next to where the messenger was standing.

Hank, the messenger extended his arms even higher as he slowly turned to face the gunmen. He dribbled the words. "Don't shoot."

One of the robbers, his head covered by a flour sack with slits cut in it for his eyes, laughed. "We won't shoot if you don't piss your pants." And then he laughed again.

The hooded man next to him uttered a harsh whisper, "Tend to business." And then to the messenger he ordered, "We want your valuables box and the mail pouch too."

Hank nodded. "Mail is up top. Don't have any valuable box."

"Don't be lying to me or you'll end up like your friend."

Hank's bottom lip began to quiver. "Hon-ho—est, we ain't got no strong box."

Thelma did not hear all of the exchange between the two bandits except the words, *you dumb shit*, stuck in her mind. Her dress buttoned to the base of her neck. She had three buttons undone just above her breasts when Hank reached the top of the stage. He threw down the mail pouch and a box of supplies destined for a barber shop in Pocatello.

The bigger outlaw, the surly one who stood to look bad if there was no strongbox as he'd been told, shouted, "That's it?"

Hank came back, his voice the epitome of fear. "It is. I swear to God it is."

The other robber laughed sarcastically. "You've been made a fool."

It was at this point that Thelma, leaning back against the seat, being not totally visible to the men outside, stuffed the bills inside her dress and began redoing the buttons. She was on the last button when a gunshot, followed by the same sickening sound of a lead mushrooming against flesh and bone, sounded. Moments later, Hank tumbled past the coach's windows and piled up next to the driver. The big guy, the one who'd just done the killing shouted. "You two, out of the coach."

The stranger whispered, "Stay calm. Not a word."

Thelma nodded, certain the terror in her eyes would give her away.

The stranger went first and then helped Thelma out of the coach. They turned to face the robbers.

The big guy stepped next to them holding his Winchester now with his right hand. "Give me your valuables."

The stranger had purposely extracted a hundred dollars from the bundle he gave Thelma and added it to the forty-two dollars already in his wallet. He acted the role of indignant victim like they'd just taken his last dollar. The big guy snatched the wallet away. He then spotted the gold chain attached to a gold-plated watch in the stranger's vest pocket. He nodded toward it. "That to."

"Please, my wife gave it to me."

"She can get you another one."

The stranger, barely two feet away from instant death, complied.

It was now Thelma's turn. The money lay flat against her chest, at least she thought it was. She held out her purse. It was cheap, black cotton that gathered at the top via a black draw string. The big guy took it and stepped back. He dumped its contents on the ground and began pawing through it. He snorted. "Two dollars and seventeen cents. This is bullshit."

From behind, the other robber reminded him, "This was your idea. And now with two men dead, we'll hang no higher than if we'd gotten a $100,000 instead of the loose change here."

The big guy stood and stared at the slits in the other robber's hood. "Don't say another word about this or you'll be on the ground with these two knotheads."

Silence briefly ensued while the agitator gaged the seriousness of the threat on his life. He then said, "Alright, 'nuff said. What about these two? We can't let'em go to town and tell on us."

The big guy turned back to Thelma and the money man. The white sack with its faded red and blue lettering hung loose on his head. His eyes were barely visible through the ragged cuts. They were like those of an animal peering out from the darkness of a cave. In spite of its apparent futility, Thelma thought she should remember all she could about the robber's appearance. *Their clothing was dark. The bigger man, six feet tall, I would guess, was wearing black boots and spurs. His friend was shorter and had brown scuffed up boots.* She would tell. Your damned right she would tell. She was still engaged in the foolish audacity of soaking up the robber's appearance when the big guy's Winchester exploded. The rifle bucked angrily in his hands. A 45-70, it was a good elk gun. Its 405 grain bullet showed no mercy. Thelma felt herself becoming sick. The impact of the big bullet lifted money man off his feet and drove him into the rear wheel of the coach. He was crumpled up there like a rag doll. No whimpering, moaning, nothing. His bright red blood pooling up in the patchy yellow grass and dirt beneath him. Thelma began to cry.

The big guy's companion called out, "Finish it so we can take our leave of this place."

Thelma shrieked and dropped to her knees, "No, please. I'm a mother. I have a family to go home to."

The robber brought the lever of the rifle down flinging an empty shell casing into the grass and then on the upswing chambered a new cartridge. He seemed to be without emotion, but then nobody could see his face. The barrel of the Winchester pointing at Thelma, no more than six feet away, was steady. Thelma's insides were not. She suddenly spewed her breakfast onto the ground in front of her. For a moment she remained bent at the waist, on her knees, retching, sobbing uncontrollably. In this frenzy, it came to her that she should give up the money. That it might appease them. But then a voice in her mind shouted. *It'll make them mad knowing you tried to keep it from them.* The voice made sense to her. She placed her hands to either side of the vomit and pushed herself up. Conscious of the wetness and odor she ran the back of her hand across her lips. She steadied her voice. "Please, I can do you no harm. I know nothing about you men."

As if things couldn't get any worse for Thelma the man behind the shooter offered, "We could take her with us. These nights are gittin' mighty cold."

Thelma was so repulsed by the thought of being passed around by these thieves and killers that she couldn't contain herself. "No, I'll never agree to that."

The man who'd suggested it laughed. "Like you have a choice?" And then he laughed some more while studying

Thelma's features. She was plump, near 40. A few strands of gray in her brown hair made it impossible to claim otherwise.

Finally, the shooter, just out of the blue, lowered the hammer on his rifle. It was like killing the money man had overwhelmed his conscience. At least for today it had. Money man had purchased Thelma's ticket to live, perhaps in more ways than one.

The robbers took what little plunder they'd gotten and went to the far side of the stage still bickering as to the wisdom of leaving Thelma alive. It was clear though, for whatever reason, the big guy was going to win out. Nonetheless, Thelma stayed on the ground. Her way of being subservient to any whim they might have to change their minds. She heard them. A third guy had come out of the trees with their horses. They were mounted, now riding south. She didn't know where the impulse came from. Brazen, careless, just plain stupidity. She looked in their direction. The recognition was instant. Before things had gone bad for the Morrows, Caleb had ridden his horse with the white star on its forehead to their place a good many times. The killers spurred their horses. Soon, Thelma could no longer hear them. She felt sick, weak, unsteady. It was an effort to get up from the ground. Sarah came to her mind. She wondered if this is how it had been for her when they took the Morrow's horses. She almost felt sorry for Sarah but then she thought, *she's a whore. They're her kind of people.*

CHAPTER TWENTY-THREE

It was fortunate that Thelma had driven their old Studebaker wagon many times over the years. Even so, given all that had happened to her this morning and there being six horses as opposed to a brace of draft horses, she had been much slower than the whip cracking driver whose body had been discovered by the ravens up on Malad Pass.

Joe Marley had readied the change of horses for the Salt Lake stage some time ago. It usually arrived at the Marsh Valley stop around 11:15. It was now almost noon. Hence the reason for his standing in front of the station staring at the road to the south. The sun was bright. He cupped his hands to the brim of his old black slouch hat to better shade his eyes. The whiteness of his hair and shaggy moustache betrayed the fact that his vision wasn't what it once was. He mentally considered the cause for the stage's absence. *Maybe a wheel come off or a horse went lame.* Robbery wasn't one of the possibilities as everybody knew there seldom was anything worth stealing on it.

"Joe, you might as well come have your dinner."

He looked to his right. His portly wife, Myrna, was standing in the doorway of their log shack She was wiping bits of biscuit dough from her hands onto a pale blue apron that hung from her waist. He was tempted. From where he stood, he occasionally detected her venison stew in the air. He came back, "Sure as I sit down to eat, they'll come."

"If they do, I'll put your plate in the oven."

"Well, I'll be go to hell, Mother, here they come."

Myrna glanced in the direction her husband was straining to see and shook her head. "Theirs' is ready too. Just need to dish it up."

Joe's voice became curious as it trailed off. "What in the world?"

"What is it, Pa?"

"I don't know. It appears old Gus has got his self a new wardrobe."

Myrna stepped from the doorway of the cabin and started across the hardpacked bare dirt towards Joe, looking south as she walked. Her eyesight, being better than Joe's, allowed her to declare, "Well, for land sakes. Those clothes are bright as a sunflower." She paused briefly. "Land a Goshen, Joe. That's a woman driving."

Joe concentrated on the yellow dot perched in the driver's seat. By and by he saw it as his wife did. "This ain't good, Mother."

"You want me to fetch your rifle?"

"No, I reckon it's too late for that."

So, they stood, side by side waiting for the yellow dot and the trouble they expected to arrive. When the stage was within a few hundred yards and it was apparent that neither Hank nor Gus was up top, Joe exclaimed, "Oh, Mother, I fear the worst has happened."

When she'd gotten on the stage this morning Thelma's shoulder length hair had been gathered and tied in back with a ribbon that matched her dress. Now, there were strands of it that had escaped. They flailed in the breeze. She saw that the old couple was staring at her. Disbelief, mild shock radiating from their eyes. She pulled back on the reins. "Whoa, team. Whoa." The stage had not quite come to a halt when Thelma shouted, "Road agents stopped us up on the pass. They killed the men folk."

Myrna gasped. "What is this valley coming to."

The team, knowing the routine, was at a standstill now waiting to be unhitched. Joe talked soft to one of the lead horses and stroked its neck making sure it would remain in place. They seemed nervous today, or maybe it was his imagination. He looked up at Thelma. "Set the brake, Ma'am, and I'll help you down."

Thelma complied with Joe's request surprising him somewhat, but no more so than her not being a hysterical mess. Her eyes were red and tired in contrast to her voice, which was strong. She was mostly down from the driver's seat before she allowed Joe a cursory grasp of her hand. The smell of vomit persisted where it had splashed on the front of her dress. It bothered Thelma more than Joe who gave no indication he'd smelled it. They were now facing one another. Joe began. "I can't feature anyone robbing the stage. Anything of value goes by train."

For almost two hours Thelma had rehearsed what she would say. With her having replaced Sarah as the Sunday school teacher, her conscience had not made it easy. She deferred, "That's not entirely true."

"How's that, Ma'am?"

The lie, as it had to be, natural and spontaneous, came forth. "A gentleman on the stage had what appeared to be a considerable sum of money. The thieves relieved him of it and a gold watch given to him by his wife just before they shot him dead."

Joe frowned. "The scoundrels. Shot him without cause, did they?"

Thelma nodded as the horse behind her began to relieve itself. The road apples cascading to the ground. Momentarily, the pungent odor floated up. Joe did not move away. His tone was even more serious, angry. "And Gus and Hank? They just shot them down too?"

Thelma was cried out as opposed to Myrna sobbing and sniffling behind her husband. She could feel the coarseness of the bills resting at the beginnings of her breasts. Her paranoia, the naysayer in her mind taunting her, *you'd better look sorry or they'll think you're a cold hearted bitch capable of stealing a dead man's money.* And so, she put both hands to her face and blinked her eyes in an effort to generate tears, but they did not come. She took a deep breath and sighed. "It was awful. Those poor men."

Joe stood quiet, processing his own images of what had happened up on the pass. He knew what had to be done but was reluctant to do it. He was an old man. After a time, he looked at Myrna and shook his head. "You know I've got to drive the stage on into Pocatello."

Sobbing a little less, Myrna nodded. "Not much choice, I guess."

"There's not." He paused before adding, "If you wanna fix this poor woman a plate, I'll change out the horses and then we'll be on our way."

Within a half an hour they were underway. Joe making light at first that his 70 year old bones might need a day or two to recover before the return trip. He then became serious promising to return tomorrow, just as soon as he could wrangle a saddle horse from the company.

Riding 17 miles in a stagecoach gives a person a lot of time to think, Thelma being no exception. *The sheriff 'll wanna know what I saw. What they looked like. I could tell him it was that Hooper bunch or at least somebody riding one of the Morrow horses.* The naysayer in her mind shouted out. *That got Orville Duke killed.* And then guilt and shame flooded her mind. She thought of her newly acquired Sunday school class. *Thou shall not steal. I'm no better than these road agents.* She looked out the window at the vast gray sagebrush flowing across the valley floor and pushing up onto the hills eventually giving way to timbered canyons. Here and there honest people, working for their money, had plowed under the sage and planted hay and grain and potatoes. Small fields struggling to survive. Thelma could see where some of the crops had failed. Crop failure had happened to her family. For a moment she felt some justification in what she'd done. Hail had destroyed their wheat crop. Never mind their prayers. God had a different plan. Her mind was in a swirl to the point she reached for the buttons on her dress. *I'll leave it inside the coach. The sheriff will think the outlaws missed it in their search.* Her fingers worked quickly towards her salvation. Four buttons undone. She pulled the bills out. Her heart immediately began to race. She'd never seen a one hundred dollar note before, let alone have a stack of them in her lap. She began to count looking up fearful that somehow old Joe had contorted himself to look down in the window while still driving the stage. *Forty-nine, fifty. Five thousand dollars. This could be a new beginning. Maybe move to town away from that vile Duke woman.* But then the stage began to slow.

"Joe, how is it you're driving the stage?"

"Road agents. Killed the boys up on the pass."

"The hell you say."

"Giddup, horses." The stage lurched. Seconds later Thelma saw a man on a buckskin horse to the side of the road watching as they rolled by. Little did he know that Thelma was about to consummate the real robbery.

As her letter had requested, Herman was there waiting for her. He got up from a wooden bench on the boardwalk in front of the stage line office. He manufactured a disingenuous smile like he was glad to see Thelma's return, while his mind's eye replayed images from yesterday's wood delivery. The school had a tiny room with a cot for a student who might become ill during the day and could benefit from rest and quiet. Herman's tryst with Irma Duke had been anything but restful or quiet.

The stage had not quite come to a stop before Joe validated the perturbed look on the station agent's face. He shouted, "Stage was held up."

As luck would have it, the sheriff was about to enter a little hole in the wall café two doors down from the stage line office. He heard Joe's announcement and was coming at a quick pace, his boots thumping out the measure of his steps on the boardwalk. When he was about on scene, the station agent, Nephi Kyle, hollered up to Joe. "Where's Gus and Hank?"

Even though the stage was now at a standstill, Joe remained in the driver's seat, perhaps soaking up the attention from the growing number of onlookers. He came back as if he were the town crier. "They're laying dead up on the pass."

The sheriff, now standing between Nephi and Joe, saw Thelma letting herself out of the coach. He immediately went to assist her.

Thelma took the sheriff's hand and stepped down. "Thank you, Sheriff."

His senses, being keen and delicate for a man, allowed him to smell the vomit, faint as it now was, on Thelma's chest. It caused his eyes to fall upon her ample bosom and the stain there. Red in color, it was most likely from the stewed tomatoes she'd had at breakfast. Thelma noticed his untoward behavior. Her knees instantly weakened as she looked down, thinking that one of her buttons had come undone exposing the money.

To his credit, Herman finally stepped up. However, he didn't reach out to touch her as the others present expected.

Instead, his voice was distant, detached. Maybe back at the school. He said, "Sounds like you've had an ordeal."

Disgust overtook Thelma's face as she stared at her husband. Her eyes spoke for her. *I've witnessed the murder of three men and been on my knees begging for my life and I don't warrant a hug? Or even an are you alright? You bastard.*

The Sheriff intervened. "Ma'am, I know you've had a pretty rough day, but I would be greatly obliged if you could indulge me for a few questions."

Thelma was hesitant to look the Sheriff in his eyes. They were hidden beneath the flat brim of a gray Stetson with a blunt peak. Dark and penetrating, they were the kind of eyes that made a person fearful their inner thoughts were on display. Her paranoia kicked in. *I should just give him the money. Oh, but how would I explain it now? They'd see me for what I am.* Aloud, she said, "Certainly, Sheriff. I'd be glad to help."

The Sheriff was wearing a black wool coat and a slick looking vest of the same color beneath it. He slid his hand under the left flap of the coat and came away with a small green notebook and pencil. He opened it and thumbed to a blank page. "Your name, Ma'am?"

"Mrs. Thelma Snyder."

"And where do you reside?"

"Grays Lake north of Soda Springs."

"Can you tell me what these road agents looked like?"

Thelma felt like she was the star attraction. Joe perched above her on the stage looking down and the Sheriff, Nephi and Herman eye to eye with her. And a growing crowd, mostly men, that had the good fortune to stumble upon a spectacle worthy of at least several days gossip. Thelma came back. "I'm sorry, Sheriff, they were wearing flour sacks over their heads."

"Did the sacks have any writing on them?"

"Yes, but I couldn't say what it said. "

The Sheriff frowned. His neatly trimmed black beard not hiding entirely the fact that he had. Thelma attempted to redeem herself. "One of the robbers was big. Several inches taller than you, I think. The other shorter by a head maybe."

The Sheriff scribbled in the notebook. "You remember anything else about these men?"

Thelma knew all along what she should tell the Sheriff. The memory, however, of her defiling herself with her own vomit and begging on her knees for her life saying that she would tell the law nothing about them, was still fresh in her mind. In fact, that image was likely never going away. It was on impulse that she finally said it. "These men are that Hooper gang. I recognized Caleb Morrow's horse. The big guy was riding it."

The shootout in Freedom, Wyoming and the circumstances leading up to it had become common knowledge in this part of the country. The Sheriff nodded and scribbled again. Paused and then asked. "What caused these fellas to kill the others on the stage?"

Thelma grimaced. "I don't know. I think they expected to get more loot. It could be they're just evil, wicked men."

The Sheriff did not scribble again but kept his pencil poised above the notebook. "Did they rob the passengers?"

"Yes. I lost a few dollars."

"And the man riding with you, did they take much from him?"

Thelma wanted to scream at the Sheriff. Lash out at him in some way for tempting her like this. In that instant she saw him as the devil incarnate. The opportunity cried out to be seized. *It will be my word against that of thieves and killers.* And so, the lie went forth. "Yes, they took a large amount of cash from him."

"Do you know how much?"

"No, but it was a stack of bills maybe a half inch thick. Abraham Lincoln's picture was on them."

Nephi threw in. "Hundreds?"

"I believe that was the amount."

Nephi looked at the Sheriff. "That was Ben Meyers that got robbed."

The Sheriff scribbled again in his book and then paused as if studying how little he had written. He frowned before shifting his attention to Thelma. "Can you tell me, Ma'am, which one of these bandits did the killing?"

Like God had willed it Thelma found herself back at the pass on her knees staring into the barrel of the big guy's rifle, crying and begging for her life. Begging for the chance to come home to her cheating husband. Assuring them that she knew nothing to tell. She played dumb. "Like I said, Sheriff, I couldn't see their faces."

"You did say one of the men was a head taller than the other. On that basis, which one did the shooting? Or did both of them?"

"I was inside the coach and didn't really see the men killed."

"So, they took Mr. Meyers out of the coach and left you inside?"

The Sheriff's words reeked of disbelief. Thelma could see it in his face, Nephi and Herman's too. It didn't make sense that she hadn't seen what happened. The truth, however, would not benefit her. When Gus and Hank were killed, she had been leaning back in the seat stuffing Meyers' money inside her dress. She really hadn't seen who killed them. Meyers, on the other hand, would haunt her nights forever. Her credibility was about to expire when she blurted out, "Well no, Sheriff, they made me get out of the stage at the same time as this Meyers fellow."

"So, you did see who shot him?"

Thelma nodded. She felt she was betraying the outlaws, at least the one who spared her life. "It was the big guy."

The Sheriff scribbled again. "That'd likely be Burt Hooper." He paused. "That is if you are correct in identifying the Morrow horse."

Thelma came back quick, almost short with the Sheriff. "Yes, I know that horse. The Morrow boy calls him Snookers."

The Sheriff scribbled again and then looked up at Thelma. "I appreciate your help, Mrs. Snyder. You're a fine citizen. Should we ever capture these rascals I hope that I can call upon you to testify at their trial."

The enormity of the sudden shock, the fear of being exposed for the thief and liar she was, caused an uneasiness in Thelma's bowels such that she was terrified she might soil herself. She said quickly. "Of course, Sheriff. Is there anything else?"

"No Ma'am, you're free to go."

Free, the word echoed in Thelma's mind. She threaded her left arm through Herman's right, not because she felt affection for him, but rather it was a show. She was a respectable married woman with a family. Certainly not the kind of person that would steal a dead man's money.

CHAPTER TWENTY-FOUR

Nobody had bothered to tell the Morrows that Caleb's horse had been used in robbing the stage from Salt Lake City. Not until they'd read the Pocatello paper, a week after the fact, did they learn about it.

After supper, Caleb was sitting next to the fireplace and a kerosene lantern reading the paper. Occasionally, the fire licked up some pitchy wood and popped an ember out onto the cobble rock hearth or sometimes the braided rug on the floor. It had just launched another ember causing him to lower the paper. The glowing particle of wood was dying on the rock. He offered up, some sarcasm in his voice. "Thelma Snyder is gittin' to be a real celebrity."

Josh looked up from where he was reading on the couch. He laughed briefly. "I suspect Herman will not be delivering anymore wood to the school now that she's home."

Caleb joined in the laughter. "If Thelma only knew, she'd box ole Herman's ears good."

The levity in Josh's face faded away on purpose so as to accommodate what was on his mind. "You know, it just occurred to me that the reason we ain't heard from Noah is because these scalawags that robbed the stage got his letter."

Caleb came back, more wishful than realistic. "Well, that makes some sense, Pa. Personal letters won't mean a thing to those vermin."

Sarah was in the kitchen feeding her sourdough. She'd heard the conversation in the living room thinking that they were just being kind, given the way things were when Noah left. Deep down she was afraid, and she suspected they were too, that Noah wouldn't write at all. Since he'd left for the Army they'd speculated at length on his decision. Tonight, however, she felt blue. She abstained from their talk lest she become more so. Staying busy was her elixir for moods like this. She measured out three cups of flour and dumped it into the big pale green bowl containing the mix. Next, she turned the handle of her new faucet not caring if any water splashed out of her cup as the white porcelain sink below would catch it and drain it away. She added three cups of the cold spring water to the sourdough and began stirring. When it was batter like again, she put a dish towel over the bowl and set it at the far end of the counter next to the wall where it always resided. Sourdough hotcakes and biscuits were a staple in their diet. Thus, the sweet, sour smell, pleasant to most folks, permeated the room year around.

The story in the paper was old news now. With the exception of Sarah, they'd read it twice and some parts more than that. For her, once was enough. She'd replayed in her mind countless times the day that Hooper and his men had come and how she'd foolishly allowed herself to be blackmailed.

Unsolicited, Caleb read aloud like they didn't already know verbatim what it said. "Mrs. Thelma Snyder, a passenger on the stage, stated that she personally witnessed the big robber, who is believed to be Burt Hooper, gun down Mr. Ben Meyers, a prominent businessman and take from his person a large amount of cash, reportedly in the amount of $5,000."

It was an effort for Sarah to suppress the urge to snap at her son. *That's enough Caleb. Keep it to yourself.* Instead, she took a cookbook from a drawer beneath the kitchen counter and sat down at the table. She pretended to read an apple pie recipe that she knew by heart. Inside, she seethed with anger and regret. *Damned Hooper. Will he never go away?*

It was clear that Caleb was hesitant, but he said it anyway. "Pa, it rankles me that these fellas has still got two of our horses."

Josh paused from his reading and glanced at Sarah for her reaction. He was not fooled by her pretending not to hear. He frowned his displeasure at Caleb for going on about Burt Hooper. It wasn't that he took offense, like Caleb was hinting he was afraid to go after Hooper. Nonetheless, he came back with agitation in his voice. "It bothers me too. And if I didn't have a ranch to run, I'd drop everything and leave your ma here by herself and go galivanting off looking for him. But that ain't how it is."

Sarah made eye contact with Josh. Always her rescuer. The affection between them was obvious. For Caleb, the emotion was different. He made a show of folding the paper and tossing it aside. "Believe I'm gonna go outside and have a smoke." And with that, he rose up and walked smartly to the door. His departure being punctuated by the silence of the crackling fire.

CHAPTER TWENTY-FIVE

In the morning they ate sourdough hotcakes, bacon and eggs and drank black coffee. Not a word was said about Burt Hooper or the holdup. For a little while it was almost like they were happy, normal people without worries or dissention in their lives. And then, when they were nearly done eating, Josh announced his plans for the day. "Been thinkin; I oughta ride the rez boundary fence over beyond Porcupine Crik. Probably wasn't the smartest thing I ever done puttin' the cattle over there this fall." He sighed and shook his head. "But that's where the grass is."

Caleb threw in, his tone respectful. "Well, the next dumb thing you could do would be going there by yourself."

Josh grinned. "I'll keep a sharp eye out."

"Lots ah places to hide and bushwhack a man over there."

A worried look consumed Sarah's face. "He's right, Josh. Please don't go by yourself."

The instinct to protect his offspring was paramount in Josh's mind. Caleb had averted death at the hands of the Indians by a fraction of an inch. The next time around God might be less kind. He held his ground, or at least tried to. "I'll be alright."

Sarah scoffed and shook her head. "Well, if you're not going to listen to common sense then I guess I'll have to go with you."

"No, you're not."

"You can't tell me no."

Josh went quiet. There would be hard feelings if he tried to stop her from going. He knew she'd as soon die with him as be without him. And he knew too that she'd give her life for Caleb. It was common sense that muddied the water. Caleb was a better hand with a rifle than she was. If there was to be a tomorrow, as things were now, he was the one that should go. Josh sighed. "Well Caleb, appears I been trumped."

Caleb laughed. "I'll go saddle the horses."

"I'll help your ma rustle up something for our dinner sacks."

When the door closed behind Caleb, Josh turned to Sarah. "You know, anymore, I don't feel good about leaving you here alone. I don't think we could count on the neighbors for anything."

She stepped closer to him and put her hands on his shoulders. "I'll be ok."

Josh put his arms around her waist and looked down into her eyes. He could see the doubt in her face. "The country's changed."

"For us it has. Maybe someday the people will learn to forgive."

Josh scoffed. "They'll have to start with themselves."

Sarah allowed the comment to gel for a moment. They both knew what he meant. And then she replied. "Hunsaker can't be so stupid as to think Herman Snyder takes firewood to the school out of some sense of community spirit. Especially when the only time he's moved to do so is when Thelma is away."

By the time Sarah had finished speaking her words were loaded with anger. Josh came back. "They'll get theirs."

Sarah stepped back from Josh. Her expression became haughty and sarcastic. "In the meantime, the sinful Irma Duke will continue to teach the children of Grays Lake." Tears welled up in her eyes. She went on, her tone even more sardonic. "Maybe an exception will be made for Irma since she likely isn't charging for her favors and I did."

Sarah began to cry. Josh pulled her to him and held her. "It's gonna be alright, I promise." Truth be told, though, he wasn't sure.

CHAPTER TWENTY-SIX

It was about an hour's ride from the home place to the open range and good grass. Most of the Morrow cattle found everything to their liking in a long valley bisected by Porcupine Creek, a little spit of water no more than six feet wide. From this valley to the reservation boundary was a mile or so. Josh and Caleb reined in their horses on a ridge overlooking the valley. Red Hereford cows dotted the yellow grass and gray sage. Others lingered amongst the willows and Quaking Aspen along the creek. Josh squinted his eyes as he poked the dots with his index finger while whispering the count. "Got 92. What'd you git?"

Caleb mouthed a few more numbers before relaxing back in his saddle causing the leather to creak. "I got 85."

Josh shook his head. "Lotta daylight between those numbers and 117. Hope they ain't drifted toward the rez."

"I reckon cows are like people, never satisfied with what they've got."

Josh sighed. "Well, I guess we better make a loop through that country on the other side of the crik and see what we can find."

They nudged their horses forward allowing them to pick their way down off the ridge. The grass being as tall as the sage caused the horses to snatch mouthfuls as they went along. At the creek they stopped to water the horses and relieve themselves of breakfast coffee. "The cows look good," said Josh as he buttoned his Levi's. "They're fat as can be."

Caleb gathered the dropped reins of his horse who was nibbling grass and willow leaves along the creek bank and stepped up into the saddle. "Be nice if we didn't have to start feedin' until Christmas."

Josh laughed as he got on his horse. "You better write Santy Clause on that one." He laughed some more as the horses splashed across the creek.

They went on admiring the good graze and the condition of the cattle until they came to the timber. There, in the shade, the grass was short and sparse. Few cows lingered here. They rode deeper into the dark green trees and closer to the reservation boundary. Josh was in the lead and first to spot it. He brought his horse to an abrupt stop. Caleb came along side of him. Josh scowled and shook his head. "The sons ah bitches. I was so hopin' everything would be alright."

Caleb studied the concentration of cow and horse tracks. "How many you figure they got?"

"Ten-twelve, hard to say. Ground's purty churned up."

"How many riders you figure?"

Josh stared at the trail of tracks crossing the mostly bare ground opening in the trees. "Ain't no shortage of horse tracks. Maybe three or four."

Overhead, two ravens began circling and calling out their presence. Caleb glanced up at them. "Our being here ain't no secret now."

"No, but these tracks is smokin' fresh. These fellas ain't far ahead of us. They'll be edgy. Feisty, I imagine, and on the lookout. Won't be easy to sneak up on 'em."

"They get across the reservation boundary we may be outta luck."

Josh's eyes suggested he was drawing on the past to deal with what lay ahead. He pulled his Henry from its scabbard and chambered a round easing the hammer down so all he would need to do is thumb it back to shoot. He then met Caleb's look. "An occasional steer I can abide. But this kind of thievery will put us in the poor house."

"You figure to go on the rez?"

"If need be. If you let 'em think they're safe there why hell, come Thanksgiving, we won't have cow one."

Caleb made no reply. He drew his rifle and did as his father had done. They fell in on the tracks. There were at least three riders. They were keeping the cattle tightly bunched moving through the scattered trees. There would be no surprising the rustlers. Steller's Jays and pine squirrels screeched and chattered Josh and Caleb's progression through the forest. But these animals showed no bias. There were no magic tricks to keep them quiet, short of just not invading their home. And so, when they arrived at the gap in the boundary fence where the wires had been cut, Josh's head snapped in the direction of a cacophony of calls from these woodland sentries. He looked over at his son, dead serious on his face, and whispered. "There they are."

Caleb nodded in the direction of the commotion. It appeared to be coming from heavier timber around 400 hundred yards deeper into the reservation. He was about to ask his father what they would do next when he saw him prod his horse through the opening. They continued single file with Josh in the lead. It was mid-morning. Blue skies. Good light for shooting. But the wind had come up in the last little bit. It caused a small patch of aspen to surrender even more of their yellow leaves. At times, the wind swayed the pine boughs. Without warning, Josh stopped and got off his horse. Caleb welcomed the move. His senses were strained to the limit searching for the rifle barrel that would end his life. He stepped close to his father. "What now?"

Josh's look was of exasperation and anger. "They're not likely to give our cattle back without a fight. Be vigilant son, or they'll bury us here."

"I know, Pa."

They tied their horses and set out on foot. Josh stayed 15 to 20 feet ahead of Caleb. *No sense giving them two targets side by side*, he'd said. The plethora of tracks and fresh, wet manure from both the cows and horses made their task easy, at least the trailing part was. Stealth and intense scrutiny of their surroundings tempered every step. They avoided openings where a bushwhacker would have a clear shot. At the same time, they never pushed through pine boughs without first peeking through to the other side. And they took care to step over the dry pine cones and sticks and go around all together the crunchy blanket of fallen leaves amongst the aspen. Their precautions, however, seemed pointless as the same forest creatures that tattled on the rustlers now did the same to them. It was causing Josh some frustration and considerable angst when suddenly those emotions spiked. He stopped dead still to listen. There were voices. Guttural sounding words he could not understand. "Hy-up. He-yaw. Yup, yup." Instantly it came to him. *We're on* 'em. He turned to motion to Caleb when a hot poker sliced through the muscle beneath his left arm. The pain was no match for his fear of dying and the adrenaline generated by that. He had only a vague awareness of the gunshot, but crowded into this second of terror his eyes had seized upon a faint puff of smoke. It was there off to his left. No more than 30 yards away, hanging on the limbs of a Douglas fir tree. The gray clashing with the green. Even before he glimpsed the blue patch of his assailant's shirt, Josh brought his rifle to bear on the smoke. He was numb to the recoil of the Henry and the noise it made. Paramount in his mind was the fear of a second bullet coming from the tree. And then he saw him, a young Indian probably Caleb's age stagger from behind the tree and collapse on the ground. For a time, he stood there watching the fallen man. Hoping that he was dead and no more threat in the fight that was coming, but regretting too that this had ever happened.

Caleb was breathless with fear. "I believe he's done in, Pa."

Josh nodded his eyes wide with excitement. "His friends will be after us."

Caleb looked at the dark red stain working its way down his father's left side. He thought to recognize it. To offer to tend to it. Common sense prevailed. *No time for that now.* Aloud he said. "They're yelling to one another, Pa. Ya hear 'em?"

Josh wondered at their arrogance, their foolishness at not being quiet. He was thankful for it. But then their generosity ended and quiet, save for the squirrels and Steller's jays, descended upon them. He whispered. "I suspect they'll try to flank us." And then he nodded towards a thick patch of pine trees some forty yards distant. "We'll make our stand there."

Again, Josh took the lead. He ran, crouched over, weaving amongst the brush. It was a struggle for him to hold his rifle at the ready out in front of him as the pain in his side was overtaking his adrenaline output. His breathing was rapid in anticipation of the Indians spotting them and putting a bullet in their backs. At last, they reached the trees and plowed into the midst of them. Limbs of the big trees began close to the ground. They presented a wall of green to the outsider, but at the same time, it was not easy to see out. And ferns, lush and green during the summer, were now brown and crackly underfoot. Movement would have to be slow and careful lest they offer their location to a sound shot. The trees were big enough to stop most bullets. Their interlocking boughs were not.

Caleb whispered. "I ain't so sure who's holding the better hand here, Pa."

Josh sat down and lay back against a rotting log. He grimaced. "If I was more fleet of foot I'd say take the fight to them, but I ain't."

Caleb knelt beside his father, not looking at him but outward peering through the limbs. "You reckon they might just push on with the cattle and leave us be?"

Josh grinned like he thought Caleb was naïve. "This is about revenge. Hate isn't so easily satisfied. They'll try hard to kill us if they can."

And then Caleb's heart jumped into his throat. He snapped his Winchester to his shoulder. It was a reflex. Impetuous, some might say, that he pulled the trigger. Others, not being in their predicament, would have called it stupid to have taken such a hasty shot. Regardless, the 210 grain bullet went on its way after having its course slightly altered by the wind's vagary in pushing a pine bough into its path. The Indian appeared old enough to be the father of the dead man lying nearby. He presented a good shot. Green Mackinaw coat. Black slouch hat. Long black ponytail escaping it. In his haste, Caleb's rifle had come to rest on the man's head. It had not been his intention to shoot him in the head as he could see his eyes, unaware as they were. But the bead at the end of his rifle's barrel had settled into the notch of his rear sight. He barely felt the gun jump back. Through the smoke he saw the Indian run, unscathed. He hissed. "Dammit."

And then providence deserted him and Josh. A bullet came crashing through the limbs somehow missing the trunks of their supposed salvation. Neither of them, as they had feared, saw the bullet's origin. And then their attackers began shouting to one another in their native tongue. Josh and Caleb strained their ears to get a fix on the voices. The conversation was brief. *Just enough for the shooter to tell his friend where we're at*, thought Josh.

Caleb whispered, "Pa, our chances are poor here."

The Indians, having coordinated with one another began firing from good cover. One to the southwest and the other northwest of the pine thicket. Their firing was not quick as they likely didn't have anymore ammunition than the white men they were trying to kill. Their intent was to draw fire and concentrate on the gun smoke produced by it. Josh and Caleb, who had crawled to the backside of the rotten log, were smarter now. Josh purposely smiled at his son. "These damned trees has gotten skinnier."

Caleb managed a grin. "I believe they're shrinkin' their way to being toothpicks."

Josh, still smiling, nodded. "I think there's just the two of them. Both of 'em is to the west of us. That leaves our back door open. We need to vamoose out it and see if we can't flank one of these fellas."

They were laying on their sides behind the decaying log. Caleb on his left sneaking an occasional peek toward the shooters and Josh, because of the pain in his left side, lay on his right looking out their back door as he called it. The roar of the Indian's rifles echoed on top of one another fading away and away into the mountains that hid them from civilization. There was no law here to check them. The parties involved would make up their own rules. Settle their differences as they saw fit. The bullets were like angry hummingbirds clipping the vegetation above them. Occasionally, one would auger into the rotten log or one of the healthy trees. They were not many in number, but only a fool would gamble on standing up to go out the back door. And so, they crawled on their bellies with Josh going first. He held his rifle in front of him alternately using his elbows to lever his body forward. The left side wriggles were excruciating. The far edge of the thicket was roughly twenty yards. By the time they reached it, Josh was sweating profusely and breathing hard. They'd gotten to their knees. Josh took a deep breath and let it out like it would fix him. He clutched his Henry by the barrel, its butt resting hard on the ground. It was clear to Caleb that he needed it to steady himself. Undeterred, Josh whispered. "Son, their shootin' tells me they're none the wiser what we've done. I believe if we was to split up and –"

"No, Pa. You're in no shape to do anything but try an' skedaddle outta here. You need a doctor."

Josh now gripped the barrel of his rifle with both hands. He was defiant. "We can't let 'em make off with those cows. All of 'em is likely to throw a calf come spring. We can't afford the loss."

"The loss, Pa, will be you. That's what this family can't afford."

Common sense had deserted Josh. Anger, ego, pride, a potpourri of emotions that would get him killed had taken over. "Dammit, Son, we can get the better of these two."

Caleb put his hand on his father's shoulder and looked him hard in the eyes. "We might. We might just put these boys under and get our cows back, but you ain't whole so that proposition appears iffy to me."

Josh went silent. His mind's eye had gone to Sarah and what would happen to her if he didn't come home. The hurt it would cause her became tangible to him. It was like he could reach out and touch it. And then they became aware that there had been no shots for close to a minute.

Caleb looked at his father with renewed urgency. "Pa, we need to make our move."

Josh sighed, "alright." He then pushed himself up with the aid of his rifle. "Let's go home."

An orange glow beyond the mountains to the west was all that remained of the sun when Sarah spotted them. She was immediately alarmed as they were riding double on Caleb's horse and leading Josh's. A couple of miles back Josh had become too weak to sit his own horse. Sarah and Buster began running towards them.

Much further to the west, the shooters drove their bounty of stolen cattle and led their companion's horse. Him being tied across the saddle.

CHAPTER TWENTY-SEVEN

The stars were still out the next morning when Caleb started for Soda Springs and the doctor. Sarah had done a good job of cleaning and bandaging Josh's wound, but it needed stitches and something to ease the pain. So it was that Caleb got to town before the sun was fully up or, for that matter, most folks. There was, however, a column of blue smoke rising from the rusty tin stovepipe protruding from the tar papered roof of the Sheriff's office. Caleb reined his horse to the left side of the street where the little rock walled building sat next to the livery stable. There was a barred window to either side of the door. Light was visible in the one to the right. Caleb tied his horse to the hitching rail in front of the door. A white sign with black lettering that read, SHERIFF, hung above it. He turned the knob and went inside. Tom Percy looked up from the newspaper he was reading. Light from the chimney lantern on the corner of his desk reflected in his wire rimmed spectacles that were perched halfway down his nose. He came to life, his tone guarded. "Well hell, the chickens is barely outta bed and here's one of the Morrow clan in my office. This can't be good."

Caleb remained standing in spite of there being a wooden chair to his right in front of the desk. He came back. "We had another run-in with the Indians."

"I told you they'd be coming for you."

"What they came for was more of our cattle."

"How many did they make off with?"

"Upwards of a dozen."

Percy whistled low and shook his head. "That'll take the profit outta things."

Caleb nodded. "Yeah, it does."

And then the obvious fact that Caleb was there and not his father prodded the Sheriff. "So, where's your pa?"

Caleb hesitated like he was about to walk out on thin ice. "He's home nursin' a gunshot wound."

Percy frowned. "So, you tangled with the Indians did ya?"

The smell of coffee was strong. A pot was simmering on the stove in the corner of the room and there was a half full cup on the desk. Caleb watched Percy take another drink while he waited for his answer. *It's cold outside. The sonovabitch cudda offered me a cup.* The thought took hold of his tongue. "We didn't have much choice seeing how nobody else wants to rein those boys in."

Percy glared at Caleb. "That's an Army problem."

Caleb took a step closer to the Sheriff's desk and looked down at him. "That's bullshit. Those boys committed a crime off the rez."

Percy, clearly angry, shot back, "This is the first I heard of it."

Caleb laughed. "We caught 'em in the act. What are we supposed to do, ride back here and tell you?"

"Might of kept your pa from getting shot."

Caleb was caught off guard by Percy's response. He had thought the same thing.

The Sheriff piled on. "Did you get your cows back?"

Caleb shook his head. He wished his father was here. He'd call Percy on his talk. He'd throw it back on him. He'd tell him that he rode his chair more than he did horseback looking for lawbreakers. But he wasn't his father. He said, "They cut the fence and took 'em onto the rez."

"And you chased right after 'em?"

"They was taking our livelihood."

"So, how'd the Indians fare in this scrap?"

Caleb thought to defend what he had to tell Percy more than what he had already, but it was apparent that it likely wouldn't change things. He just put it out there. "Pa killed the one that bushwhacked him."

Percy closed his eyes briefly and shook his head in disgust. "That probably won't be the Indians take on what happened."

Anger overtook Caleb. "For hell sakes, Tom. They stole our damned cows. I'd like to know how they'll spin that tale so as to make them look good."

Percy smiled wryly. "The rez is another world."

"So, we're to just let them keep our cows?"

The Sheriff gauged the anger in Caleb's eyes before purposely taking another drink of coffee. He sighed. "I got no authority on the rez. Best I can do is send a telegram to the U.S. Marshal in Pocatello. Maybe he can work some magic with the Indian agent at Fort Hall."

"And the guy Pa killed?"

"If it was self-defense like you said he may be alright. Where there might be a stink is your pa taking it upon his self to go on the rez after these fellas. It's common knowledge amongst most white folks they ain't allowed there without permission."

Caleb scoffed. "Well Tom, it's common knowledge too that stealing another man's livestock is against the law."

The Sheriff went quiet, just staring at Caleb, saying nothing. His look of indifference was unwavering. Only now did they hear the old clock on the wall behind him and a dog barking in the distance. Caleb considered, even regretted for a moment, the damage his sarcasm had done and then he walked out. He'd told his father early that morning, when it was still dark outside, that it would do no good to tell Tom Percy what had happened. But he was insistent that Caleb go there first.

The November air was cold and still. Smoke from breakfast fires hung over the town like a layer of fog. Main Street was deserted, save for the owner of the mercantile who was out front with a pitchfork and wheelbarrow cleaning up the patron's horse manure from the previous day. As Caleb rode by he looked at the man. "Mornin'."

The storekeeper looked up, his breath pulsating steamy clouds in the frigid air. He acted like he was going to return the greeting before abruptly tossing his forkful of manure in the wheelbarrow, like Caleb wasn't there. Caleb rode on. Since his mother had been shunned, people who they had known for years felt no obligation to be civil, unless they were in the mood.

Through the window, Caleb saw movement in Doctor Hale's office. He tried the door and went inside. The doctor was standing across the room next to a bookshelf that covered most of the wall. He turned while supporting an open book with the palm of his right hand. Concern came quickly to his face. "Never a good sign someone coming into my office before I'm open. Especially someone who lives as far away as you do."

Caleb was bundled against the cold. Heavy dark coat. Brown cotton gloves. A good-sized blue neckerchief and an old black slouch hat that he thought warmer than his usual Stetson. He took the hat off. The doctor's education intimidated him. He was respectful of the fact Doctor Hale had the power of life and death. More so than God if people were honest about it. He said, "Pa's been shot."

Doc Hale frowned. "You Morrow's seem to have a propensity for that."

"Well, if the Indians would leave our cattle alone, we'd quit pestering you."

Hale looked out the window. Seeing only Caleb's horse his expression darkened. "Is your father outside?"

"No Sir, it's 30 miles round trip to town. We figured that wouldn't do Pa any good."

"Probably not, but I can't go to your place today. Maybe not even tomorrow."

Caleb's first inclination was to put the doctor in the same category as the storekeeper shoveling manure. However, he had no trump card to play against a man with almost the same footing as God. He came back, respectful, hat in hand, "He's hurtin' purty bad, Doc. He's got a helluva hole where that bullet came out."

Hale shook his head. "I can give you something for his pain and something to clean the wound with, but that's as good as I can do."

Caleb looked at Hale, less respectful now. "Doc, I ain't no medical person but I believe his wound needs sewed up."

An angry, annoyed look came over Hale's face. "Son, I've got a patient here in town who is in the early stages of labor. It's not going well. Sometime today I expect to perform a caesarean operation on her. Now, that's about all the explanation I figure I owe you."

Caleb wanted to come back at Hale with another plea, but the futility of that was clear in his face. He was set on delivering this baby. Caleb understood that reasoning. It was the doctor's refusal to commit to coming tomorrow or the next day that bothered him. Eighth grade education or not, he thought he was in the right to expect that. Had he known the woman in question was Pastor Tom Combs' wife it might have rankled him more. What with the pastor being the one to start the hatefulness towards his mother. But Caleb did not know that Laura Combs had come to town for the last week of her pregnancy as the Morrows no longer attended church. He just knew for certain that his father had lost a lot of blood and was hurting bad. So, he argued no more. He paid his three dollars and took the laudanum, with Hale's instructions, and went on home.

CHAPTER TWENTY-EIGHT

It had taken nearly a week for the edition of the Pocatello paper that told about the stage holdup on Malad Pass to make its way down to Preston, Idaho, but finally it did. A drummer left his copy on a cafe table. The headline, in bold black letters an inch high read: MURDER! ROBBERY ON THE PASS! A secondary headline in smaller but dark print stated: Road Agents Make Off With Large Amount Of Money. It was the big headline that had drawn Burt Hooper and his associates to that particular table. The smaller headline had them struggling to contain their anger amongst the decent people surrounding them. Eventually, however, the husband and wife at the table next to them finished eating and left. Hooper read the front page article while they were waiting for their food. He then folded the paper neatly and laid it on the table. Pete started to reach for it. Hooper said quietly but with authority, "Leave it be."

Pete gave Hooper an angry look. "You read it."

"I don't work my jaws like you do."

Frank Taylor, who'd tied in with them after Walter's demise in Freedom, nodded towards the smaller headline and whispered. "I don't consider a hundred and eighty-seven dollars a large amount of money."

"Something's not right," added Pete.

Hooper had not wanted to have this conversation here. There were still people eating who looked different than them. They were dressed better, and their eyes did not have that look of someone who has killed another person. Hooper could see it, or at least he thought he did. It may have been his conscience reminding him of who he was every time he looked in the mirror. It had gotten worse since he'd killed this Meyers guy on the Pass. He found himself constantly looking at good people's eyes and envying them. It grated on what conscience he had. He liked it better when he was camped in the mountains with Pete and Frank. They were no better than him. He said to Pete, his voice careful, "We've been fooled."

Pete whispered. "It wasn't on that dapper fella. We looked him over right good."

A woman three tables away looked over as Pete was speaking. Hooper caught her eye and smiled. She smiled back before abruptly turning away to her husband lest he detect her embarrassment. Hooper leaned in and whispered, "Either this Meyers fella hid the money in the coach or that woman had it."

Frank chastised them. "You shudda searched her."

Hooper, in a rare moment of self-deprecation, came back, "I just didn't think she had the moxie to do something like that. You saw her. She was throwing up on herself."

Frank and Pete exchanged a knowing look like they'd bested their leader before Frank snorted and nodded towards the newspaper. "Maybe this is why."

Hooper saw their faces and growled. "That money ain't gonna be hers for long."

CHAPTER TWENTY-NINE

The wound in Josh's left Latissimus dorsi muscle was ugly. More so on the back side where the soft nosed bullet, having expanded some, tore open a silver dollar size hole in his flesh. However, on the bright side, it didn't appear to be infected likely due to Sarah changing the dressing on a daily basis. The healing process, now in its fifth day had been made tolerable by liberal amounts of laudanum. Nonetheless, the narcotic couldn't prevent Josh from fretting over the cattle still being on Porcupine Creek "No tellin' how many more they've rustled."

Caleb offered again. "Pa, I can make a swing through that country today. Just let the Indians know we're watching over those cows."

Josh shook his head emphatically. "No sir, you ain't going up there by yourself. Ravens 'd have you picked clean by sundown."

Sarah said, knowing the response she would get, "I'll go with him."

"Like hell you will." Josh paused purposely allowing his agitation to show before adding, "The both of ya, just settle yourselves. All I need is one more day and I'll go my own self."

"That'd be smart," said Sarah. "Go bouncing up there and break open your wound. You're lucky to be getting by without it being stitched up."

Josh came back even more angry. "Well, maybe next time we'll just take our doctor business to Eagle Rock."

"I'm hoping there won't be a next time. At least not for this sort of thing."

And then it came out. Likely what all three of them had been thinking. "Damned Noah. He's left us high and dry."

Sarah gave Josh a harsh look. "He did what he thought he had to."

"He could have done it differently. It didn't have to be the way it was."

Anguish spread over Sarah's face. "I don't care. I just miss him. He's been gone over three weeks and we've heard nothing."

"Maybe that's the way he wants it."

"I don't believe that."

From where he lay on the couch, Josh looked up at her. For a moment they silently shared their misery, their missing Noah in the solitude of the fireplace popping and cracking. And then he said, "It'll get him in some trouble, but if you write his commanding officer you'll get your letter."

"I don't know who that is."

"You don't need to. Just Commanding Officer – Fort Douglas, Utah will do."

"Maybe since you were a soldier once you should write the letter."

Josh snorted. "Well, I guess since I'm stuck ridin' this couch it's the least I can do."

Sarah turned and started towards a drawer in the kitchen. She called over her shoulder. "I'll get you writing material."

With some difficulty, Josh got up from the couch and trailed after her. "I'll sit at the table."

Caleb could see the change in them. Just the possibility they would hear from Noah seemed to lift their spirits. He was hopeful too that this letter would force Noah to write them. At the same time, he was angry with Noah. *Purty damned sad when parents got to twist their son's arm to get a letter from him. It'll make him mad being ordered to write home. They'll get their letter but what about after that?*

In the morning, the task of riding to town and mailing the letter fell to Caleb, as he knew it would. It was biting cold. Lasting snow had still not come to the valleys yet but with Thanksgiving just two days away it wouldn't be far behind. Sarah, who had walked to the barn to see Caleb off, now looked up at him sitting on his horse. "Don't forget, if you want sweet spuds on Thanksgiving you'll need to stop by the Merc and get them. And some sugar and molasses too."

Caleb smiled. His mother made sweet spuds mostly for him as everyone else in the family only tasted them to be polite. "Anything else?"

"No, I don't think so."

He laughed. "Well, you remembered the important stuff."

Sarah smiled. "Be safe."

For a short time, while she'd talked with Caleb, the constant worries that plagued Sarah had faded. They'd been replaced by the promise of a letter from Noah. And Thanksgiving, it had always been a good time for them. In the past they truly did give thanks for what they had. This year would be different. She tried to not think about that as her and Buster plodded up the road to the house.

It was about noon when Caleb got to town. He went straight to the post office which was nothing more than a tiny room attached to the postmaster's clapboard house. It was a white structure with the American flag flying from a metal pole that was more than twice as tall as the house.

Occasionally, a breeze would cause the flag to unfurl and ripple. Mostly, like this morning, it hung limp. Caleb stepped inside the room similar in size to a prison cell. To his left was a cork board with some wanted posters and other government things of public concern. Straight ahead was an oak wood shelf for writing and such. And to his right, embedded in the wall, were brass mailboxes for town people who could come every day to pick up their mail. Country folks, who might only come to town once or twice a month, called for their mail at the little window to the left of the mailboxes. A frumpy woman, with graying hair piled high with the aid of bobby pins, was visible through this portal. Caleb stooped slightly so he could look her in the eyes. He addressed her like he would a schoolmarm. "Good morning, Mrs. Beal. Got any mail for us?"

She stared at him for a few seconds like he was bothering her before sighing. "You're one of those Morrow boys, aren't you?"

"Yes Ma'am, I'm Caleb. My brother Noah joined the Army. I was hopin' you might have a letter from him."

"No, I don't."

The woman's abrupt response angered Caleb. His response was flavored by it. "Well, do you suppose you could take a look for it?"

"I don't need to."

"You know without looking, do you?"

"It's not been a week since you were here last."

Caleb stared at the woman. She was wearing a dark blue dress. A frilly white hanky protruded slightly from the neckline. She casually removed it and dabbed at her nose, the end of which was red. She remained silent, unphased by her rudeness. Caleb knew she was probably right. That she made it a point to know everybody's business was common knowledge. *Be a feather in her cap to substantiate the gossip that the younger Morrow boy ran off to the Army rather than live in the valley with the shame of his mother being a whore.* But it occurred to Caleb too, that if there was a letter from Noah it would make his mothers' day. They would have reason to be thankful two days from now. A letter would make it easier for all of them to look at Noah's vacant spot at the table. Unfortunately, the words escaped him when the anger within him had peaked, "Dammit, Mabel, I rode four hours horseback to get here. And I don't know when any of my family will be back to town. It won't take you but a minute to check for our mail."

Mabel Beal, already thinking how she would tell it, *that insolent Morrow boy swore at me demanding mail he didn't have,* licked her lips just barely with the tip of her tongue. She said with a smug tone, "I know what I know and you're not going to tell me my business."

Caleb looked at the old woman. Her green eyes never had been friendly but now they were downright hateful. It came to him that should Noah ever write Mabel might see to it that his letter got lost. He thought to apologize to her but, as he formed the words in his mind, he saw her there sitting not ten feet from the stove. And, in the same instant, he felt the cold on the long ride home and saw at the end of it the disappointment on his parent's face when he had no letter from Noah. He looked away from her to the brass slot beneath her window and slid the letter to the Army in it. He said nothing as he walked out. It irked him that she was probably already speculating on the contents of the letter.

Caleb couldn't help but look up. Clouds, big clouds with dark bottoms and whipped cream tops were coming together overhead. *Gonna snow. I need to git on the road for home.* It was good advice he gave himself. Nonetheless, his common sense surrendered to the growling of his stomach and the irritation that Mabel Beal had caused him. Big Jim's

Place, a drab red brick building, was just across the street. For fifty cents a person could get a roast beef sandwich and a dill pickle slice. For a nickel more a cup of coffee to go with it. Caleb tied his horse out front with several others and went inside. He paused to let his eyes adjust. Natural light from outside was severely limited by the small, dirty windows to either side of the door. The room was long and narrow. To the left was a black, slick top bar with a plethora of liquor bottles reflected in the mirror behind it. On the wall opposite the bar and above an idle pool table was a multitude of animal heads and hides. Mule deer, elk, antelope and tanned hides with the heads attached of black bears and mountain goats. Some people came to Big Jim's, as opposed to the other bar in town, because they never tired of looking at the dead animals or the animals looking at them. Others came there because of the poker game at the far end of the room. An ornate kerosene lantern hung from the high ceiling over the card table. Its glow did not extend much beyond the surface of the dingy green felt of the table and the players. There were five of them. Four were dressed like they worked for a living while the fifth appeared to be a dandy out to sell you something, at least in Caleb's estimation he was. Directly across from the poker table, on the end of the bar right above a brass spittoon, were the sandwiches. Caleb placed his right boot on the brass foot rail and leaned on the bar. Up to this point, the bartender, a skinny bald-headed man in a long-sleeved white shirt and black vest, had said nothing, even though he eyed Caleb all the way to where he now stood. He took a step towards Caleb as if to put his hands on the bar in a friendly way but stopped short. "What it'll be?"

Caleb looked at the man's brown eyes, dull and un-interesting, like he was elsewhere. "Came for one of your sandwiches."

The laconic man nodded towards a white platter where several sandwiches remained. "Be four bits."

Caleb slid a silver dollar across the bar. "Need a cup of coffee too."

The bartender took a brown ceramic mug from the back-bar and set it in front of Caleb. He nodded again towards a pot-bellied stove halfway across the room. "Help yourself."

Caleb followed the man's gesture. A large blue porcelain pot simmered on the stove's flat top. Steam and the accompanying smell of fresh coffee drifted out of its spout. When he reached back for his cup, the dollar was gone and so was the bartender. The dark wooden floor, stained over the years with tobacco spit, liquor and blood creaked under Caleb's weight. He poured his coffee, mostly oblivious to the banter at the poker table and went back to his place at the bar.

A voice at the poker table suddenly rose above the others. "I'll tell ya, that schoolmarm they got out there at Grays Lake is a real looker." He paused, studying his cards and then added. "My missus would cut me off for a month if she was to hear me say that." There was more laughter, some polite and some genuine.

A different voice belonging to a husky man with red whiskers seated across the table from the talker sounded off, "Well, you know why it is they got that schoolmarm they do don't ya?"

Caleb felt his heart trip as it tried to catch up with the sudden surge of adrenaline that flooded his system. *Don't pay it any heed. Don't turn around.*

"No, we're new to this country"

And then it came. Laughter. "The teacher before this one got fired. Turns out she was a whore back in her prime."

"The hell you say."

"God's truth. Rumor has it she gave fresh horses to the outlaws that robbed the bank here last summer."

"And she was the schoolmarm?"

"Yes sir, that's a fact."

Caleb laid his sandwich on the bar. It had come more than once to his mind that night he and his folks had met Irma Duke and Herman Snyder coming late from the school. He thought to tell about it now but the naysayer in him shouted, *You got no right to do that.* He let go of that impulse in favor of rational thought. *You can't fight 'em all. Leave. Just walk out.* But he was frozen where he was.

The husky man went on. "I'll tell ya, I've seen this old whore. She's easy on the eyes." He took a drink of his beer and laughed. "I'd give two dollars today for a roll in the hay with her."

Caleb lost control of himself. Before he knew it, he was standing over the man. He looked up. Confused at first, then arrogant after recognizing the anger in Caleb's eyes. He said, still holding his cards, "What can I do for you, Mister?"

"I'd be obliged if you'd keep your mouth shut in matters that you have been ill informed."

"I don't know that what we talk about at this table is any of your business."

And then it came to Caleb that he was ashamed to reveal up front that the man was talking about his mother. It made no sense for him to be standing there in a threatening posture unless he was willing to claim, *this whore*, as his mother. The game had stopped. All eyes were on him. Waiting for him to justify his behavior. He was in it now, like having to ride out a scree rock slide or lose his reputation. There was only one way to go with his words. "That whore you're talkin' about is my mother."

Everyone at the table but the husky man went dead silent, embarrassed to be part of the conversation now. Husky man, however, was in the same predicament as Caleb. He'd lose face to apologize. He snorted, "Well, I reckon that's your bad luck." And then he laughed, seeking approval of the others at the table. Their faces were rigid. Eyes fixed on the meager pile of chips in the center of the beer-stained felt, like it needed to be counted. The tension in the air was palpable. It was clear, husky man was hoping to be rescued.

Caleb looked down at the top of the man's black slouch hat. Several green, hay leaves clung to its crown. He said, his voice rock steady, "No, Mister, the bad luck is all yours today."

Husky man regretted saying what he had. It wasn't that he didn't believe what he'd said about Sarah because he did. Getting in a fistfight over it was another matter. Just like saving his reputation was. His hands, cupped around his cards, rested on the table in front of him. He collapsed the five cards and placed the stack next to an ash tray with a smoldering cigarette. Husky man appeared older than Caleb. He said as he pushed back from the table, "You're a smart pup that needs his comeuppance."

Caleb gave the man space to stand. He said, eye to eye, "Apologize for your remarks and we can let this go."

"Like hell I will."

And with that, the dam broke. Caleb punched the man in the face causing him to stagger backwards into the poker table. Money, cards and beer skidded across the felt and onto the floor. Players turned spectators stumbled out of the way as Caleb charged their friend throwing punches into his ample belly. But husky man, probably twenty pounds heavier than Caleb, would not go down. Blood trickled from his nose and lower lip. In the background someone hollered, "Get the Sheriff." Caleb looked in that direction. Then it came. The punch jolted his entire head. He saw stars. He staggered back several steps. Husky man was on him. Trying to grab him around the head and shoulders so as to throw him down. But he'd misread Caleb. Underestimated his strength. Caleb gripped him beneath the arms, stepped through on his right side and shoved him to the floor. The sound of husky man's head smacking the brass footrail was loud and sickening. It was like a bullet striking flesh. There was no doubt that the impact had done damage. Proof of that was in the stillness of husky man's body. He lay there on the floor. Eyes wide open but rolled up so only the whites showed. Next to him, an overturned spittoon irrigated the hardwood.

"You've killed him."

Caleb looked to his right. The bartender, the person who had legitimate reason to stop the fight before it began, the man who could have allowed the combatants to save face, now stepped up to condemn. Caleb took his assertion to be true. Fear gripped him hard. His knees weakened and his insides quivered. He wanted in the worst way for husky man to wake up. Daylight and cold air poured in the front door. With it came Tom Percy. He studied the man on the floor for a moment and then frowned at Caleb. "You got tired of killing Indians so you come to town for some white men did ya?"

Caleb was taken aback. Anger strengthened his trembling body. "The man insulted my mother."

Percy shook his head. "Do you think he'll be the last man to do that?" He did not wait for an answer turning instead to one of the poker players. "Has anybody gone to fetch Doc Hale?"

Caleb stared at Percy. His sarcasm and indifference ringing in his ears. He made no effort to hide his hatred. Percy suddenly turned back to him. "Who started this?"

Caleb nodded towards husky man. "He did."

A voice behind Caleb shouted, "That ain't so. We was playin' cards and just shootin' the shit and here comes this fella all worked up."

Caleb glared at the stranger. "Your friend could have apologized."

"And you could have just let it go."

"Is that what you would've done if he'd called your mother a whore?"

The man's face was covered with gray stubble. Obviously, no match for Caleb but cocky now in the presence of the Sheriff, he came back, "Facts is facts. Some of 'em ain't so easy to swallow."

And then the front door opened again. Another one of the poker players followed by Doc Hale and a swirl of snowflakes came inside. Caleb could see several more people with their hands cupped to the sides of their faces peering in the flyspecked windows. *Damned circus and I'm the star attraction.*

Doc Hale immediately knelt beside husky man and felt for a pulse. He then looked into the man's eyes. The room was lonely quiet, save for the wind outside that had blown in a snowstorm. After a time, Doc Hale announced, "He's alive but for how long, I don't know." And then Hale noticed that some of the spittoon contents had seeped under his right knee. He scowled and lowered his voice, "Sonovabitch." He then stood, the stain on his right knee clearly evident. To no one in particular he said, "Could I get some of you to carry this man to my office?"

The poker players, the same ones that hadn't suggested to their friend he apologize, a viable face saving alternative if it had support of the group, now picked up his limp body. The entourage with the unconscious man had barely made their exit from Big Jim's Place when Percy said to Caleb, "Give me your six-shooter. You're under arrest."

Caleb shrieked. "Arrest, for what?"

"Right now, assault and battery. But if this fella dies, that could change."

Caleb looked at Percy. Reluctant to give him his pistol. Even more so to go to his jail. He pled his case. "You know,

Tom, it ain't been all that long ago that I was a deputized member of your posse."

Percy was puffed up with agitation. "That don't mean you get a free pass to beat a man senseless."

"He took an unlucky fall."

"With your help. Now, gimme your gun."

Caleb snorted and shook his head as he handed his pistol over. "This ain't right."

"You can tell it to the judge tomorrow morning."

Shock came to Caleb's face. "What?"

Percy's demeanor hardened. "The judge 'll tell you how much it's gonna cost you to get out of jail."

Caleb raised his voice. "I can't spend the night in your jail. My folks is expecting me home today."

A smug grin, supported by the fact he wore a badge, came to Percy's face. "You got no choice. Now let's move along as I have grown weary of this conversation."

Caleb gave Percy a disgusted look before shaking his head and starting toward the door. The Sheriff trailed after him clutching Caleb's pistol in his right hand. It was snowing hard outside. Persistent gusts of wind took the snow sideways. Caleb stopped at the hitching rail. "I need to take my horse to the livery."

Percy squinted his eyes against the blowing snow. "I'll do it just as soon as I get you settled."

Caleb patted his horse's neck. "You'll be out of this in a little while."

From the warmth of the various buildings, people stood at the windows and watched the two men trudge through the wind driven snow. It was obvious to most who they were and where they were going. As they walked by the bank it occurred to Caleb, *If only that damned Hooper hadn't robbed the bank, this wouldn't be happening.*

CHAPTER THIRTY

It was one of those decisions that was slow to develop because Josh and Sarah kept thinking, or hoping mostly, that Caleb, in spite of the storm, would get home by dark. There'd been no discussion between them. Out of the blue Josh gave a long, worried sigh. "I believe I'm gonna ride part way and meet him."

Sarah, who had been peeling spuds near her new sink abruptly paused and turned around. Her look was incredulous. "You think because you milked the cow tonight that you're fit to ride?"

Josh shifted his attention from the living room window to Sarah. "Snow's easing up."

Sarah laughed sardonically. "At least it's not coming down sideways." She paused. "You're on the mend, Josh. Why push it?"

"I'll take Boots. Ride till the daylight gives out and then come back. I'm bettin' this storm will be done by then and there'll be starlight to come home by."

"All of this, to what end?"

"We'll know where he is, or he isn't."

Sarah wanted to make a stronger case for Josh not going but her worry, her motherly concern, wouldn't allow it. "You know if you go, I'll have twice as much to fear."

Josh laughed to reassure her. "I think you've mistaken me for some pilgrim."

Sarah smiled. "Never in a thousand years would I do that."

It took Sarah's help to saddle Boots. The pain on Josh's left side being too great for him to lift the saddle. She now stood near the barn, the feel of his goodbye kiss lingering on her lips and watched him go. The wind had died away. Snow fell as it should, light and fluffy. About eight inches was on the ground. From nowhere, it flashed in her mind. *The cows will have to come home. We'll have to start feeding.* She struggled to see Josh, due not so much the distance as it was the encroaching darkness. And then she was alone, save for Buster. She reached down and tussled his ears. "Let's go to the house, Ok? Let's go to the house." And so, they went toward the comfort of the house. Their footfalls barely audible in the dry powdery snow. And Josh went, unaware, toward the calamity that awaited him.

If there was anything good to come the Morrow family's way on this night, it was that about three miles into Josh's ride the storm broke up. He'd seen nothing of Caleb, or for that matter, anyone. Not a soul was out. In the distance across an expanse of sagebrush snugged up next to the timbered mountains he could see a speck of yellow light. Herman Snyder's place. *This close to home it wouldn't make sense for Caleb to go there unless he was bad off.* Josh rode on. *I'll go till it's full on dark and then go home by starlight, just like I told Sarah I would.* The air was stinging cold. His ears were painfully numb. It made him wish that he'd worn Sarah's stocking cap, as she suggested, instead of his Stetson. Nonetheless, conditions weren't bad enough for his common sense to overrule concern for his son. On he went. Close to eight miles, he guessed. The stars, thousands of them and a sliver of the moon were out. Where sagebrush dominated it was a sea of white. Rolling, endless until it ran into the trees. It was at one of these unions that a rider appeared on the road just coming out of the trees. Josh's first impulse was joy, relief that it was Caleb. But then nothing in the dark outline of the rider matched. Not his hat, body size or horse. Maybe most telling was that he didn't call out upon seeing Boots' distinctive white feet. Soon, they came to within easy shouting distance. Josh was first to call out. "Evenin' to ya."

The stranger came on a short ways and stopped. "Thought I was the only one fool enough to be out ridin' in a blizzard at night."

Josh obliged the man and laughed. "No, I don't reckon you've got a cinch on that."

"Damned snowstorm caught me in town."

In the starlight they could not see one another's eyes, especially tucked back under the brims of their Stetsons as they were. "My boy went to town today. I'm thinkin' he musta decided to overnight there."

"Wished I'd done that, but to be honest I'd had my fill of that place and their nagging sheriff."

The mention of the word sheriff caused Josh to be on edge. "You have a run-in with Tom Percy did ya?"

"Not exactly, but I had the misfortune to be playing cards in Big Jim's when some fella came over from the bar and picked a fight with one of the players."

"He just picked a fight for no reason?"

"Oh, he was mad cause the fella at our table called his mother a whore. Course the guy doin' the name callin' was confident in what he was saying was true so he wouldn't apologize, and then the fight was on."

Josh was sick with fear. There was little doubt in his mind who the man was talking about. He didn't let on though. "So, the sheriff was twistin' yer tail over this deal?"

"Oh, hell yeah. Made me write down on paper what I saw. Said I might even have to go to court and tell it there."

Josh's apprehension jumped up several notches. "Court?"

"Yeah, this fella died."

Josh came back quick. The alarm in his voice clearly evident. "Died, which one?"

"The guy we was playing cards with."

"What about the other guy?"

"The sheriff's got him locked up."

Josh's mind went to what he had to do. *Sarah will be worried if I don't come home but I'm halfway to town and I know that I gotta go there in the morning.* To the stranger he said, "Helluva note that fella getting' locked up."

"It was just words. He cudda let it go."

"Yeah, and I reckon the other fella could have done the same." And with that, Josh urged Boots onward into the darkness of the trees and the uncertainty of what awaited him in town.

CHAPTER THIRTY-ONE

Frank Taylor had only recently tired of working for a living. As such, he did not have the notoriety of a well-known outlaw like Burt Hooper. He could go with impunity into town and inquire where the Snyder ranch was located. *My ma corresponds with Mrs. Snyder. She said they might have need of a hired hand.* The man at the Mercantile gladly gave Frank directions and off he went just before the storm set in. They held up a time or two in thick trees to let the gale play out. As luck would have it, they turned off the town road to the Snyder place not more than fifteen minutes before Josh came along.

If it hadn't been such a miserably cold night, Patches, the Snyder's black and white dog, might have been out front snooping around as she was wont to do. Tonight, however, she was laying on the rug in front of the fireplace. Her snout was resting between her outstretched front paws giving the impression she was sound asleep. Herman Snyder, who was laying on the couch with the Pocatello paper collapsed on his chest, was snoring lightly. Thelma was doing the supper dishes.

Pete and Frank waited in a small stand of trees about a hundred yards from the Snyder's log house. Smoke, with the promise of warmth and hot food floated out to them.

Hooper, on the other hand, rode right up to the house and knocked on the door like a decent person would. Inside, he could hear Thelma.

"Herman, get up. There's somebody at the door."

Rousted from a deep sleep, a fantasy land where nothing made sense and glimpses of the past and future were seen, Herman managed a groggy, "What?"

"The door. Somebody's at the door."

Herman pushed the newspaper off, more or less in a wad, and got to his feet. An awareness of how it was outside come back to him. "Who in the hell would be out on a night like this?"

Thelma sensed the droplets of dishwater on her hands and began drying them on the apron hanging from her waist. It was cheerful, white with red and yellow flowers embroidered on it. Her words were cautionary. "Got to be somebody in trouble."

Hooper smiled at hearing this through the door. *Yes, Thelma, somebody is in trouble.*

Herman was to the door with Patches just behind him. His gun belt hung on a peg at eye level. The impulse to take his pistol from it before he opened the door came to him. He started to reach for it.

Thelma hissed, "What are you doing? This person likely needs help."

Herman frowned and dropped his hand away to the doorknob. The door was barely open when he realized his mistake, or maybe his good fortune, to not be armed. There stood Hooper, Colt in hand. A wry smile struggled through a week's worth of whiskers. "Am I too late for supper?" The smile graduated to a laugh as he stepped inside.

Thelma gasped. Even without the flour sack, there was no mistaking the voice. Gravelly and cruel. She'd feared this day ever since the story in the paper. Her eyes were locked onto Hooper's when Herman shouted, "If you've come to rob us, you'll get little for your effort. We're poor people."

Hooper looked away to Herman. "Don't start in lying to me mister. Nuthin pisses me off like a liar. I won't abide it."

In his ignorance, Herman pleaded, "I'm being truthful with you. We have little money. Not even in the bank. We lost our savings last spring when it got robbed."

Hooper snorted. "Well, you're about to lose again."

Herman spate the words. "Fine. We've got less than twenty dollars in this house."

Without warning, like a blue sky unleashing lightning, Hooper smacked the side of Herman's head with the barrel of his pistol. An Army Colt. Seven and half inches of hard steel. Herman dropped like the floor had been jerked out from beneath him.

Thelma screamed and ran to where he lay. Patches began barking angrily, baring her teeth to Hooper.

"Call your dog off or I'll shoot it."

Thelma shouted, "Stop Patches. Stop. Come here!"

Patches reluctantly obeyed, going to Thelma's side. She sobbed, she wailed, "You've killed him."

Hooper snarled, "I warned him I've got no patience for liars."

Thelma looked up. Tears streaming down her cheeks. Snot running from her nose. She blubbered, "He doesn't know."

A few seconds went by while Hooper processed the meaning of what Thelma had just said. He then laughed. "I guess $5,000 can make a liar out of anyone."

Thelma looked down, gently stroking Herman's head. A good amount of blood was working its way from his right temple through dark hair and onto the wood floor. She could see his chest moving. It was close to a reality check for her. Life without Herman. That's what it would have been if she'd been able to execute her plan to go visit her mother in California and never come back. Now she was stuck playing second fiddle to Irma Duke.

Hooper said, cold and threatening, "I want the money you let everyone believe we took."

Thelma did not look at him. She nodded, "Alright, I'll get it." She got to her feet and started toward her and Herman's bedroom. Hooper followed, still brandishing his pistol. In the center of the room was a neatly made four poster bed. A red and blue block quilt with little yellow yarn ties in each block adorned it. To the right of the bed was a closet and to the left of it a cheap looking pinewood dresser. A mirror hung above the dresser. Thelma went to the top right drawer. She looked back at Hooper. "Please turn your head. I keep my unmentionables in here."

Hooper laughed before saying, "I've seen those things before."

"Not mine you haven't."

Hooper snorted like she disgusted him. "Get the money."

Thelma thrust her hand into the undergarments and pulled out Ben Meyers' money neatly wrapped in a powder blue hanky. She handed it to Hooper. "It's there. All of it. I didn't dare spend it. Not here."

He scowled. "Just gonna let the law think me and my boys was off having a good time with it was ya?"

Thelma thought to say she was sorry, but the words wouldn't come. Instead, she said, emboldened by their frank exchange, "I wish you would go now."

"I'll go when I'm damned good and ready."

And then the front door opened. Frank and Pete could be heard questioning what had happened. Hooper appeared to briefly listen before seemingly succumbing to an epiphany. He set the handkerchief and his pistol on the dresser. He became almost frantic, his fingers fumbling to unwrap the bills. He left ten of the hundred dollar notes and stuffed the rest into his shirt. Hastily folding the hanky around the money that remained, he whispered, so only Thelma could hear, "Play along and you and your husband will survive this night. Don't, and my boys will have their way with you before you die. Understand?"

Before Thelma could even nod, Frank filled the open doorway. "Did ya get it?"

Hooper gave Thelma one last knowing look. He turned back to Frank and held out the bundle. "Right here."

Frank's eyes settled on the hanky, suspicious already. "Doesn't look like much."

"Well, let's go out to the kitchen and count it. Divvy it up right there."

Frank backed out of the room almost running into Pete. "She had it. Just like we figured."

Thelma was terrified. Sick to her stomach almost. She made eye contact with Hooper. His look was stern, mean, arbitrary. It would be his way, or she would die. Herman too. Thank God the kids had gone to Grandma's. From nowhere the naysayer in her mind shouted, *maybe this is how it had been for Sarah, Hooper gave her no choice.*

Hooper pointed his gun at her and motioned towards the door and mouthed the words, "Play along."

Thelma nodded and started immediately for the door lest he just shoot her to ensure her silence. It sickened her that she'd become his ally. She wished she could turn back time to before tonight, before Irma Duke. Back to when things were pure and simple and Herman loved her.

Frank placed the blue hanky on the kitchen table and waited till Hooper and Thelma emerged from the bedroom to begin unwrapping the money. They arrived at the table just as the last fold of the hanky revealed a stack of crisp one hundred dollar bank notes. Thelma looked down at the tiny, perfect pictures of Abraham Lincoln. Even now, with Herman lying unconscious in their front room, the money had a narcotic effect on her. She went back to that day in the stage when Meyers had insisted she take it. *You will be rewarded.* It galled her to have risked lying to the sheriff and now have these thugs take what was hers.

Hooper played his part. "Don't look like much."

"Ain't nowhere near $5,000," said Pete looking at Thelma.

In the short time they'd been alone they had not devised a lie to account for the missing money. Thelma stepped up to the task. "I sent all of the money but $1,000 to my relatives back east. They were facing bankruptcy and used it to satisfy their debts."

Frank gave Thelma a hateful look. "I believe as sure as the sun is gonna come up tomorrow, you're lying. I know you've got the rest of the money somewhere."

Not that it would have done Pete much good to have thought about it beforehand, he challenged her, "You put it in a bank?"

Thelma, bold, almost to the point of being impertinent, came back, "Yes, that's what I did right after the paper gives the details of the holdup, I walk into a bank and deposit $4,000 cash."

For a few seconds they showed Pete no mercy allowing the embarrassment of his apparent stupidity to hang over him. Hooper, maybe not much smarter than Pete, naively put forth, "Well, I reckon this is all we're gonna get."

Frank exploded. "Are you shitin' me? Just like that you're going to let this go. She's lying, Hooper."

Hooper responded, smug to have come up with what he thought was good logic. "No, what she says makes sense. She lied to her husband about the money because she knew he'd never go along with sending most of it to no account relatives."

Frank glared at Thelma and then Hooper. "What about the thousand dollars. Her husband didn't know about that?"

Hooper appeared stymied. Thelma jumped in, "My husband is an honest man. I was waiting for a better time to tell him about the money."

Trying to redeem his earlier faux pas, Pete declared, "I don't believe a damned word she says."

Thelma now recognized that Hooper was her salvation to this night which was early in its consequences. She pointed to the money on the table. "So help me God, that's all there is."

Hooper threw in, maybe too quick. "This woman is a church going person. She wouldn't say that unless it was true."

Frank snorted. "You're a fool, Hooper."

Anger flared in Hooper's eyes. "You might wanna go easy with that kinda talk, Frank. I'm in no mood for it tonight."

It was clear there was more sass loaded on Frank's tongue but whether it was divine intervention or him coming to his senses he swallowed it and said, respectful in his tone, "Maybe we should divide this up and be done with our quarreling."

Hooper reached down and took up the money. He began sorting the bills. "One for you, one for you and one for me."

When he had done this three times there were three piles of $300 each with one, hundred dollar note leftover. He held up the extra bill and looked them straight in the eyes, "I'm keepin' this one since it was my idea to rob the stage."

It was an effort for Frank and Pete to suppress their anger, but they did. Both of them knew that to quibble over the odd bill might mean they wouldn't live through the night. Frank, however, ventured into what he figured was safe territory.

"Well, Hooper, if you take that extra me and Pete will split the $20 her husband said they had. That sound fair to ya?"

Hooper could feel the $4,000 resting against his chest. It was hard for him to not grin. "Well, I reckon that'd be alright." He paused and then nodded towards Thelma. "Why don't you get that $20 for the boys?"

Thelma looked at Hooper but not in the eyes. She stared at the slight bulge beneath his shirt that only the two of them knew about. She recalled the paranoia of having that money against her breasts while answering the sheriff's questions. She said, on purpose, "Don't you have enough already?"

Hooper gave her a dirty look before laughing. "Tell you what. You fix us something to eat and I'll give the boys $20 out of this extra hundred."

Thelma thought to say something uppity, but it flashed in her mind how Hooper had been talking to Ben Meyers one second and in the next casually killed him. She came back, "Can I tend to my husband first?"

"No Ma'am, we been a long time without decent grub. Your husband will be just fine when he comes to."

Thelma looked over at Herman's body. He gave the appearance of being dead. She thought to say something threatening like, *if he dies the law will hang you.* But then it occurred to her that Hooper had done enough in just the past few months to warrant hanging several times over. She said aloud, "I've got venison stew and sourdough biscuits."

It went unnoticed, Frank stepping behind Thelma just before another bolt of lightning came down from that pro-verbial blue sky as his hand slapped her butt. He laughed. "Maybe after supper I'll have some dessert."

Thelma spun around poised to slap Frank. Fortunately for her a flicker of common sense grabbed her hand. She stood there, awkwardly, hand raised, staring at Frank's yellow teeth. She could smell the plug tobacco on his breath.

She thought to cry. Just do it on purpose. Playing that out in her mind, she saw him laughing.

"Frank, behave yourself."

Thelma looked over at Hooper. A hint of gratitude radiated from her eyes. At the same time, though, they both knew she'd tell about the money before she'd let Frank rape her. Like it or not, Hooper was to be her protector on this night.

Oblivious to the relief in Thelma's eyes, Frank scowled at Hooper. "You don't wanna make a habit of talking down to me like I'm some schoolboy, Hooper. I won't tolerate it."

It didn't come as a total surprise what came next. That same Hooper from Malad Pass pulled his Army Colt and thumbed back the hammer in one smooth, slick as you please, movement that instantly caused Frank to tremble. Hooper had his arm in an outstretched position so there was no doubt he was aiming for a spot between Frank's eyes that had now teared up considerably.

Frank, no longer cocky as he was a few seconds ago, whimpered, "I'm sorry, Hooper. I sometimes get too brash for my own good."

Hooper seethed the words. "You damned sure do." He then started around the table holding his pistol out in front of him. Thelma stepped back from Frank to make way for Hooper who pressed the barrel of his Colt to Frank's forehead. "You've bucked me one too many times, Frank. And that's what I won't tolerate."

Thelma's mind went to the shocked look on Ben Meyers' face when Hooper killed him. That image had been a nightly visitor, sometimes even in the daytime when it had no business being there. She'd be peeling spuds or scrubbing clothes and there'd be Ben Meyers, uninvited. Wanting his money back. She closed her eyes lest she have Frank right there with Ben.

Of its own accord a .45 Colt makes a lot of noise. Outdoors, that sound can bleed off pretty quick because it has someplace to go. But inside a log cabin is another story. However, louder than the .45, to Thelma anyway, was the sound of Frank's body hitting the floor. She could hear that over the ringing in her ears. It competed with Hooper commanding Pete, "Drag his ass outta here." Still, she kept her eyes closed, even cupping her hands over them. She could smell the gun smoke. Feel the cold air of the door opening. Hear Frank's boots scuffing across the floor until at last the door closed.

"Open your eyes."

Thelma did as Hooper ordered. From the corner of her left eye, she could see Frank's blood on the floor. She looked away towards Hooper. He still held his pistol. Half expecting, she thought, for Pete to burst through the door and shoot him. Being a logical person, she wondered too why he didn't kill her. His conscience was obviously no deterrent. She said, trying to act like she'd not judged him for what he'd just done. "I'll fix your supper."

Hooper caught her eye. "With him alive it wouldn't have been good for you. You know that don't you?"

Thelma nodded and then seeing the expectation in his face, said it, "Thank you."

From across the room Herman groaned. Thelma did not ask for permission. She went to him. Hooper said nothing. Herman's groan turned to a mumble. Thelma looked up from the floor. Her face scrunched into a plea, "Can't we at least put him on the couch?"

Hooper showed no emotion. "Alright."

Together they lifted him onto the couch. Thelma said again, "Thank you."

Hooper nodded. And like he could atone for killing Frank, he allowed, "Go ahead and tend to him before you fix our supper."

The door opened to Patches barking. Pete looked first to Thelma and Hooper standing near one another and then to the bare table. He dared not say what he was thinking.

Hooper called out. "Better put the horses in the barn, Grain 'em good. Supper 'll be ready when you get back."

Pete said simply, "Alright," and then he was gone.

By and by Pete returned. The smell of the stew permeated the room. He and Hooper ate mostly in silence while Thelma tended to her husband. He was not lucid which may have been his good fortune. Later in the night as Pete snored loudly in front of the fireplace, Hooper crept from the Snyder boys' room to their parent's bedroom. Thelma did not cry out and protested only enough to tell herself that she'd tried to save her honor. That, *what choice did she have? He'd kill her if she resisted.* But the naysayer in her mind spoke the truth. *Sleep with Irma Duke will you. I'll show you.*

In the morning the road agents left. Frank went too, tied across his saddle. Later on in the morning, Herman was able to make some sense and hobble along with Thelma's help. She bundled him up on the buckboard for the trip to town. They agreed on several things. He'd injured his head when he fell off the hay wagon and hit it on a sharp rock. That Burt Hooper and his men had never been there. And that it would be bad for her if Hooper was ever caught. Thelma's night however, with Hooper, was her own little secret.

CHAPTER THIRTY-TWO

Having a prisoner in his jail meant Tom Percy or his deputy had to spend the night there. The fact smoke was drifting up from the jail's stovepipe suggested to Josh that whoever was inside was vigilant in tending the fire. He tied Boots to the hitching rail. The windows were dark. *Gonna make somebody mad*, thought Josh. He turned his gloved hand sideways and hammered on the door. For a short while, he listened. *C'mon, Percy, git yer ass outta bed.* With the stars and the snow had come bitter cold. A combination of moisture from his breath and snot had frozen in Josh's moustache. It looked like heavy frost. He dabbed at it with the back of his hand. Instantly, he grimaced and recoiled from his touch. It was frozen solid. There was no give to it. Josh banged on the door again. "Tom, it's Josh Morrow. Open the door."

Silence, Nothing, And then, "You come back in the morning."

"Like hell I will. You got my boy locked up. Now open the door."

Momentarily, there was a glimmer of light through the window to the right of the door as Percy struck a match. The light grew in response to the lantern's wick being turned up. A brief coughing fit accompanied the sound of the door being unlocked before it opened. In his haste, Josh nearly impaled his self on the barrel of the Sheriff's pistol. He blurted out, "What the hell is this?"

"Like I told you, come back in the morning. It's just north of midnight and I ain't debatin' this with you at this hour. Now get out."

From beyond the Sheriff, a voice called out sounding like it was beneath bed covers. "I'm alright, Pa. Don't get yourself crosswise with him."

Josh looked beyond Percy to a closed door that led to the two cells the county had. It eased his mind a little hearing Caleb's voice. He came back calmer. "What are you charging him with?"

"Voluntary manslaughter."

"What? I heard this was a bar fight that another fella provoked."

"Depends on who you talk to."

"Well, let me talk to my boy. I need to get the straight of this."

Percy poked toward Josh with his pistol. "You come back eight o'clock in the morning. You can talk to him then. Nine o'clock he gets arraigned so the two of you better have your minds made up how he wants to plead."

"Tom, I know my boy. He didn't kill anyone on purpose."

"Tell it to the judge." And with that Percy closed the door and turned the deadbolt. Frustration descended on Josh like a collapsed tent. He was still standing there, not sure of what to do when the light inside went out. Unconsciously, he sighed heavily causing a stab of pain where he'd been shot. Even in the cold he sensed the renewed bleeding.

As a paying customer, Josh got a better reception at the livery than he had from Percy. The owner of the stable was an ex- cavalry trooper. In the old days, he had fought in the

Indian wars just as Josh had done. It was their bond. He'd said, *Most folks ain't seeing it your boy's way.*

It was early. Before six and still dark. From his bed of straw and blankets in an empty stall Josh stared up at the floor of the livery's loft, wondering, but mostly dreading, what the day would bring. He'd wrestled all night with how to advise Caleb. There were no good answers, especially when it didn't seem right that he should be in jail for defending his mother's name. By and by there was light in the window of his friend's tiny room near the entrance to the stable. Soon the smells of horse manure, hay and sweaty saddle blankets gave way to coffee. Not much later, the door to the liveryman's quarters opened. He called out. "Got a pot on if you're ready for a cup."

Josh sat up and shouted toward the shaft of light coming from the open door. He laughed on purpose. "I was hopin' to get some room service."

From the light came laughter in kind. "You need to go outside and duck your head in the snow cuz yer still dreamin'."

Josh laughed again. "Be right there." The friendly banter temporarily diluted the worry crowding his mind. Lately, it was a foreign feeling to be free of it. Kind of like fresh air to a drowning man.

Over the years, Jack Purcell had always treated Josh right. Especially after Sarah's past had become common knowledge. He was not like others who let their moral indignation flavor their behavior. It was the Morrows' record, as he knew it for the past twenty years, that mattered to him. Their familiarity with one another was such that Josh did not knock. He opened the door slowly and stepped inside the light and warmth of Jack's room. Jack handed him a cup of steaming coffee.

"Barn rats keep ya awake last night?"

Josh looked at his friend, older by ten years. Gray hair and moustache, he looked every bit of it. Josh lied. "Slept like a bear in January."

Jack grinned, just enough to expose the ends of his tobacco stained teeth. "That straw bed and horseshit suited ya then?"

Josh snorted, "Better 'n Army days being on the march and sleepin' on rocks."

They laughed hearty before Jack went on. "I figured we'd have a cup or two of coffee and git our minds de-fuddled and then have us some sourdough hotcakes and eggs. Sound good?"

Josh nodded. "It does." He then hid behind a long sip of coffee as his mind's eye tried to reassure Sarah that he'd survived the storm ok. Her and Buster would be up now fixing breakfast before going out at sunup to do chores. And then along came Caleb, waiting to be judged.

Jack invaded his silence. "So, you're going to court with your boy?"

"Nine o'clock."

"It don't surprise me them wantin' to blow this outta shape."

"It's just how they are, don't you reckon?"

Jack shook his head. "I think Percy and that prosecutin' attorney would be more clear-eyed about it if Willy Thomas' old man wasn't a big shot rancher."

"Willy Thomas is the fella that died?"

Jack took a drink of his coffee and nodded. "Don't mean to speak ill of the dead but that boy had an opinion on everything. That fight he got into with your boy wasn't his first by a long way."

"This is good to know, Jack, but it sounds like this Thomas fella has got far more sway than I do."

Jack had no reply. The silence, save for the ticking of a wind- up alarm clock sitting next to the salt and pepper on the table between them, poured into the room. Finally, Jack said, are you ready for some hotcakes?"

CHAPTER THIRTY-THREE

At 8:30 they stepped out of the jail. Caleb, in handcuffs, walked between his father and Percy. The courthouse was nearly two blocks away. Time enough for a fair number of townspeople to see the killer on display. Judging by the faces in windows along the way a person would have thought a flyer giving the time of their walk had been posted. There was plenty of head shaking and excited talk behind the glass that didn't take an expert lip reader to decipher. As they neared the Mercantile Caleb noticed the owner and another man staring at him through the glass half of the front door. He raised his tightly joined wrists overhead and gave them a mocking wave. He shouted, so they could hear him inside where it was warm and comfortable, "Mornin'." Instant disgust came to their faces, but they did not turn away.

Percy said, arrogant in tone but prophetic nonetheless, "You know if you go to trial you might just have cinched a couple of votes against you."

Unphased, Caleb came back, "Shit, Tom, you think there's anybody in this town that won't vote against me."

Josh said, looking straight ahead and low enough to warrant being called a mumble, "No need to badger him."

They walked on. Dead quiet now except for the snow crunching under their feet and Percy huffing and puffing.

Soon they came to the courthouse, a two-story red brick building surrounded by leafless cottonwood trees twice as tall as it was. About 30 paces worth of sidewalk and a short flight of cement steps provided access. Percy stopped short, staring at the drifted in walkway. He shook his head. "You'd think they'd have at least one flunky in the place that could be spared to come clear the snow so's a fella doesn't bust his ass gittin' in there."

Josh eyed how the snow was laid down and offered. "If we gotta post-hole it, I'd say let's cut across the grass. Looks to be boot-top deep there."

Percy, in as cordial a tone as he'd struck since Josh got to town, came back, "Well, alright friend, lead the way."

Josh broke trail, followed by Caleb with Percy bringing up drag. They high stepped through the crusted snow and ascended the steps. Josh opened the tall half wood – half glass door and went inside. They stomped their feet leaving bits of snow on the pale green tile that defined the passageway.

Percy nodded into the tunnel of closed oak doors in a sea of flowery green wallpaper that was intended to compliment the tile. "Big doors at the end of the hall."

Josh went on. In all his years at Grays Lake he'd never had occasion to go into the court room. He paused in front of the oversized cherry wood doors. They were intimidating. It was an ominous feeling like no good could come from going through them. Percy's voice sounded behind him, "Go on in."

The room reminded Josh of church. Hardwood floor, pews, aisle up the middle and a pulpit for the judge. But it was different too. An American flag and the state of Idaho's flag hung on the wall behind where the judge would sit. And there was a chair, another uncomfortable oak chair to the right of the judge's pulpit for those people who would be required to tell what they knew. More importantly, though, were the tables and chairs to either side of the room in front of the pews. The table on the right was occupied.

Percy paused their entourage and called out. "Good morning, Mr. Quinn."

Harvey Quinn, middle aged, blonde and clean shaven twisted in his chair. His eyes, slightly magnified through his wire rim glasses, briefly roved over Josh and Caleb. Then, like they didn't exist, he said, "It's here, Tom. Like it or not, winter is here."

Percy laughed. "Maybe somebody should tell the folks that run this joint it snowed. Damned near needed snow-shoes to get to the front door."

Like he hadn't heard or was bored with fluff talk, Quinn came back, "I guess you know Judge Reed won't be here today."

"Yeah, I heard. Judge from Pocatello is supposed to fill in for him."

Quinn nodded. "Judge Scardino. Had dinner with him last night."

"What'd you think?"

Quinn frowned. "I'm sure you've heard the stories."

Without warning, one-half of the two big doors at the back of the room swung open. Gerald Thomas, and his remaining son, Leonard, pushed past it. The rowels on their spurs singing as they came forward. Quinn was quick to get on his feet. He started toward them hand outstretched. "Glad you could make it."

Gerald, who had several days' worth of salt and pepper whiskers, scowled, "Did you think I would miss this?"

Josh knew of Gerald Thomas, but with Grays Lake being about 30 miles north he had never met him. The man looked different than he'd imagined he would. Not smartly dressed. Instead, he wore a tattered red mackinaw and Levi's that had been patched and a gray, wide rimmed Stetson heavily stained with sweat. But he had money. Rumor had it that he ran a thousand head of cows. Josh made eye contact with the man. As he expected, his look was hateful.

Sensing the hostility in the air, Percy nodded to some empty chairs at the table across from Quinn's. "Let's sit down."

Caleb sat at the table by himself with his father and Percy directly behind him in the first pew. The clock on the wall to their left read ten till nine. Caleb turned to Percy. "That lawyer fella that came to see me yesterday, isn't he supposed to be here?"

Percy frowned. "He's not the cream of the crop."

Josh knew a little about James Pearson. He'd been in town about three years barely surviving doing wills, divorces and filling in as the public defender when needed. He'd heard too that the man had a drinking problem. Josh whispered, "What if this fella doesn't show up?"

Percy shrugged. "Be up to the judge, I guess."

"He talked yesterday like we could cut some kind of deal," said Caleb.

Percy shook his head. "Well, he ain't here."

They sat, alternately, watching the big clock on the wall and the doors at the back of the room. Across from them, Harvey Quinn and Gerald Thomas had their heads leaned together whispering. Occasionally, Thomas' voice got away from him and the defendant's table could hear him. *That sonovabitch needs to go to Boise for a long time.* This would be followed by Quinn shushing him. And so it went, until nine o'clock when the door behind the pulpit marked, JUDGE'S CHAMBERS, opened. Everyone stood as the black robed-gray haired man took his place looking slightly down on them. With a wave of his hand, they took their seats. He said, his voice deep and calm, "Judge Reed has been called out of town on a personal matter. I'm Judge Scardino." He paused, looking briefly at Quinn's table before coming back to Caleb. He said rhetorically, "Who are we missing here?"

Percy offered, "James Pearson, Your Honor."

The judge glanced at the clock and frowned. He then looked directly at Caleb. "Mr. Morrow, have you and Mr. Pearson talked about your situation?"

Caleb's heart was beating so fast it hurt. His voice was shaking. "Yes Sir, for a little while yesterday."

"And what did you decide?"

"That he was gonna try and get me a better deal."

Percy leaned forward and whispered, "Your Honor."

Before Caleb could correct his self, the Judge came back, "And just what was that deal going to be?"

"I think he called it a plea bargain, Your Honor."

Scardino looked at Quinn. "Are you aware of this deal, Mr. Quinn?"

"No, Your Honor. I've not had any conversation with the defendant's counsel. As far as I'm concerned, the charge of voluntary manslaughter stands."

"I see."

"Your Honor, Mr. Morrow started the fight."

The Judge, cognizant of the hospitality Quinn and his wife had shown him the night before, did not say what he was thinking but his eyes gave Caleb reason to be hopeful. He said, "Mr. Morrow, I read before retiring last night the witness accounts of what happened in Big Jim's Place. It seems to me you had a choice in this situation."

"A choice, Your Honor?"

"Yes, you could have ignored Mr. Thomas and either remained at the bar or leave."

The hopefulness that had welled up in Caleb just a moment ago now began to quickly fade. He came back, his tone on the verge of disrespect, "Is that what you would have done, Your Honor? Just walk away after a man calls your mother a whore?"

For a time, the Judge gave no indication that Caleb's words had affected him. It was like he was visualizing Big Jim's and what had happened except he was the one standing at the bar. He could feel their eyes, the dead man's kin, just daring him to side with the killer. And Josh, just wanting common sense to prevail. Scardino came back, satisfying none of the eyes. "According to what I read Mr. Thomas stated your mother aided some bank robbers this past spring. Any truth to that?"

Caleb obviously did not tell all that he learned about that day. He started into a look of incredulity but cut it short of insulting the Judge. "She didn't have a choice, Your Honor. They had guns."

"And to the rumor of being a prostitute?"

Caleb was taken aback. He wanted to yell at the Judge. *Does it give you pleasure rubbing my nose in that?*

It did no good that Percy grabbed Josh's arm. He stood behind his son and called out in a loud voice. "Your Honor, I'm this boy's father."

Percy now took hold of Josh. "You gotta sit down and be quiet."

"It's alright, Sheriff. Let the man speak."

Josh nodded his appreciation to Scardino. "Your Honor, it is true that twenty-two years ago my wife was, for a brief time, a prostitute. At the time, that was the choice that life gave her. But I don't fault her for it, not like all of her so-called friends and neighbors do. Caleb and I know her as nothing but a wholesome God-fearing woman. So, I hope you can see, Your Honor, how it could have riled my boy for someone to have criticized his mother for what she did a long time ago."

It was now Gerald Thomas' turn. He jumped to his feet in spite of Quinn admonishing him to the contrary. Scardino reached for his gavel and was about to bring it down when he suddenly realized how it would look not letting the victim's father have his outburst. Thomas looked at Josh no less hateful than before he'd spoken. He stabbed the air with his hand in Josh's direction. "This man has admitted what his wife was. From his own mouth, it's a fact. So, if people in this community want to repeat that fact, which they have many times over, I would reckon that is just human nature. My boy was no different." He paused for a couple of seconds before giving a dismissive backhand toward Josh. "They can't kill everybody."

Scardino now banged his gavel perfunctorily. "Alright gentlemen, you've both said your piece. The intent here today was to arraign Mr. Morrow. Advise him that he's being charged with voluntary manslaughter and hear his plea to that charge. However, without him having legal representation I am inclined to either reschedule this proceeding or strike a plea agreement right here and now. Does that sound amenable to you, Mr. Quinn?

Quinn knew, to keep the peace, he should ask for permission to consult briefly with Gerald Thomas. At the same time, he knew too, without a doubt what Thomas' response would be. He was still pondering when from behind him, Thomas shouted, "No damned deals. This boy's a killer and he needs to go spend time in Boise."

Scardino banged his gavel. "Mr. Thomas, I made an exception to your speaking out of turn. No more or you'll have to leave the court room." Scardino did not wait for Thomas' acknowledgement. He looked at Quinn. "I think what we're dealing with here is a fistfight started in the heat of passion that resulted in a freak accident."

Quinn felt anger. Maybe some embarrassment too as he knew what was likely coming. "So, what are you thinking, Your Honor?"

Scardino appeared stern, inflexible. "Simple battery. Thirty days in jail."

Gerald Thomas was instantly on his feet. He shouted, "That's bullshit. Thirty days for killin' my boy. No sir. I won't have it."

Quinn now slid his chair back, stumbling before finally standing, much too late, to try and calm Thomas. "Gerald, Gerald, we can't have this kind of behavior."

"Like hell we can't."

Scardino yelled. "Sheriff, arrest this man."

Percy reluctantly got to his feet trying to drum up courage to replace what was clearly showing on his face. He started toward Thomas speaking in a voice like a person would use to reassure a horse before slipping a halter on it. "You gotta settle down, Gerald. Things 'll turn out. You'll see."

Thomas, however, was not to be taken in by soft talk. "Stop where you're at, Tom. I'll not allow you to arrest me.'

Percy stopped. His insides were churning. Regretting the badge on his chest. "I got no choice, Gerald. Hell, I'll turn you loose in an hour or so."

Thomas snorted. "I ain't nobody's fool. I'll not spend a minute in your jail."

Percy looked at the Judge like he should relent. His eyes screamed. *Can't you see what is about to happen?*

Scardino frowned at Percy's cowardice. He said calm and indifferent to Percy's fear. "No one takes control of my court. Now do your job, Sheriff."

In his haste to distance himself from Thomas, Quinn backed into the wooden table. It skittered loudly for several feet across the floor. Initially, Caleb thought it would be wise if he moved too as he was in a direct line with Percy's back.

But then it came to him that if Percy went down, Thomas would likely try to shoot him wherever he was in the room. And then it happened, like jumping off the courthouse roof, Percy could not take back his step toward Thomas. And Thomas could not pull back his hand as it fumbled under his too long mackinaw for his pistol. Percy, however, had unbuttoned his coat some time ago which was very fortunate as his pistol rode high on his hip. Equally fortunate was the fact it was a double action revolver. His trembling hand needed only pull the trigger and that's what he did while Thomas' arthritic thumb struggled to cock his Colt. God, or maybe pure luck, smiled upon Percy as he didn't often attend church. His .45 Caliber bullet struck Thomas in the center of his chest while his dying impulse discharged a bullet into the brass framed picture of President Benjamin Harrison on the wall beyond Caleb. It may have been shock at what he'd just done, but Percy was seemingly paralyzed looking down at Thomas struggling to keep hold of his life. Through the gun smoke and ringing ears, Josh shouted at the Thomas boy, "Drop yer gun on the floor or I'll be obliged to shoot ya."

It was only now that Percy saw he was about a second away from joining Thomas wherever he was going. Fear of that happening caused him to jerk the trigger of his smooth double-action six shooter. In that very instant, Josh yelled in response to seeing the boy's gun falling from his hand, "No Tom."

Percy's bullet spun the boy around. Josh hollered again. "Hold yer fire, Tom. He's done."

The Sheriff did not lower his gun, but it was apparent in his face that his fear of dying had eased. The boy, clean shaven, baby-faced almost, collapsed back onto the pew from which he had risen moments ago. Tears had begun to spill down his cheeks. There was blood, not a lot, seeping through a new tear in the right arm of his coat. Percy looked back at the Judge. "You want me to arrest this fella?"

Scardino sighed and shook his head. "No, send him to the doctor."

The boy sobbed to the Judge. "What about my Pa?"

"We'll tend to him, son." Scardino paused and then added, "I'm sorry it turned out this way."

The boy snarled hatefully, "To hell with you and your court."

Percy started toward the boy.

Scardino called out. It's alright, Sheriff."

At the rear of the room one of the big doors peeked open just as the wounded boy pushed through. A man in a dark coat with a sharply peaked black Stetson and an Army Colt in his hand stopped the boy. Percy shouted, "It's alright, Zeke, let him get to the doctor."

Zeke Jensen, the Sheriff's deputy, stepped inside. He was halfway to the front of the room when Scardino started again. "Mr. Quinn, are you amenable to amending the charge against Mr. Morrow?"

Quinn looked at the Judge in almost disbelief. A dead man lay not more than three feet from where he stood. Blood had crept out from beneath Thomas. His eyes staring up at the ceiling like it was intensely interesting. Quinn wanted only to be free of this room. "That would be fine, Your Honor. Simple battery. Thirty days in the county jail."

Scardino turned to Caleb and Josh. "How do you plead to the charge of battery?"

Caleb didn't feel that he was deserving of jail time. He wished that none of this had happened. That the Thomas's were not dead. And all the others that had been killed since Burt Hooper showed up at their ranch. He said to the Judge, "Guilty, Your Honor."

CHAPTER THIRTY-FOUR

Gerald Thomas was a big man. It had taken Percy and Zeke on his arms and Josh and Caleb his legs to carry him out of the courthouse. They left a trail of red drops on the green tile and across the still un-shoveled snow to the street. Caleb's earlier walk to the courthouse in handcuffs paled in comparison to the spectacle they made trudging through the snow with the hatless body of the area's most prominent rancher. A young woman who was approaching the courthouse with her husband became faint at the sight. Already out of breath from laboring through the snow, her knees began to fold. Had it not been for her husband taking hold of her around the waist and pivoting her away from the scene, she would have gone down right there. Word of the courthouse shootout had spread up Main Street like a grass fire in August. Who lit that fire was not known, but the version they gave went something to the effect of, *that new judge gave that Morrow boy a slap on the wrist for killing the Thomas boy. The old man and his youngest son pulled their guns. The Sheriff shot the both of them. Killed the old man. Can you believe it? All of this over that Morrow woman being called a whore in Big Jim's.*

Josh knew the chances of it being a happy Thanksgiving for Caleb sitting in Tom Percy's jail tomorrow were slim to none. To that end, he went to the Mercantile to get Caleb something to occupy his time short of laying on his bed and studying the size and shapes of the rocks used in making the wall. When he walked in Mrs. Halverson, a middle-aged woman who clerked at the store, looked up from behind the counter but said nothing. The woman was no stranger to Josh. She'd waited on him for about seven years. Sarah's past coming to light had caused her to cool toward him, but not like most people that he knew. Today, however, Gerald Thomas' body, shaking and bouncing on the back of the undertaker's buckboard as it worked through the ruts and potholes hidden beneath the snow exhausted her sympathy for the Morrows. Josh set a newspaper, several dime novels and some hard candy on the counter. The woman refused to look at him as she began writing the items and their prices on a ticket. Josh thought to engage her in conversation. Like they usually did. Her kids. The weather. What they were doing for Thanksgiving. To say these things now, he knew, would appear trite. To not accept some blame for putting a pall on everybody's Thanksgiving that knew Gerald Thomas, and there were many, would be akin to blasphemy in the eyes of Mrs. Halverson. At last, she finished her list. "That'll be seventy-eight cents." Her voice was cold and indifferent.

Josh's demeanor stiffened. *Does she not think I regret what happened today? To hell with her.* He set a silver dollar on the counter saying nothing. She took it, rang up the sale and turned back with the change, all the while maintaining her silence. She ignored his outstretched hand and set his twenty-two cents on the counter. Josh looked her hard in the eyes so she would know her behavior was hurtful. And then he piled on, what he hoped would be her guilt, "Happy Thanksgiving."

After what had happened and the sentiment that was growing in town, Josh found the door to the jail locked. He applied a couple of loud knocks to the door and shouted, "Tom, Josh Morrow. I need to see Caleb for a minute." Silence, save for the melodic call of a mountain chickadee perched in a nearby cottonwood tree, came back at him. He sighed, irritated, just wanting to get home to Sarah and ease her worries. He knocked again and the door opened. Percy snarled. "This ain't good, Josh. You need to go home. People ain't happy about today."

"It was outta my hands. Caleb's too."

Percy snorted. "Well, it's got people riled up."

"Well, Gerald Thomas brought this on himself. His boys too."

Percy shook his head. "Zeke tells me there's already talk over at Big Jim's of evening the score."

"Meaning what?"

"I'm not sure. They're pissed at me, Scardino, Caleb. Hell, anybody named Morrow."

Josh' mind went to a worst-case scenario. He edged up to just short of questioning Percy's courage. "I don't think they'd shoot a judge or you, but what if they come for Caleb?"

"He's under lock and key."

"What if you're forced to shoot another upstanding citizen, would you do it?"

"Would you?"

"If it was my job, I would."

"Well, it's what I get a hundred dollars a month to do. Maybe tonight I can count each one of those dollars to help me sleep when Gerald starts pestering me."

"I'm sorry, Tom. Killin' a man is no easy thing."

Percy frowned. "Why don't you gimme what you got for Caleb and be on your way."

Josh handed the paper sack to Percy. "Tell him I'll be back in two weeks to get our mail and pay him a visit."

Percy nodded and shut the door. Josh could hear him turn the key in it.

CHAPTER THIRTY-FIVE

Josh paid Caleb's livery bill and borrowed a halter and lead rope from Jack Purcell with the promise he would return it in two weeks. He would be back then, he told him, not only to visit Caleb but get their mail. *We're hopin' Noah will write us by then. The little cuss is worrying his ma to no end.* And so it was, a little past noon, he headed out of town leading a saddled horse with sweet spuds in the saddlebags but no rider. People stopped and gawked at him. None waved. Their looks were cold and disapproving. Still, they soaked it up. This odd sight, this reminder of how the calamity at Big Jim's had ended this morning. Josh rode on absorbing the stares, unpleasant as they were. Like angry hornets coming out to attack him.

At last he cleared town, but it did not bring peace of mind. He was worried about Caleb's safety should agitators at Big Jim's get liquored up and decide to correct Scardino's mistake. He was not certain that Tom Percy would stand up to them. And Sarah, all she knew was that he had ridden off into a blizzard to find their son and didn't come back. He hoped that she would not come looking for him.

The ash-colored clouds of the big storm had dropped their burden mostly during the night. This morning they had lingered making idle threats of what their empty shells might do. By and by the sun put the run on them. It brought too, its ally blue skies. The air even warmed enough that Boots' breath was no longer visible. "Gonna be a good day after all," said Josh as he patted his horse's neck.

They went on in the creamy white snow. Devoid of any disturbance, it glistened in the bright light such that Josh occasionally squinted his eyes against it. To either side of him were sage covered hills with patches of dark timber on north and east slopes. Here and there, creeks like veins of blood coursed down canyon bottoms giving rise to aspen and willows. It was just after Boots had labored out of one of these creek bottoms that Josh encountered Herman Snyder's blue Studebaker. The sight of Thelma holding the reins caused him instant alarm. He came to a halt across from her. "Good morning, Mrs. Snyder."

"I can't say that it is." Her tone consistent with the concern in her eyes. "Herman took a tumble off the feed wagon this morning. Hit his head on a sharp rock. Got a nasty gash."

From his vantage point sitting on Boots, Josh could see Herman laying in a bed of quilts in the back of the big wagon. His eyes had been open when he rode up. Now, they were closed. A fact that had not escaped Josh's observation. He came back, not letting on in the least that he was wise to their deception, "Sorry to hear that. Old Doc Hale 'll fix him up."

Thelma gathered the reins more tightly. "Yes, I'm hoping he can."

In an odd way Josh felt like he was the deceiver in not telling her of the ruckus the Morrow family had caused in town. *It'll turn her against us more so than she already is.* He said aloud, "I'll let you be on your way, Thelma. Hope everything works out for Herman."

Josh expected her to right away snap the reins and leave, but she did not. Instead, she said, her look peculiar beyond his ability to figure, "If it's alright with Sarah, I'd like to drop by in the next week or so to visit."

It was difficult for Josh to suppress the shock he felt. It caused him to stammer. "Well, yeah, I reckon she'd like that."

Thelma's face was absent any shame or embarrassment for her part in the ostracization of Sarah these past months. To the contrary, she said simply, "It's been so long since we've talked."

Josh searched her eyes for what motivated her to the point it became awkward between them. His silence caused her to say at last, "Tell Sarah that I'm sorry for my part in all of this."

Josh sensed the contrition in her voice as sincere. He nodded. "I'll tell her."

And then Thelma toggled the reins. The old Army wagon, the same one Herman had hauled wood to the school in, jolted forward. Herman's eyes were wide open.

Besides giving Josh something to ponder the remaining two hours until he got home, his chance meeting Thelma would be a bright spot in what he had to tell Sarah about his trip to town. It would likely be overshadowed really quick once it came out about Caleb and all that had transpired after he went into Big Jim's Place. But when the futility of second guessing those events had exhausted itself and they were left with nothing but reality, then Thelma's apology would look good.

Josh was close to home. The sun had gone beyond the timbered mountains to the west. Their place was in deep shadow. To the east, a full moon was edging up over those mountains. Kind of like a teeter-totter with the sun being on the heavy end, at least for now it was. It was in this light that Sarah stepped from the barn with a brass bucket full of warm milk. She'd just finished milking Flowers, their Guernsey cow, so named because of her fondness for wildflowers. The weight of almost two gallons of milk had her walking lopsided. Not more than a minute ago she had studied the ocean of white towards town and came away with nothing but snow and trees. Now, however, Buster was barking in the direction of the house. She'd lit a lantern before coming down to the barn and she'd had a fire going all day long. In short, it looked like someone was home. And then she saw him. She gasped. A rider was coming around the south end of the garden. His head and shoulders just visible above the dead corn stalks. Her heart was pounding hard. She'd not brought 'Skunk Getter' as she sometimes did when going to the barn, especially when she was home alone. Then she saw it. A single feather sticking above the crown of a black slouch hat. Fear stabbed her in the chest. *Oh Josh, where are you?* Buster charged up the slope, bounding through the snow while barking wildly. Sarah cried out, "Buster, stop. Get back here." Reluctantly, Buster turned back. The rider, however, was coming following the dog. Sarah set the bucket on the ground and tried her best to act unafraid. The rider's horse, sorrel in color, picked its way through the foot deep snow. Sarah could see the butt stock of a rifle pointing forward from the scabbard beneath the man's right leg. And then he was before her. His black eyes purposely not menacing. His voice was of the same tenor. "I am Tony Bear Killer. Your husband knows me."

Sarah nodded. "I know your name."

"Your husband and me, we've had our troubles."

"Yes, you and your friends took our cows. That's not right."

"We had no choice. We were hungry."

Sarah shook her head. "There is wild game and lots of land on the reservation to graze your own cattle and grow crops. I think you took our cows because it was the easier way."

Tony gave a laugh that ended almost before it started, "You don't know how it is."

Sarah was surprised at her boldness. "I know the Lord doesn't want us to steal from one another."

Tony went quiet. He looked at her for a time before finally saying, "The day is not long enough for us to talk this out."

Sarah nodded. "Probably not. So, why have you come here?"

"I come to tell you that we brought seven of your cows back."

"I don't see them."

"They are where we took them from."

"My husband said you took ten."

"The others are no more."

Sarah looked up at Tony searching for a sign of what motivated him. In the stillness between them a sudden, but soft, pulse of wind brought the smell of wood smoke and sweat from him to her. She let go of the three good mother cows that would likely have thrown calves come spring. "So, why do you bring our cows back?"

"Indian police arrest my brother. Say he steal cattle and try kill white man. You have cows back. You tell BIA. Maybe they let my brother out of jail."

"I'll tell my husband. He may want the other three cows, though."

Tony raised his voice slightly and touched his hand to his stomach. "They are gone. Indian belly."

Sarah nodded. "He'll understand."

"Him tell BIA all cows come back."

"But they didn't."

"Tell anyway."

Lie to the BIA, thought Sarah, *or maybe they'll take these cows back and more.* She said aloud, just wanting to appease him. "We'll tell them but there's no guarantee the BIA will let your brother out of jail."

"You tell them good. I tell you secret."

"Secret?"

"You tell first."

Tony reined his horse around in the direction he'd come from. Over his shoulder he called out, "You tell."

Sarah thought to shout back, *what secret?* At the same time, it came to her that he wasn't going to tell. Recollections of kids on the playground taunting one another came to her. *I know something you don't.* For a moment she watched him go, certain, almost, that he was trying to trick her. *What could he possibly know that would be worth three cows?* She sighed and picked up the bucket of milk. "C'mon, Buster, let's go to the house."

CHAPTER THIRTY-SIX

Tony Bear Killer had not been gone long when Josh got home. His request they tell the BIA that they had all of their cows back, and his promise to reveal a secret if they did, and Thelma Snyder's apology and her request to come visit, all of it, got lost in the deluge of disbelief surrounding Caleb being in jail. They held one another in bed and talked to no good end. Finally, fatigue and the laudanum Josh had taken for the pain in his side left Sarah staring out the window. The moon, big and bright, filtered through the mostly naked aspen trees along the creek. Somewhere amongst them a Great Horned owl hooted. Buster raised up from the rug beside their bed and shook his head, rattling his ears. Sarah whispered, "No Buster. That owl is fine where it's at."

After a time of fidgeting and licks, Buster laid down resting his head on his paws with one last long sigh.

The stars were just evaporating when Josh returned with Flowers' milk. He was walking through the kitchen with the bucket when it occurred to him what day it was. "Happy Thanksgiving."

Sarah's eyes, still red from crying last night, looked up from the hotcake batter she was stirring. "You still wanna have it?"

Josh knew what she meant. Without the boys it would be hollow, just another day. He came back, "Let me think about it while I take the cream off this milk." And then he went on out the back door to the porch where the separator was located. He poured the bucket into the biggest of the three metal bowls attached to the machine and began to turn the crank. The round wooden knob fit his hand good. In no time he had the gears of the separator purring smoothly. Fatless milk was trickling into a smaller second bowl while cream was going into an even smaller third. The screened in porch offered little warmth. His breath being visible in the cold air. He'd not gotten into any serious thinking when the door behind him opened. Sarah came out. She went right to it. "I can't do Thanksgiving. Not this year."

Josh let go of the crank and stood up straight. The handle went around several more times on its own before the hum of the separator died. He looked at her wondering if not having Thanksgiving was the right thing to do. He put forth a grin. "Might do us good to stuff ourselves and fall asleep in front of the fire."

Sarah came back, somber in tone. "I'm sorry, Josh. I don't mean to ruin your day."

"You're not. Maybe next year the boys will be here."

"It's more than that."

"I know. I wish I could change how things are."

Sarah shook her head and sighed. "These people, I sometimes think the human tongue has got to be the most destructive weapon known to man."

Josh stepped to Sarah and put his arms around her. "Maybe Christmas will be better. Caleb will be home then and the Army might allow Noah some leave. It'll be grand you'll see."

Her words came out muffled into Josh's chest. "I hope so."

After breakfast, they saddled their horses and started for Porcupine Creek. Without the boys, it would be far more difficult than usual to gather their cattle. It would be like the old days when it was just the two of them building their ranch. They'd done it then and they were sure they could do it now.

The day turned out sunny and warm. It worked their horses hard searching out the draws of timber and aspen to either side of the big grassy basin that was now under a foot of snow. As they came upon cattle, they pushed them towards the creek and open country. It was tedious, exhausting for the horses. Time and again, Josh found himself cursing at an uncooperative cow, *Why you sorry old blister, I've a notion to put a loop on you and drag you home.* Idle threats such as this did not improve the cow's behavior, but it helped ease Josh's frustration.

In spite of Tony Bear Killer's peace offering, Josh refused to let Sarah search on her own. *We'll work it together. Stay in sight of one another.* They gathered the east side of the creek first, pushing the cows into a loose bunch in the big meadow. They paused at the head of the valley near a big spring that birthed Porcupine Creek. Their horses snorted wearily, appreciative of the rest. "Let's git a count," said Josh. "See what we're short."

They counted only the east side of the creek. Sarah's pointing and whispering ended first. "I got 51."

Josh eased back into his saddle from having stood slightly in his stirrups to see better. "Well, I reckon it must be a fact, cuz that's what I got too."

Sarah looked almost festive with her red stocking hat pulled down around her ears. "Long ways from 114."

Josh frowned as he instantly recalled the Indians had butchered three of their cows. He sighed and glanced up at the sun, high overhead to the south. "I guess we'll see what this afternoon brings us."

They nudged their horses towards the creek. Their hooves crunching the snow as they went. Two ravens perched in some tall willows watched their approach and cawed their disapproval. Sarah invaded the lull between them. "Are you curious as to what Tony Bear Killer's secret is?"

Josh snorted. "A ploy, I reckon, to sweeten the pot so I'll ride the 30 miles to town and back and tell Percy we got all our cows back and those poor fellows the BIA has got locked up are actually some fine men. Never mind the fact they tried to kill me and Caleb."

"So, you're not going to talk to the Sheriff?"

"Well, let's see what the count is on the west side."

Sarah went silent, as she was of the same mindset. And then they came to the creek. Thin ice crept out from each bank. A ribbon of deeper flowing water, two or three feet wide in most places, separated the ice. Josh went first. The ice immediately crackled like glass beneath his horses' hooves. Within seconds they were across the tiny creek. Josh paused looking at the country they had to work. "If the boys were here, I'd leave one of 'em to keep these cattle on the other side of the crik from roamin'."

Melancholy haunted Sarah's voice. "Maybe next year."

Josh nodded without looking at her. "Yeah, maybe so."

They rode downstream, working the big meadow west of the creek. As they went, they pushed everything they found to the other side of the creek. By and by they came to where the dark timber pinched off the meadow. Josh stopped his horse next to Sarah. "By my count we picked up another 47 head."

Sarah nodded. "We're short 16 then."

Josh wiped at the moisture collected in his moustache with the back of his dark cloth glove. He said in a voice that hinted at what they were both thinking. "That's a lot to be out."

Sarah wanted to believe Tony Bear Killer. That there was some remorse in this country, even if it was for selfish reasons. *What unlikely sources*, she thought, *Tony and Thelma*. A grin of absurdity started to appear on her face before she caught herself. She said aloud, "Maybe they're in the timber."

Josh looked at the thick pine trees. They appeared cold and undesirable compared to the tops of the yellow grass sticking above the snow, sparkling in the sun. Josh shook his head. "'Bout the only place we got to look I reckon." He paused and snorted. "But you know how cows are. Lot of 'em ain't gonna win any contest for being smart."

They started into the shadowy woods tromping through virgin snow. At times they brushed past boughs that showered them and their horses with even more of the white stuff. It was cold and slow going. After a while, the sun no longer cleared the tall trees. It was as if they were riding in a trench that, at any moment, would be filled in with dirt. Sarah was first to suggest it. "Maybe we should take what we've got east of the creek and start for home."

Josh looked up between the trees like he was double checking that the sun hadn't come back. He sighed and shook his head. "Sixteen cows is a lot to leave behind."

"We can come back tomorrow."

Josh could feel a trickle of blood from the pain in his side. Truth be told he didn't want to come back tomorrow. But he had no choice. Just as he wouldn't have a choice to start feeding these cows once they got them home. Forking that hay on and off the wagon would aggravate his wound. He said aloud. "You're right, Hon. I figure we got two hours 'fore dark."

Sarah came back, her body aching from fatigue and well aware of how the sky had been last night. "We'll have moonlight. It's full you know."

Josh teased. "Nuthin' like a romantic moonlight ride."

Sarah's cheeks were rosy and her eyes a bit watery from the cold. She smiled. "I guess we better get started then."

Josh returned the smile. A feeling of affection swept over him. This challenge, the adversity. It would bring them even closer. He caught her eye in a knowing way. "Well, let's vamoose outta these miserable trees and make tracks for home."

They rode single file until they broke into the big meadow whereupon they went next to one another even splashing across the shallow creek that way. To their relief, the cattle had stayed loosely bunched, pretty much where they'd left them. They began walking their horses to the closest ones. Some of these were laying down chewing their cud and watching the approach of these intruders. Others, standing, staring wide-eyed at the horses, appeared ready to bolt. Josh brought his horse to a halt, as did Sarah. He pointed. "You see that old, crooked horn cow?"

Sarah's eyes looked off the end of Josh's outstretched arm to a cow well into the herd. "Yeah."

"Well, that old gal knows the way home. She's done this plenty times before. If we can git her in the lead, I'm hopin' these others will act more like sheep than cows and follow her home."

Sarah nodded. "I remember that cow. I believe she will do what you want."

Josh pointed again. "See those bug- eyed heifers on the right side there? The ones that look like they're just lookin' for an excuse to head to the hills?"

"Yeah."

"Well, I'm gonna take up a vigil on that side. See if I can't keep them in check."

Sarah jumped in knowing what the plan would be. "I'll let you get over there next to them and then I'll start pushing the others."

Josh smiled warmly. "You know, I think I'll keep you."

Sarah came back. "I love you too."

CHAPTER THIRTY-SEVEN

Old Crooked Horn did not let them down. It was like the cows sensed they were going to an easier place. Nonetheless, it was fortunate that there was a full moon as they did not get to the fenced pasture until almost 8:30. The day had been exhausting and they still had to ride another half mile to the house, tend to the horses and milk Flowers. And in the morning, while the stars were still out, they'd repeat much of what they'd done the day before.

Buster paced and yipped nervously near the barn where they were saddling their horses. Sarah was first to dash his hopes of going. She looked at the dog like it was a child she loved. "No, you can't go. It's too far and there is too much snow."

Josh turned away from tightening his cinch and petted the top of Buster's head. "He don't understand being left home two days in a row."

Sarah collected her reins from where they hung in front of her horse. "He's an old dog."

Josh grinned playfully like he expected sympathy. "So are we."

Sarah scoffed. "We're not as old as Buster."

"Damned near."

And so they rode out, admonishing Buster to "stay" several times. They were on fresh horses. Ones that Burt Hooper had swapped out last spring. Until now, Sarah had avoided riding any of them. Her association with Hooper was far different than the rest of the family. It was an emotional scar that would never heal. Now here she was straddling his horse. The image of him and his men riding in that day played over and over in her mind. And tumbling too in that kaleidoscope of unpleasantness was an image of that night in Bear Creek when, for two dollars, she had surrendered herself to him. She could still smell the whiskey and tobacco on his breath and his body odor. She could feel the roughness, the cracks filled with black grime on his fingers as he grabbed at her breasts. Had Josh not been riding next to her she would have allowed herself to cry.

The way back to the big meadow on Porcupine Creek was now well defined due to their having trailed 98 head of cows over it the day before. They'd just started down off the ridge overlooking the meadow when Josh called out, "Well, hell's bells, Christmas has come early."

Sarah caught sight of Josh's reason for joy. "Eleven head by my count."

"Leaves five more."

"Well, maybe today we can have supper on time instead of a bedtime snack."

Josh shook his head. "That'd be welcome but I ain't gittin' my hopes up."

It wasn't so much that Sarah felt sorry for Tony Bear killer and his friends as it was adding to the positive vibe of seeing the cows down in the meadow had brought them. "These cows give us 109." She let the number simmer in Josh's mind without looking at him.

A breeze, just enough to rustle the ends of Josh's blue neckerchief, played as he offered, "Maybe the Indians did bring back some of our cows."

In the sky, high above them, two ravens chastised them for coming back today. Sarah nodded, blending her voice with the ravens. "It appears they did."

"So, you're thinkin' I should speak up for 'em?"

"Might go a long ways to ending the rustling and gun-play in the future."

"Maybe so."

"You gonna do it then?"

"Let's see if we find the other five."

They then went down off the ridge saying no more about it lest it become a sore spot between them. Sarah wanted peace between them and their Indian neighbors before they were the ones doing the crying and burying. Josh wanted the same, but not at the price of three mother cows and the fat calf they had butchered earlier. In his mind it was real simple. A person didn't take what wasn't theirs.

By three o'clock a shadow that defined the cut of the mountains to the west lay over the little creek and the mead-ow surrounding it. The eleven cows had not wandered far from where they were when Josh and Sarah had disappeared into the timber. Now here they were coming out of the trees empty handed, so to speak. They paused to look at the cows and count them again. Sarah aired what they had resigned themselves to. "Those five cows aren't in this basin, Hon."

Josh sighed. "I suspect they went to roaming before the big snow thinking they were gonna find better feed than this." He paused. "Or Tony Bear Killer is lying."

Sarah was hesitant to dispute Josh, but he'd not heard the sincerity in Tony's voice. The promise he'd tell them a secret. She came back, "It could be that-"

Josh cut her off. "Let's just take these and go home." He did not wait for her response.

CHAPTER THIRTY-EIGHT

There were a number of factors that led to the discovery of Frank Taylor's body. It was snowy and cold. The top two or three inches of soil were frozen and beneath that there was more rock than dirt. And as much as anything, Hooper just plain didn't care if Frank got a decent burial. So it was, he and Pete invested minimal time in digging a grave. Instead, they piled rocks and tree branches on Frank. This, of course, was no deterrent to coyotes. In due time, ravens joined in dining on Frank. It was their noisy squawking that attracted Phil Giles, out hunting deer, to the site not more than a mile from the Snyder place. Hence the presence of Tom Percy and Giles at the Snyder's front door.

Herman, who was now fully lucid and ambulatory, greeted them. There was some trepidation in his voice. "Mornin'. What brings you fellows our way?"

"Business," replied Percy.

"Well, come on in." Glancing at Thelma, Herman added, "Thelma pour these men a cup of coffee."

Thelma's hands had already begun to tremble. She set mugs, heavy, brown porcelain with fat loop handles on the kitchen table before the men. And then she took the coffee pot, big, heavy, equally good to disguise her fear, from the stove and poured the black as tar steaming liquid in their cups. The men nodded their thanks.

Herman went on. "So, what's the nature of your business, Tom?"

Percy almost smiled. It registered with him how civilians, as he called them, got real cordial or overly respectful when they thought they might be in trouble. He slurped the hot coffee before answering. "Phil here, found a dead man just up the canyon from your place. I was hopin' maybe you'd seen or heard something peculiar that might shed some light on this matter."

Thelma jumped in. "It's been quiet for some time now with the big snowstorm and all. I don't recollect seeing anything out of the ordinary, do you Herman?"

Herman's answer came like cold molasses. "Well, let me think. I was kinda goofy for a while. Fell off the feed wagon. Busted my head on a rock. But, no, no, nothing odd comes to mind."

Percy looked at Giles. "Mr. Giles tells me on the day of the big storm he saw three men on horseback come down to your place. You don't recall that?"

Thelma feigned wholesomeness against the suspicion that was evident in Percy's eyes. "Land a Goshen, Phil, what were you doing out on a day like that?"

Phil was uneasy with implicating his neighbors in anything to do with the dead man up the canyon. They attended the same church. He came back. "If you recall, Thelma, that day didn't turn sour until afternoon. I just got caught in the storm."

It was obvious to Percy and Giles that the Snyder's were lying. An air had come over the room like an intense chess match was underway. Each of them was processing what their next move might be when Percy's eyes dropped to the floor near his chair. A dull green braided rug had shifted slightly partially revealing a discoloration of the wood. With the tip of his boot, he folded the corner of the rug back. And then he may as well have called checkmate. "What happened here?"

Although Thelma had scrubbed what she told the kids was chicken blood, an outline of Frank Taylor's blood remained on the floor. In her desperation for credibility, she switched lies. "Oh, clumsy me, I spilled a pan of boiled chokecherries. I scrubbed until the cows came home and for the life of me, I couldn't get it all up."

Percy nodded like he believed Thelma. "Such a waste. Chokecherry syrup is one of my favorites."

Thelma looked at Herman for support. "It's Herman's favorite too. Isn't it, Dear?"

Herman remained silent. He was no quitter, but it was clear to him that Percy was going to be the victor in this exchange. The question in his mind was whether he should abandon Thelma's ship now or go down with it. And then Percy fired a broadside. "Phil tells me he's purty certain one of the men that came to your place during the storm was riding a horse that belonged to Josh Morrow. One of those that Burt Hooper's bunch took last spring. Do you know the Morrow horses?"

The color left Thelma's face. She looked again to Herman for support, but he sat stone faced and quiet. Not even under her pleading stare did his demeanor change. She knew, right then and there, that Irma Duke had won. Her thoughts had become jumbled, distracted with anger. *That hussy. That worthless slut passing herself off as some virtuous schoolmarm.*

Percy fired again. "Thelma, did you recognize any of the horses?"

Thelma suddenly boiled out of her trance-like digression. Riding her lie to the bottom. "I told you, Sheriff, I don't recall any visitors during the big storm."

And then it happened. Casual, indifferent to their 18 years of marriage. Herman said, in a calm voice, "I do."

"You do what," shrieked Thelma.

Angry life now came to Herman's eyes. "I recall that Hooper fella clubbing me with his pistol. Damned near killed me. And I recall them dividing the money that you kept from the stage. And I got my suspicions where that fella slept that night too."

Thelma pretended shock, outrage. "He's lying, Sheriff. He was unconscious."

Herman snorted. "So, you thought."

Thelma looked hatefully at her husband before surrendering her lie to retaliation. She seethed the words, "You pretended to be knocked out and left me to fend for myself? You coward. You worthless two-timing coward."

Percy pointed towards the floor. "And these stains, they belong to the dead guy Phil found?"

Thelma nodded. "Hooper got in an argument with one of his men and killed him. Frank somebody."

"What about the money? They get all of it?"

"Yes."

"Five thousand dollars?"

Thelma's anger finally gave way to sadness and painful regret. She began to cry. Percy did not press her for an answer turning instead to Herman. He'd heard the rumors. It was his business to know what went on in the county. He studied the man. Middle aged. Not overtly good looking so as to catch a woman's eye. Certainly not a beautiful married woman like Irma Duke, but he had. And that, he suspected, had caused Thelma, a portly, devout, church-going woman to stray. There would be no new start in life for her, at least not as she envisioned it. Percy said, at last, "Herman, you're about a coin toss away from me taking you to jail with your wife."

Thelma gasped and began to sob into her hands. Herman cast a cold look at his wife before coming back to Percy. "So, what's it gonna be, Tom?"

Percy had no use for someone who would cheat on his wife or hide the fact she had stolen $5,000. At the same time, he had no desire to completely destroy their family. He came back. "The District Attorney is gonna want you to tell in court what happened here. If you do, I suspect he'll not charge you with being an accomplice to your wife's goings on."

Relief swept over Herman's face. "Thank you, Sheriff. I appreciate you seeing this for how it is."

Percy frowned before turning to Thelma. "Ma'am, you're gonna have to go to town with me. You can either go horseback, or buckboard if your husband is willing to drive you there."

Before Thelma could answer, Herman cut in, "Tom, it'd make for an overnight stay if I was to set out this late in the day. Don't know that I really want to do that."

Thelma shook her head in disgust. She thought to call Herman vile names. Label him as the adulterer he was, but she did not. She composed herself and said calmly, "When the boys come in from feeding you tell them what happened. Give them a fair accounting of things because you know there'll come a time when I will. And tell them I love them."

CHAPTER THIRTY-NINE

It was mid-morning, about a week after it became common knowledge that Thelma Snyder had gone to jail when the Miller boy showed up at the Morrow place. Josh and Sarah were in front of the barn unharnessing the team that pulled the hay wagon. Josh looked over, squinting against the acrid smoke of a freshly lit Bull Durham cigarette that dangled from his lips. His mind was searching for a possible reason to justify the boy being there. Nonetheless, he called out like they talked on a regular basis as neighbors do. "Mornin' Fred. How are you this fine day?"

Fred Miller was 17, without a hint of a whisker on his heavily freckled face. His outward demeanor, awkward and nervous, suggested he was embarrassed that his family had not talked to the Morrows since Sarah lost her jobs at the church and school. He went right to the message he was sent to deliver. "Mr. Morrow, there's five of your heifers over in the bottom of Snowslide Canyon."

"The hell you say."

"Yes Sir, Pa and me saw 'em 'bout sundown yesterday."

"How they farin'?"

"They're a bit gant but alright. Me and Pa wudda pushed 'em this way but it got dark on us. And then this mornin' we had to feed and then Pa and my brother went to load the wagons for in the morning and we still need to chop ice. We was just bogged down and then Pa says I better come tell you 'bout those heifers 'fore the day is shot."

Josh, and Sarah too, savored the boy's guilt like the first day of a spring thaw coming out of a bad winter. Josh removed the cigarette from his mouth with his gloved right hand. He couldn't help but smile at the boy. "Well, Fred, I appreciate yer lettin' us know about them heifers. Be sure and tell yer Pa thanks."

Fred nodded. "I sure will." He paused and then added like he'd not satisfied the debt his family had incurred in five months of ostracization, "I'd lend you a hand but like I said, we're purty bogged down."

"Not a problem, Fred. We just appreciate yer stoppin' by."

Sarah put in, "Yes, Fred, we thought we were out those cows. This is such good news."

Fred beamed, proud of himself. "Well, I'll sure tell Pa."

They watched in silence until Fred was beyond hearing. Josh was first to speak. "Maybe things are changing."

Uncertain if she should bring it up, the smile on Sarah's face began to melt. "So, are we going to tell the Sheriff we've got our cows back?"

Josh snorted and shook his head. "You're determined to know Tony Bear Killer's secret."

"Aren't you curious?"

"I'm more curious that when we tell the BIA they owe us for three cows, if they'll pay."

"The money would be nice but at what price?"

"Are you afraid of the Indians?"

Anger came to Sarah's face. "Yes. I want to be able to ride over our range without fear of trouble. I don't want to worry about you or Caleb getting in another gunfight with them and this time their aim is better. If three cows will buy us peace, I say, lie to Tom Percy. Tell him we have all our cows back and they should let those Indians out of jail."

Josh thought back to his days in the Army fighting Comanches. They'd nearly killed him and now the Shoshone had too. To give in on the three cows made him feel like he would be losing. He came back. "You know last year I caught Tony butchering a calf and I let him take it on the promise there'd be no more. Now here they are for another calf and gunplay. And then they come back for more. Why do you think these three will be different?"

Sarah shook her head. "You may be right or maybe not. We're rolling the dice, I guess. But I like our odds better giving them the three cows to help them get out of jail than I do the prospect of their relatives getting revenge."

Josh took a final draw on his cigarette before throwing it down in the snow. He expelled the smoke from his lungs in a forceful, irritated rush. "Alright, Sarah, if we git all the heifers today we'll go see the Sheriff tomorrow."

She said, barely above a whisper, "We gotta try."

CHAPTER FORTY

They rode horseback to town. The heifers had been right where the Miller boy said they'd be. Their nomadic ways had put them in a canyon grubbed out during the summer. As a consequence, they were receptive to being driven from Snowslide Canyon to the home place and a ration of green grass hay.

They were coming up on the jail. Sarah twisted slightly in her saddle towards Josh. "He's gonna be surprised to see us, don't you think?"

Josh looked at Sarah, his excitement almost as keen as hers. "I've no doubt he will be. I was thinkin', though, we should go to the post office first. How grand would it be if there was a letter from his brother."

Sarah flashed a smile. It being framed by her red stocking cap that was tugged down around her ears such that she looked like a boy from afar. She had knowingly dressed that way. Dark cotton pants. Loose fitting, baggy almost. Leather boots. A splotchy red and black mackinaw. She came back. "You think? A letter from Noah this soon?"

Josh laughed. "Commanding officers don't like gittin' letters from upset mothers. I reckon some first sergeant saw to it that the boy wrote a letter right pronto."

Sarah was already visualizing what it might say. "What a treat this will be. We'll read it together."

Josh grinned. "Yeah, right there in the county jail."

Sarah ignored his tease. Her attention having been diverted to the gray smoke lolling above the old rock building. It spewed from the stovepipe in copious amounts. *Maybe Thelma's cold blooded,* she thought. *Keep Percy or his deputy busy splitting wood.* A smile came to her face. Involuntary or not, she wasn't certain. After a time, it went away.

By and by they came to the post office. Sarah made no motion to get off her horse. From the ground, Josh looked up between their horses at her. "She's a hateful woman."

Sarah shook her head but said nothing.

Josh went inside. A little brass bell attached to the top of the door jingled. Shortly, Mabel Beal's face appeared in the rectangular window. Upon seeing who it was, her expression went to one of being inconvenienced. She frowned. "Just a minute."

Josh could see her back as she rummaged through packets of mail mumbling in a bitter tone as she did. Finally, she came up with two letters. Studied the return addresses more than who they were to before turning around and placing the letters, without a word, on the window's tiny shelf.

Josh picked up the letters averting his eyes from Mabel's condescending stare. He started to leave when, on impulse, he turned and ginned up a smile, "You have yourself a good morning, Mrs. Beal."

It caught her off guard, but not to the point she would reciprocate.

Josh laughed to himself. *Old bitty is dug in on being how she is.* The brass bell rattled again behind him. It was only then that Josh noticed the letter beneath the one from Sarah's sister in Boston was from the Army. Concern instantly came to his mind. From her saddle above him Sarah sensed something was wrong. "Noah didn't write?"

"No, the Army did."

A fluttery fear began to build in Sarah's stomach. "Guess we better see what it says."

Josh sighed. "I reckon so." He stepped between the horses and tore open the envelope. His intent was to read it aloud, but it was so brief that his eyes scanning ahead had absorbed its contents in seconds. He snorted as he handed the letter up to Sarah. "He ain't even in the Army."

Sarah read the sentence several times. *We have no record of your son, Noah Morrow, having ever enlisted in the Army at this location.* Sarah handed the letter back to Josh. "I don't know what to think."

Josh shook his head. "Wouldn't be the first time a fella has gone off to join up and lost his nerve. Could be that's what happened and he's ashamed to write home and tell us."

"There's no shame in that."

Josh grinned in deference to her. "You ain't a man." He then handed the other letter up to her.

Normally Sarah would read her sister's letter right away. Looking upon it almost like an early Christmas present. Today, she stuffed it in her coat pocket.

There was no way to not look at them, Zeke and Thelma coming along the worn down path in the snow from the privy back to the jail. Sarah could tell that Thelma did not want to make eye contact, but they did, uncomfortable as it was, just before they went in the side door.

Josh and Sarah, being members of the public went in the front door. Tom Percy was seated at his desk cleaning his pistol. He looked up. "Mornin'. Come to see your boy?"

"We did," replied Josh stepping closer to Percy's desk. "Need to conduct a little business first."

Percy looked back to his gun. "How's that?" He then threaded a clean strip of white cloth through the eyelet of his cleaning rod and inserted it into the barrel of his pistol and began working it back and forth.

"The Indians, they brought our cows back."

Percy paused and looked Josh in the eyes. He said emphatically, "Well, I'll be go to hell. I'd sooner bet on Santy Claws comin' in July than them bringing yer cows back."

With Sarah's left arm intertwined in Josh's right he replied, "I'm with you on that score, but they did."

"Gottem all back, huh?"

On the ride to town, they'd wrestled the matter of the three butchered cows until it was as dead as the cows were. Josh came back quick like it was the truth, "Yes Sir, surprised hell out of me but we did. Ten head."

Percy pulled the swab of blackened white cloth from his gun barrel. His voice was casual, bordering on inconsequential. "I'm assuming you're telling me this cuz you think it'll have some bearing on those Indians they got locked up at Fort Hall?"

"We struck a deal, Tom. They give our cows back and we don't press charges."

Percy went quiet, looking at Josh like he was a Quaker preacher or some such. He snorted while shaking his head. "For someone who came within about two inches of dying you're mighty forgiving."

Sarah intervened, "Sheriff, we don't want anymore trouble with the Indians."

Percy picked up his pistol and began taking the cartridges from his desktop and reloading. "Well, I'll let those folks over there know of the change in the circumstances here. What they'll do with that information, I can't say."

Josh nodded. "Thanks, Tom. Appreciate it."

Percy turned the cylinder of his pistol and inserted the last bullet like he hadn't heard Josh. He then turned to his deputy sitting across the room next to the stove, "Zeke, you wanna take these folks back to see their boy."

The deputy, a skinny guy not much older than Caleb, got up from a straight back wooden chair. He went to the door behind Percy's desk and took a key ring from a hook on the wall next to it. He pulled the door open being respectful of Sarah, "Here ya go, Ma'am."

Sarah smiled, genuinely appreciative of his politeness. A simple common courtesy, but so rare in her world since last spring. She purposely looked the young man in the eye. "Thank you."

The door, heavy and thick with wrought iron strapping binding its planks together, closed with a thud of finality behind them. Caleb's cell was the first one. He was standing, his hands grasping the bars. "Hello, Ma. It's good to see you. It's good to see you both."

For a while they talked comfort things, sleeping, eating, boredom but not a word about how defending his mother's reputation had caused him to be in there. He lied on the sleeping part telling them that he slept just fine, and not a word about the loud mouth Thomas boy laying on the floor of Big Jim's. And he neglected to tell them of the nightly visits of Tony Bear killer's friend, the one he had killed. And he did not tell them of Thelma's whimpering and crying in the night. Soft at first. Barely audible. She rambled. *Damned Herman will get his. Irma too. And that despicable Hooper. Ride me like a whore, will he. They'll all burn in hell.* Her shame too great to share with him. After a while, she could not bear it alone. They agreed there would be times when Thelma should lift the blanket hanging between their cells. That she should tuck it into the bars so they could see one another. That a 22 year old boy, who'd been with only one girl in his life, couldn't explain why her husband went to Irma Duke caused Thelma to drop the blanket for a night and a day. And so, it had not been a good time for Caleb.

"Have you heard from Noah?"

Sarah glanced at Josh. "No, nothing yet."

"Well, that scalawag. With us writing his boss, I figured sure he'd write by now."

Josh, letting the façade stand, came back. "Could be they sent him east for his training."

From beyond the blanket, Thelma interrupted. "They're still riding your horses, you know."

The look on Caleb's face said that he knew. Josh stepped to where he could see Thelma. Her hair was not done up in any way. Not even brushed. He felt sorry for her. "Are they taking good care of them?"

Thelma sat on her bed. Her knees tucked up against her chest and her back against the wall. She said, her voice sullen, devoid of spirit, "Good as killers do anything that lives."

And then salvation in the form of Zeke sounded behind them. "Time to go, folks."

Sarah looked to the side of Josh. She struggled for something positive to say, finally settling on, "Maybe we'll see you another day, Thelma."

Thelma smirked. "If it's in here, that wouldn't be good for either of us."

CHAPTER FORTY-ONE

On December 24th they had their breakfast of a biscuit with a dollop of strawberry preserve, a cold fried egg, and a reasonably hot cup of black coffee. After they'd had time to eat, Percy himself, as opposed to Zeke, came back to let Caleb out. He said in a loud voice, almost jocular, "Well, here's the day you been looking for." He rattled the key into the lock, twisted and swung the door open. "You're a free man."

Caleb was uncertain if he should wish Thelma a merry Christmas. She'd not yet raised the blanket this morning. Nor had she said a word during breakfast. He supposed envy of him going home had caused her to be this way. He stood still. Staring at the blanket. Cheap, thin, gray wool. Dead silence. And then a slurp of coffee. Percy's impatient sigh. At last Caleb spoke to the blanket, "Good luck to you, Thelma." He paused. Then came a sniffle. Caleb shook his head and trailed after the Sheriff.

Percy locked the big wooden door behind them like Thelma was some escape risk. He nodded to a small table with Caleb's personal belongings while going to his desk. "There's your property. Tell your Pa that the Indians that shot you two are still in jail."

"They're not gonna let 'em out?"

"Stealing cattle is one thing. Trying to kill their owners is another. That's causing real concern to some important folks."

Caleb picked up a letter sized white envelope containing what little money he'd had when he was arrested and stuffed it in his coat pocket. He looked over at Percy, sitting behind his desk taking a sip of coffee. "I'll pass that on, Tom."

Percy lowered his cup. "You have yourself a merry Christmas."

"Same to you, Tom." Caleb went out the door. He hoped that Thelma hadn't heard him and the Sheriff's last words. It was like she was in a place where there was no Christmas.

Caleb shuffled through the snow, now rutted and churned up with mud and horse manure on his way to Jack Purcell's livery. His 30 days in jail and the editorial harangues in the local rag had made him a celebrity. Most town people did not know enough about the Thomas boy that died in Big Jim's to form an opinion as to his character. More to the point, they didn't know enough about him to say whether or not he got what he deserved. So, they erred on the side of what they did know and that was his father had contributed a lot to the building of the school and Baptist church at the edge of town. And now they were both dead due to, as they saw it, getting crosswise with the Morrows. So, they felt at liberty to stare. Others whispered and pointed. After an eternity Caleb completed this gauntlet of shame and self-restraint.

Jack Purcell called out from the shadowy depths of his stable. "Saw you coming. Got a horse saddled."

Caleb walked on past empty stalls and those with horses patiently standing. He was not yet there when Jack gathered the reins and held them out. "Here ya go."

Caleb's paranoia kicked in. *He wants to be rid of me.* Aloud, he replied, "Appreciate your helping me out."

Jack glanced at the sorrel horse." He's a good animal. I call him Rusty."

Caleb stepped up into the saddle. "I'll get him back to you first chance I get."

Jack nodded. "That'll be fine." He then started to walk off towards his one room quarters.

Caleb thought to call out, *Merry Christmas*. But in that instant, he took note of Jack's dreary quarters and there being no sign of Christmas. He nudged Rusty' sides and went on home.

CHAPTER FORTY-TWO

It was still dark outside when Caleb woke up. He'd slept hard. It felt good to not be surrounded by rock walls, steel bars and the gray blanket. And to know that he was square with the state. He could not help how town people were. That 30 days of his freedom in exchange for the Thomas boy's life was not enough in their eyes. A sliver of light was visible beneath his door. He could hear his mother's soft steps in the kitchen. *No doubt fixing breakfast and working on Christmas dinner too.* He dressed in the dark, save for his muddy boots which he'd left at the front door, and padded out to the kitchen. A pan of bacon sizzled on the stove. Its smell permeated the air. Sarah was forming a pie crust. She looked up. "Merry Christmas, son."

"Merry Christmas, Ma. I overslept. Pa doing the chores?"

"He is, but he said for you to not fret over it and stay put."

"Well, I'll help feed."

"That you can do, while I finish getting Christmas dinner ready."

Caleb picked up his mug from the table, which was already set, and poured himself a cup of coffee. He immediately took a noisy sip. "Nobody makes coffee like you, Ma."

Sarah smiled and continued crimping the edges of her pie crust.

Caleb took another sip and laughed. "You could give Percy's deputy a lesson on coffee makin'. The stuff he makes would peel the paint of a lard bucket. But that's the way the Sheriff likes it, I reckon, so you'd probably be wasting your time." He started to laugh again but cut it off when he saw the look on his mother's face. The abrupt silence between them prompted her to air her mind. "I'm sorry you had to spend time in jail." She paused and shook her head. "That entire affair at Big Jim's happened because of me."

The culmination of 30 days of staring at the rock wall and talking late into the night with Thelma, poured out. "No, Ma. I could have just walked out."

"And the Thomas boy could have apologized."

"It's done, Ma. It's over. Six days from now will be a new year. A clean slate as far as I'm concerned."

Sarah nodded. "You're a good son, Caleb." She held up her hands covered with flour and bits of dough, as if wanting to hug him and smiled.

Caleb smiled back.

It was late afternoon. Josh and Sarah were sitting on the couch. A chess board between them. Christmas was largely over. Ham dinner. Cards opened to each other. A new shirt for Caleb and two slices of ham for Buster. Flames licking the inside of the fireplace. It was hard to stay awake. And then the lull, the illusion that things were good, ended. Buster ran to the door barking wildly.

Josh got up from the couch. The Christmas tree was blocking his view of the window and who or what was out front. Given Buster's excitement, he pulled his pistol from its holster where it hung on the wall. And then he opened the door. Surprise, mild shock confronted him. Stocking feet, pistol in hand, he stepped out onto the front porch closing the door behind him. "Hello, Tony. I didn't figure you'd be coming. Especially today."

Tony Bear Killer had not come under the influence of missionaries. He held a pagan view of how the world and all that was in it came to be. He said, still on his paint horse, "This white man's big day. Nothing to me."

Josh allowed his hand with the gun to hang, non-threatening, straight down at his side. "Your friends. They're still in jail?"

"I know you say ok they get out. BIA no do."

"Then why are you here?"

"Tell the secret. It no good."

"So, what is this secret?"

Tony's voice did not break stride. "Tony hunting. Hide in trees. See bad man kill your son."

Josh suddenly felt sick, weak. Through the door he heard Sarah scream. He came back, "Are you sure? You saw this happen?"

"I see your boys plenty times. It him. He try take horses from three men. Claim they belong him. Bad man shoot him."

And then the door opened. Sarah's crying had evolved to deep sobs of grief. Her body trembled. With Caleb's help she stepped out onto the porch next to Josh.

Josh struggled to endure Tony's secret. Tears puddled in his eyes. "Where'd this happen?"

"Other side mountain. Road to big town."

"Pocatello?"

Tony nodded.

"Can you take me to where my son's body is?"

Tony shook his head. "Bad man throw him river."

Josh grimaced. He wanted to shout at Tony, *why didn't you help him*? The reality of how things were checked his impulse. He said aloud. "When did this happen?"

"Long time back."

"Before our troubles on Porcupine Crik?"

"Not long before."

"Can you show me where this happened?"

Tony crossed his fingers. "It where Crow Creek go in Portneuf."

Josh had no doubts, but he asked anyway, "The man who killed my son, what did he look like?"

"Him big. Mean look."

"Was he riding a black horse with a white star on its forehead?"

Tony nodded.

"And one of the others, was he riding a buckskin?"

"That him."

Josh went quiet as tears finally escaped his right eye. Tony looked back at him, not indifferent to his pain. He said simply, "I go now."

The enormity of Sarah's sadness and guilt stole away her strength. She dropped to her knees trembling and crying. The stoic woman who'd dealt with all that had come of the day Burt Hooper came back into her life, was spent. Josh helped her up. "Let's go inside." They collapsed onto the couch, her leaning against him. His arm around her.

Sarah sobbed. "I should have shot him that day he came here. I could have you know. I could have killed him and none of this would be happening."

Josh was quick to point out the absurdity of what she'd said. "His men wudda killed you in the blink of an eye."

Sarah sniffled. "Maybe so, but Noah would be alive and instead of people shunning us they'd pity you. They'd say, oh, there goes that poor Morrow fella. He was widowed at the hands of outlaws. And they'd say of me, she died trying to capture bank robbers. No, Josh, it would have been for the better if I'd killed him."

Caleb had taken a seat on a plain wooden chair near the fireplace. He knew as sure as the sun going down what his father would say, but he had to try. "Pa, we need to report this to Tom Percy."

Josh snorted. "Percy has had ample time to catch Hooper and his bunch. But what does he do, sit by the stove and drink coffee. I believe in law and order but when it's not working and it's personal like this is, a fella has got to deal with it his own self."

Sarah raised her head up from Josh's chest and looked him in the eyes. "No, Josh. Caleb is right. Let the Sheriff deal with Hooper."

"I'll not debate this. So, the both of ya can save your breath."

"But where would you start? It's winter. People freeze to death in these mountains."

Josh sighed. "I know this causes you worry but I'm no tenderfoot, you know."

"I'll go with you."

Josh looked at his son and scoffed. "And leave your mother here alone to feed the cows and do all the other chores?"

Caleb sunk back in his chair. Defeated as he knew he would be.

Josh went on. "I'll ride Boots and pack Gus with about ten days worth of provisions."

The anguish in Sarah's face was clear. "But to go where?"

"Wyoming, I reckon."

Sarah snorted and tossed her head. "Well, that narrows it right down."

It was not like Caleb had a sudden epiphany. Rather it was something Thelma had said to him in her rambling quest to determine why Herman had sought out Irma Duke's company. It had played in his head like the catchy part of a song ever since Thelma had told it to him in the dark, with the blanket down no less. The reason it had stuck in Caleb's mind was Thelma seemed to take some satisfaction, if not pride in it. The color came up in Caleb's face. "You know, Thelma told me something that Hooper told her in bed." He paused wishing that his mother wasn't in the room.

Sarah cut into the awkwardness. "For land sakes, Caleb. Just say it."

He came back quick so as to be done with it. "She said Hooper told her she was better than any of the girls at Gerties."

Sarah's face was still searching Thelma's words when Josh probed, "Did it sound like, to Thelma, that Hooper was a regular at Gerties?"

"I believe that's the way she took it."

Sarah asked, "You know this place?"

"I know of it. It's about 15 miles south of Jackson Hole next to the Snake River."

"That's a long way to go in winter on the chance that Hooper is there."

Josh sighed. "Where else am I gonna start?"

CHAPTER FORTY-THREE

Throughout the night Josh wrestled with what he was about to do. The hard fact of the matter was he was going in search of a man to kill. He would be judge, jury and executioner. Burt Hooper had it coming, of that he was certain.

The sun was teasing just beyond the mountains to the east. It was cold, really cold, even for the day after Christmas. Josh was not more than a mile from home and already his ears were stinging numb. He wished, almost, that he'd taken Sarah up on her offer of a stocking hat. And he found himself tempted by fleeting thoughts of acquiescing to her tearful, last minute plea this morning, *let Tom Percy go after Hooper.* Her plea, however, could not stand up to his conscience. *You should have gone after those horses a long time ago. Noah would be alive now if you had.* But here he was, his mind in turmoil. Boots dutifully trudging through the snow and Gus, their 1,200 pound black mule, trailing less enthusiastically behind. He turned north on the main road out from their place. In two days time it would take him to Gerties.

He was a good way down McCoy Creek when the gnawing in his gut convinced him that the sun overhead was not lying about it being noon. Boots snickered wearily, causing Josh to lean forward and pat his neck. "I know boy. We're gonna stop here real shortly and have a bite to eat." Up ahead the canyon bottom widened revealing a patch of rye grass sticking above the knee deep snow. Like he said he would, Josh gave Boots and Gus their freedom to graze. He, on the other hand, took a seat on an aspen tree that beavers had downed but, for some reason, had not yet incorporated into their dam. Sarah had made him two bacon sandwiches on thick slices of her sourdough bread. She'd wrapped each one in a page of the Pocatello newspaper reminding him, *you can use this to start your fire tonight so keep track of it.* He bit into his first sandwich savoring its flavor. Not far away Boots and Gus tore off mouthfuls of the tall grass. It was dry and coarse, and he could hear them work it between their teeth like it was oats. In the aspen branches above him mountain chickadees called out their serenade. Across the meadow near the creek, gray jays made no bones about their desire to share his sandwich. It was peaceful, soothing. For a brief moment, the nagging angst within him had gone away. And then down the canyon where the trail and the creek jogged left, a rider and pack horse emerged from the trees. The animals were laboring in the nearly virgin snow. Josh continued to sit on the log and eat as he watched the man approach. He appeared to be a trapper. Heavily clothed against the cold. Full black beard. A red cloth hat with earflaps that were presently turned up in the bright sun. As the stranger got close, he eyed the last of Josh's sandwich. He shouted in a friendly tone, "Bean time I take it."

Josh continued the banter. "Well, if yer a mind to, sit yerself down. I got another sandwich in my pocket."

The stranger stepped down from his gray horse. He was a big man, the snow striking his legs about five or six inches below the knees. "Name's Homer Woods."

Josh shook the man's gloved hand. His eyes were dark like he might be part Indian. "Josh Morrow. You doing some trapping?"

Homer went several feet down the log from Josh and brushed the snow off before taking a seat. Josh leaned toward him with the other sandwich. "Here ya go."

"Much obliged. I generally have a few pieces of elk jerky to last me till supper, but I went off this morning and forgot it."

"You got a place up here?"

Homer finished unwrapping the sandwich and paused, "Got a little place down on the Snake." He then took a big bite.

"You run any cattle?"

Homer's right cheek had puffed out like a squirrel with a mouthful of nuts. He chewed several times, swallowed and then came back, "No, I trap. Pan a little gold. Sometimes I hire out logging or driving a buck rake during haying." He laughed. "Mostly, I just try and keep from starvin'." He paused and took another bite, smaller this time. "And you, what brings you up here?"

Josh could not help that his expression went dead serious causing Homer to follow suit. "I'm lookin' for some men. They stole my horses and one of 'em killed my boy."

Out of respect, Homer stopped chewing. "Sorry to hear that. I guess you know better 'n anybody the country is alive with scoundrels these days."

Josh nodded. "These fellas are ridin' a buckskin and a big bay that has a white star on its forehead. You seen any horses like that? Maybe on up the Snake around Gerties' place?"

Homer was not an experienced liar. Josh had watched his face as he described the horses. It was like a still beaver pond on a hot summer day. Occasionally, a trout will sip an unsuspecting insect from the surface leaving a faint ripple.

There were ripples in Homer's eyes. He came back pretending to be distracted with taking another bite of his sandwich. "You know, I can't say that I recall in recent times seeing any horses around here quite like that."

Josh reached in his coat pocket and took out a couple of oatmeal-raison cookies. He purposely extended one to Homer so that he'd have to look at him. "I'm sure if you'd seen these horses, you'd remember them. They're good-lookin' animals."

Homer took the cookie. He started to set it on his thigh but suddenly became aware of the dried blood and bits of flesh and hair from the animals he'd skinned and set it in the snow on the log beside him. He dodged, "Your wife fill your feed bag did she?"

Josh came back so as to let Homer know he was tired of the dance. "You should know, the stage line put out a thousand dollar reward on this Hooper fella. As near as I can gather, he's the one that rides my bay."

"The hell you say."

"The money is not my interest. I'd be willing to give that up to anyone that could point me in the right direction."

Homer said nothing, putting the last of the sandwich in his mouth. He chewed several times. "Thousand dollars. That's a lot of money."

"You could take the winter off. Sit by the fire."

Homer's expression did not change. He seemed to accept that Josh had seen through him. He sighed and reached for the cookie. He took a bite and began to chew. His eyes fixated on the aspen across the meadow. After a time, he sighed even more heavily like it would expel his fear. "You know, they'll probably kill the both of us."

"I ain't asking you to come with me."

"The man is like the devil his self. He'll find out."

"If he's dead it won't matter."

Homer scoffed. "Yer purty cock-sure of yerself, my friend."

Josh forced a wry grin. "A person set on killing another person has no room for doubts or he'll be the one dying."

Homer shook his head and took another bite of cookie. "He ain't far from here."

"You mean he ain't up around Gerties' place?"

"Don't need to be. Word I heard is he gave Gertie two spankin' new hundred dollar notes for her best girl. She lives with him and another fella over on Fall Creek." Homer paused and laughed. "Kinda funny that bunch living over there right under the noses of all those Mormons."

"Can you show me where his place is?"

Homer snorted. "I'll draw you a map for my thousand dollars, assuming yer alive to collect it. But ain't no way in hell I'm going over there. Hell, you stop in Swan Valley. Most anybody can tell you where the Bob Smith place is."

"Bob Smith?"

"That would be Hooper. Told people he got an inheritance from his father."

"So, how is it you know all this?"

"One of the girls at Gerties that is friends with the gal Hooper bought swore me to secrecy. And then, as luck would have it, a fella I was workin' for this fall sold Hooper a load of hay. I was the one to haul it over there. Pitched it all off myself. Lazy scoundrels sat on their porch drinking whiskey and watched. But I saw yer horses. They was in a little pasture next to the barn and corral."

Josh shook his head in disgust. "They got any law in Swan Valley."

"Nope. Have to go to Eagle Rock for that. It's a long day's ride."

"Well, I reckon you better draw that map so I can be on my way."

Homer reached in his coat pocket and took out an envelope. "Got a letter from my sister. She never uses the back sides of her pages. Wasteful, but it's handy for us that she didn't this time." He balanced the paper on his leg and began to draw. "Gonna make you two maps. Second one is so you know where to bring my money."

Josh finished his cookie and rolled a smoke. When the cigarette was burnt half down Homer looked up and handed him two pieces of paper. "It don't matter to me if you read the dribble my sister wrote."

Josh studied the maps pulling on his cigarette as he did. He smiled. "I believe the promise of a thousand dollars has sharpened your pencil mighty fine."

"Well, if I don't see you again, thanks for the grub."

Josh smiled. "Next time dinner is on you."

CHAPTER FORTY-FOUR

Josh forded the Snake a little way upstream from where McCoy Creek dumped into it. Boots had no problem with the icy belly-deep water. Gus, on the other hand, was less confident. Mid-stream, Josh had been forced to dally the mule's lead rope around his saddle horn to overcome his resistance. Had Gus pitched a fit it could have been bad for everyone, but he did not.

The road next to the Snake was well traveled. Josh made camp in a stand of cottonwood trees a few miles south of Swan Valley. Everything he did, unsaddling Boots, unpacking Gus, graining them, pitching his lean-too, fixing supper, it all had a sense of finality. Like after tomorrow he would never do these things again. It hung on him like a wet blanket. In his mind's eye he could see too, someone, probably Tom Percy, going to tell Sarah that she was a widow. And so went the night. Fitful. Shivering against the cold. Playing over and over in his mind how it would go tomorrow. *You kill those fellas they're gonna call you a vigilante. They won't appreciate the grief Burt Hooper has caused our family.* And then none of that mattered. He could see himself laying there dead in Hooper's front yard. The talk would be different. *The damned fool rode right in there. Went up against Hooper and another fella.*

Throughout the night he could hear the wind course through the trees. About dawn it died away. He used his remaining page of newspaper to rekindle the fire. By and by, the coffee began to boil. He fried some eggs and ate them with Sarah's sourdough biscuits and chokecherry jam. The feeling of doom was still with him. It brought back memories of his time in the Army fighting the Comanches. Back then he knew it for what it was, fear.

Most people were up and about when he rode into Swan Valley. Smoke lay heavy over the little settlement crowded next to the river, as it was. It had occurred to Josh on the way there that if he rode Boots into Hooper's yard he might not live to step down from the saddle. He reined in at the Livery Stable. A burly man wearing a gray flat cap and green mackinaw was standing out front. He looked up squinting his eyes against the morning sun. "Howdy. What can I do for ya?"

"Need to board these animals and rent a saddle horse."

"For how long?"

"I'm not sure. Maybe today or maybe however long it takes for a letter to reach my wife and for her to come get 'em."

The livery man looked bewildered. He spit tobacco juice in the mud and horse manure and then raked the back of his hand across his salt and pepper moustache. "You don't know if you're coming back?"

"It's in my plan to, but you know how plans are."

"Well, I'll sell your animals for what's owed against 'em if you don't come back but I don't know about renting you a horse. That'd be a sizeable loss to me."

Josh grinned. "If I don't come back, you send the sheriff out to Bob Smith's place for your horse. Tell him to go well heeled as things aren't what they appear to be out there."

The livery man scratched the back of his head in a thoughtful way. "You know, Mister, the more you talk the less inclined I am to do business with you."

Josh looked down locking onto the man's eyes. "Just trying to be honest with you."

The man appeared to wither. He sighed. "Alright, Mister. I ain't never claimed to be the brightest star in the sky."

Josh nodded, "Appreciate it."

In about a half hour the livery man had situated Boots and Gus. He'd saddled a plain looking sorrel mare. A horse that would not alert Hooper to danger. On borrowed paper, Josh wrote to Sarah.

Dear Sarah,

Please know that I love you and the boys more than life itself. The years have been good to us. Today, however, is one of those rough spots. If you get this letter, you'll know things didn't work out for me. Boots and Gus are at the livery in Swan Valley. Please come fetch them home.

Your loving husband,

Josh

Josh folded the letter and put it in an envelope addressed to Sarah. He then handed it to the livery man. "If I ain't back by sundown I'd appreciate it if you'd mail this."

The livery man looked uncomfortable. "Alright." He paused and then added, "I don't know the nature of your business at the Smith place, but it sounds to me like you might be well advised to get the sheriff."

Josh snorted. "The law's had their chance."

CHAPTER FORTY-FIVE

A bridge made it easy to cross back over the Snake. According to Homer's map, the Smith place was about an hour's ride from here. He'd penciled an X where a squiggly line labeled, 'S. Fork Fall Crik' intersected the main creek. Josh rode on. His rented horse being sound but not the equal of Boots in the rutted snow. Overhead there was sunshine. To the west, however, dark clouds were coming together. He'd been watching them since crossing the river. Little by little they were patching the blue cracks and moving en masse toward him. He whispered, like it mattered, "Gonna dump on us later today." High above him, ravens tracked his progress. They darted one way and then another cawing loudly as if they had something important to say. Occasionally, some of them would land in the aspen and pines to either side of the road. It put them closer to eye level with Josh. If he'd been rounding up cattle, he would have thought their behavior as, *just what ravens do.* Today, his paranoia likened it to a warning. Maybe another one of those things he'd never hear again after he tangled with Burt Hooper.

After a time, he could see up ahead a stringer of yellow leafed aspen threading its way down the bottom of a shallow canyon to the main creek. Black timber crowded it hard. Right where he figured Homer had intended the X to be, was a cabin that backed up close to the creek. Blue smoke was coming out of a rusty stovepipe like someone inside was extra cold. *That whore has got a chill on*, thought Josh. The sound of steady chopping coming from an open face wood-shed on the upstream side of the cabin seemed to confirm that notion. Josh stopped at the turn that led to the Smith place. He could see better from here. A small barn, its weathered boards having grayed a long time ago, stood maybe fifty yards east of the cabin. A pole corral was attached to its south side. There stood Snookers, Baldy and two other horses that Josh did not recognize. And then it happened. They began to whinny at Josh's livery horse. Shortly, the chopping ceased. A stocky man, older than Josh came to the doorway of the shed. He was wearing a black slouch hat and dark coat. He was unarmed, except for the double bitted ax that he held at his side. Josh waved and rode toward the man. His adrenaline pumping faster now than the smoke coming from the cabin. He called out, "Mornin'. Looks like we're in for more snow."

It was clear that Walter was suspicious, as a wanted man might well be. But at this point it was in his best interest to continue the ruse he and Hooper were perpetrating on their neighbors. Walter looked up at the storm clouds. "Yeah, I'm tryin' to git the wood box filled 'fore it gits here."

"Well, that's a smart idy. Keep the missus happy."

"Ain't my woman. She belongs to my brother."

From the corner of his eye, Josh saw the curtain part in the cabin window across from him. A blonde woman in a blue dress showed herself. She mouthed the words, "Help me."

Walter, oblivious to the woman's plea, nodded. "So, what brings you our way?"

Josh's heart was hammering in his ears. He had visions of being shot at any second. *Where's that damned Hooper. He came back.* "Mind if I step down?"

Walter said as he watched Josh dismount, "Mister, I don't know you."

Josh dropped the reins of his horse on the ground so his hands would be free. He said with a wry smile, "But you do know me. You've been to my house and terrorized my wife. You've got my horses in your corral. And your *'brother'* killed my youngest son. So, yeah, we've got plenty of history don't ya reckon?"

The sudden realization of who he was talking to caused Walter's eyes to be gripped by shock. His next action was definitely on impulse. No doubt from his fear of hanging, of having the State of Idaho snap his neck like a matchstick. He raised the ax and lunged at Josh.

It being about 20 degrees it would've looked odd for Josh to have ridden into Hooper's yard bare handed. So here he was struggling to push his coat out of the way and draw his Army Colt with a gloved hand. He'd barely gotten a grip on his pistol when the ax handle, just below the head, struck his uplifted left hand. However, the momentum Walter wielded drove the ax onward striking Josh a glancing blow on the shoulder. The impact caused him to stumble backwards. Walter was raising the ax a second time when Josh's gun finally roared. Walter immediately hunched up like a mule had kicked him in the stomach instead of a .45 Caliber bullet. Although his knees had buckled, he still held onto the ax. Josh's breathing was fast and excited. He thought to shoot Walter again but saw by the look in his eyes that he was done. *Hooper's got to be coming now.* Indeed, he was. At that very moment he was leaning against the barn's open doorway to steady the aim of his Winchester. Had it not been for the rented horse bolting and temporarily obscuring Josh, he would have been dead. Luck had saved him. Still unaware of Hooper's presence, instinct told Josh to take cover. He began to crawl away from Walter's body and the chopping block both visible in the large opening to the woodshed. He was nearly to the wall and out of view when the vagaries of the livery horse caused it to trot off. In that instant, Hooper's rifle belched smoke. The sound of the shot reached Josh a split second after the bullet punched through the crown of his Stetson. A sudden, massive surge of adrenaline enabled him to catapult his body against the wall. Within seconds the inch thick board above Josh's head splintered in response to the sound of Hooper's rifle. Instantly Josh buried his face in the dirt, sawdust and sloughed bits of bark. Under other circumstances, the smell of the freshly cut pine would have been pleasing. Today, it represented his proximity to dying. And then came another shot and more splintered wood and if not for a chunk of firewood not yet split, Josh would have had a .45 Caliber bullet embedded in the top of his head. He felt as if he was playing Russian Roulette. At some point, one of the big bullets coming through the wall would find him. Josh thought back to his time in the Army. *Hooper's gotta know he's got the upper hand. As long as he keeps shootin', I don't dare raise my head. He'll walk right up and shoot me point blank.* Hooper's rifle sounded again. Different this time. Closer, like he'd read Josh's mind. Trembly fear seized Josh. He seethed the words. "Sonovabitch is coming." On the heels of the epithet came the advice of his old first sergeant, *there's times when a fella ain't got no choice but to go on the offense. It's either that or die hunkered down.* And then another gunshot, closer still, and wood chips flying. Josh obeyed his sergeant. With his arms extended out in front of him and a two-handed grip on his pistol he rolled toward the opening. There was Hooper twenty feet away. Surprise. Terror. Frantic to realign his rifle. Second roll. Hooper fires. A big piece of aspen to Josh's left absorbs the bullet. Josh's elbows came to rest just to the right of Walter's still boots. The Army Colt bucks. Hooper's eyes flare big with regret and anger. The rifle falls from his hands cascading down along his body as he pitches over backwards. For a time, Josh stayed where he was, hammer back, finger on the trigger until he was certain that Hooper had no life in him. It felt good to lay there in the softness of the sawdust and let the adrenaline bleed off. Snow began to fall. Random. Unorganized. Like it was a tease, a warning of what tonight would bring.

"Hello, out there. Are you alright?"

Josh looked over to the cabin. The whore in the blue dress was standing in the doorway. He got to his knees and waved. "I'm ok."

The girl started toward him carefully placing her ankle high shoes in the steps of others. She stopped midway between Walter and Hooper. For a time, she looked at them. Indifferent. Finally, she looked at Josh. "Thank you. I've been waiting for this day for a long time."

Josh came back, "So, have I."

EPILOGUE

It turned out the sheriff from Eagle Rock had spent the night at a ranch just outside of Swan Valley. As was his custom, he stopped by the livery the next morning to get a pulse of who was coming and going in the valley. It was then that he learned of Josh's letter and his quest. About an hour after the gunfight, he showed up, his horse lathered in frothy sweat, and verified Hooper's identity. *Why there's a thousand dollar reward on him, don't ya know? Can't say for sure when you'll get your money. Things like this take time. Maybe next spring, I reckon. It'll go along with the stage company being able to recover almost $3,500 of the money that got stole on Malad Pass. These boys must have had a fine time with that other $1,500.*

At this point, the girl in the blue dress had looked at Josh for fear he'd change his mind about the $500 she rifled from Hooper's pockets. But he did not. She rode to Eagle Rock, along with him and the Sheriff. She was 19 years old. Younger than Noah. He said to her just before she boarded a train to her sister's place in California. *Just know the past is past to people who care about you. So, cultivate those folks. Someday you may need them.*

In the spring, Tom Percy brought the reward money for Hooper out to Josh. A few days later when some of the mud had dried, Josh and Sarah rode over McCoy Creek to the banks of the Snake River to deliver the money to Homer. He insisted that they split it, but Josh would have none of it. They did stay, however, for supper. Beans, sourdough biscuits, strawberry jam and black coffee. And there were oatmeal raisin cookies made by a Mormon lady downriver. Not as good as the one Josh had given Homer that day on the log, but they were alright.

It was several weeks after they'd returned from Homer's that Tom Percy rode out to inform them that the spring thaw had gave up Noah not far from Pocatello. They buried him, just the three of them and Buster in attendance, on a little rise overlooking the house. By and by there were neighbors who paid their respects.